"GOOD MORNING," SHE OFFERED WITH AN EASY SMILE.

She ignored the faint fluttering in her stomach and remembered her resolutions when those intense, disturbing amber eyes of his locked with hers as he lifted a wet can of cola to his lips. He took a long swig, and she watched him drink his fill, lower the can, then continue to clutch it as he leaned his shoulder against the doorway. His message was obvious. She wasn't getting in.

"I thought I made myself clear the other day. Nothing you have to say interests me, lady."

"Believe me, detective, I know how you feel. If I could just—"

"Lady, you can't have the slightest notion of how I feel. Don't stand there insulting me, pretending you do when you're here to do a job. Cut to the chase. I'm in no mood to indulge you." She looked so cool, so composed, so damned beautiful . . . and his brother's neck was on the line.

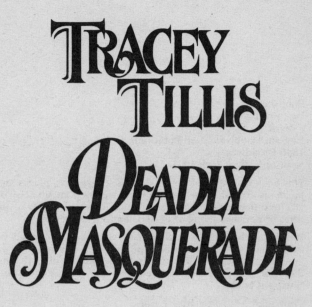

TRACEY TILLIS

DEADLY MASQUERADE

A DELL BOOK

Published by
Dell Publishing
a division of
Bantam Doubleday Dell Publishing Group, Inc.
1540 Broadway
New York, New York 10036

ISBN: 0-440-21547-1

Printed in the United States of America

Published simultaneously in Canada

June 1994

10 9 8 7 6 5 4 3 2 1

OPM

ACKNOWLEDGMENTS

Mom and Dad, my love always;

Ray Walton, your patience and insight were invaluable. Thanks;

Ginny Walton and the Paperback Shoppe crew, ditto for your support;

Mark G., same goes for your candor;

Pewgwy, thanks; (it's late)

And Natalie, Alicia, Mary W., and my IRWA family, you're the cheese, guys.

Prologue

———⟡———

The boarded tavern sagged into the assassin's sight. He slowed and took a moment to scan his surroundings with a casual glance.

Hell's Acre. No one lurked along this gutted-out, abandoned strip. No one came here after dark except the rats. Long observation gave him that assurance. The unexpected luck of this drizzly, steamy night reinforced it. He walked on, glancing once at the sooty sky as a faint rumble of thunder shuddered in the distance.

Keeping his steps measured and even, he closed in on the tavern and the alley beyond it. There was no real reason to hurry. Cain wasn't going anywhere. Careful planning had him sure of that. The assassin smiled thinly. He passed the tavern and rounded the corner.

Two feet within the mouth of the bordering alley, he stopped and dipped his hand into the colorless folds of his damp cotton coat. The smooth butt of his pistol felt cool, welcoming against his fingers. For brief moments he stood motionless, savoring the warm swell of anticipation. This was almost too easy. Still, the thought did nothing to dilute his rush.

Suddenly a jagged bolt of lightning flashed across the alley, illuminating two men. *Two*— what the hell? Another bolt of lightning flashed and the assassin stopped thinking. Instinct told him where there was one glitch there could be two. The upswing of his pistol was swift and sure.

The flash of lightning and a residual glint against the gun's dark metal were the only warnings Cain's young companion got. He moved a second too late.

"Cain!" the young man shouted, shoving his companion to the side.

"No! God, *no!*"

The shocked words were Cain's last. Two spits of the assassin's bullets flailed him backward, the impact contorting his body like a rag doll.

Stunned, the younger man drew his own weapon and fired. The shot went wide as he backpedaled blindly toward the alley's rear exit. He turned and almost rounded the corner when his wrist slammed against the sharp edge of a metal trash Dumpster. He felt his flesh rip, and the pain was excruciating as his thin silver bracelet snapped and gave way, sliding to the pavement.

He couldn't retrieve it. The assassin was in fast pursuit.

Two sets of footsteps pounded through the gravel and garbage lining the twisting network of empty back streets. Two sets of lungs labored for air. Somewhere in the distance a siren wailed.

Then there was one set of footsteps, one set of heaving lungs; the young man realized he ran alone.

He jogged to a stop and started to shake, just dimly aware of the crumbling abutment against which he stood. Even less aware of its location or of the shadowy river slushing beneath it.

The deal had gone down. But death hadn't been in the plan; Cain was dead!

The man's eyes slid closed as fear battled remorse. He could do nothing for Cain now. Not when he had just become the hunted. Tonight, in their eyes, he'd become a traitor. In his own he'd become a survivor who must keep running to live.

He stumbled to his feet but was knocked to his knees by a rush of nausea that doubled him over, leaving him coughing and gagging into the rain-scarred night.

1

"Nick! Over here!"

Detective Sergeant Nicholas Abella squinted against the sun, trying to target the voice hailing him through the mob of excited reporters flooding the front steps of the Sedgwick City Police Department.

His height of six feet two and the imposing grimness that sharpened his aquiline features had little effect in parting the sea of hysterical media hot on the scent of a sensational murder.

In fact, he looked very much like one of his fierce Roman ancestors as he battled the hordes of reporters to push his way to the revolving glass doors barring the entrance to the building. He thought he'd made it when the wave of questions hit.

"Detective Abella, is the department any closer to discovering the identity of Peter Cain's murderer?"

"Is it true that Prosecutor Cain was dealing drugs at the time of the shooting?"

"Detective, sources inform me that this isn't the

first time police have linked Cain's name with illicit drug trafficking in this city—is that true?"

"No comment. No comment . . ." The headache at Nick's temples intensified to a vicious pounding as he reached out and smacked through the doors, effectively shutting out the din of reporters.

"Nick, Sheriff Brower's screaming." Detective David Robbins moved closer to Nick to make himself heard against the bustling crowd flooding the corridor. He had to hustle to keep pace with Nick's long stride.

"Who the hell isn't? And why's the sheriff here at city headquarters giving orders? Why isn't he at his own headquarters at County?"

Robbins shrugged. "I hear he's being based here in the chief's old office for this one. Executive orders or something."

"Or something," Nick repeated, barely breaking stride. "You should be out there with that mob. They can't get their facts straight either."

The officer flushed and Nick sighed. "Sorry, David."

"Forget it, we're all feeling the heat."

"It wasn't your fault," Nick said, impatient with the younger officer's subdued tone. "There was no way you could have anticipated what was going down."

It was common knowledge around the precinct that Cain's death had hit Robbins just about the hardest. Robbins had been one of Cain's personal bodyguards, and he'd been dismissed for the night by Cain just hours before the prosecutor had been gunned down. The irony was that only six months before, Robbins had been the one to take a bullet meant for Cain during a political rally.

"I wasn't just his bodyguard, Nick. I was his friend. Don't you see, if he was involved in something serious enough to get him killed, I should have known it. I should have listened to my gut and kept a watch last night in spite of my orders. Maybe I could have—"

"Bullshit," Nick said. He paused to lean against a water fountain and pinned the subdued officer with a cool amber gaze. "Don't give me that I-could-have-prevented-it crap. You're only human like the rest of us. You weren't dealing with any death threats or other warnings, so why are you standing here second-guessing yourself now? You know how much good it does—Christ, all of us do."

Robbins stared morosely at the floor and Nick sighed again. He understood the man's pain, the crushing guilt, even if it was misplaced. "We've all been there. And you know something? It never changed a thing. It never will. Hindsight may be twenty-twenty, my friend, but it's a bitch."

Another moment passed before David looked up. "Thanks, Nick."

Nick nodded, running a weary hand along the back of his neck. "Who else is up there?"

"The mayor just left. Now Brower's screaming for you. He knows you're the best we've got, buddy." The gibe was sardonic.

"And you know where you can go." Nick tempered his sarcasm with a faint smile.

Ever since the media had bestowed glamorized notoriety on him during his investigation of a string of serial killings a year ago, Nick's fellow officers had gently ridden him about it. Usually he indulged their teasing with tolerant amusement. Right now his nerves were too thin and it just irritated him.

"That's not all, Nick," Robbins said. "Some of the men are saying . . . they're saying—"

"What? Spit it out," Nick's tone was distracted. He was squinting past David, down the distance of the corridor, to see if another barrage of enterprising reporters awaited.

"—that it was a cop. They're saying a cop killed Cain, and that there's evidence."

Nick's head snapped around. "Where the hell did you hear that?"

"Thompson heard it from Bellows and Bellows heard it from McElroy in forensics. A cop, Nick. Jesus, they wouldn't be saying that if it wasn't true, would they?" Robbins glanced around, belatedly realizing how his voice had risen.

Nick had no answer. The idea was too outrageous to consider, let alone accept. Evidence? What the hell did that mean? He pushed away from the fountain.

"Are you here for the day?" he asked Robbins, who kept step with him as he headed down the hallway. Now that he thought of it, he was surprised Robbins was here at all. He would have expected him to take some time off.

"Yeah," Robbins answered. "I guess I just want to stick around. It helps, you know?"

Nick gave him a considering look. Yeah, he could imagine how it must. He squeezed David's shoulder. "Hang in there, man."

Angling left, he headed for the private-access elevator that would take him up to the third floor. A cop. Damn. Wasn't this thing messy enough without rumblings of police corruption?

He lifted his hand to jab the third-floor button on the panel inside the elevator, considered Brower's summons, and jabbed the one that would take him to the second-floor cafeteria instead. He wanted a cup of hot caffeine. It didn't take a psychic to figure out that things were going to get worse before they got better. A minute's detour from the inevitable wouldn't matter much.

The cafeteria was uncharacteristically empty, even for seven thirty in the morning.

Glancing at his watch to see how long he could legitimately stall Brower, Nick headed straight for the row of vending machines against the far wall. He was distracted as he noticed David stroll into the room, so he nearly ran into the woman who stepped swiftly into his path, beating him to the coffee machine.

Her back was to him and she'd angled in so quickly he hadn't gotten a full view of her. But his imagination was thoroughly captured by what he did see.

Classy. His preoccupied gaze widened enough to appreciate the sleek luster of her appearance. The cut and fabric of her pastel summer suit was very chic, very professional, very modern. She wore it with a careless ease that suggested despite its expense, she'd selected it for comfort, not effect. He liked that. He also liked how the ultrafeminine image she projected was all the more potent for her disregard of it.

Nick dug in his pocket for change, appreciating the soft way her auburn hair brushed against her shoulders. No artifice there either. The slightly curling fullness of it was the product of nature, not the latest trendy spray out of a bottle.

The square dove-gray shoulder bag she wore neatly over her shoulder swayed as she bent to insert a quarter into the machine. Nick tracked the bag's movement as it bounced back to rest against a softly rounded hip that casually shifted to bear her weight while she waited patiently for the cup to drop and the coffee to fill it. A slow smile curved his lips as he let his eyes travel over an endless length of shapely legs. One small, dove-gray leather-shod foot was tapping impatiently. It was the incongruity of that restive movement that sidetracked Nick's concentration enough for him to register what the faceless beauty had just uttered.

"Damn." Her soft expulsion contrasted with the hard whump she dealt the machine that had smoothly swallowed her quarter.

"Can I help?"

Heeding the low, deep voice behind her, she turned. "No, thanks," she murmured, while continuing to look at him.

Her lovely brown eyes had widened briefly when she'd turned to face him, and Nick pursued that flare of awareness. "Usually takes a swift kick, but since it's a little early in the morning to get physical, we'll try plan B."

"Hey, it's okay. I—"

"No problem." He flashed her a confident smile and popped his quarter into the slot. Nothing happened. "Son of a bitch," he murmured. A swift kick still failed to elicit the desired result.

She tried tactfully to suppress a chuckle. She didn't succeed.

At the delicate sound, Nick caught her eye. His consternation at being outwitted by the hunk of junk faded. It was replaced by something less discernible but more potent, and it struck him squarely between the eyes. Did she work here? How had he missed her before this?

"Pretty funny, huh? You know, I'd be offended if I were trying to impress you." He hoped his smile wasn't as foolish as it felt.

"Yeah, well, don't let it distress you. I wasn't that impressed."

"So give me a minute, I'll think of something else."

She leaned against the machine and smiled. Nice. All the same, she tensed slightly when he moved a little closer.

"Listen—" Nick began.

"You through here, Nick?"

She turned at the same moment Nick did.

"No, I'm not through," Nick answered evenly. "What do you want?" He wondered at David's bad manners and the grim resignation that had sobered the woman's lovely features so suddenly.

"I want to talk to you," David said. He glanced

at the woman's back, then gestured at his table. "Over there."

A cool response was on the tip of Nick's tongue, but he held it. He knew David could be blunt, but he had never seen him this blatantly uncivil in a situation seemingly not warranting it. What was between these two? he wondered, looking over at the woman, then back to the officer. She didn't say anything, didn't even turn away from the machine. She just stood there, calmly drinking coffee she had finally gotten with yet another quarter.

"I'll be over in a minute." Nick's steady gaze held David's until the latter wavered. Mumbling a response, David turned away, but not before he'd tossed another unreadable look in the woman's direction.

"Don't mind him," Nick said, stepping around to shield her from the curious stares that had perked up a couple of tables away. "He's only a jerk sometimes."

She turned to face Nick fully. "It's no big deal. No harm done."

"So, you had better luck this time," Nick said inanely, nodding at the cup of coffee she raised to her lips. He didn't know why he was so reluctant to leave. Maybe it had to do with the withdrawal he sensed beneath that easy smile.

The subtlety of it intrigued him. He'd seen it in punk street kids who adeptly concealed their wariness behind arrogant, cocky masks. There was nothing arrogant or cocky about this woman. But there was an inner something she'd shut off from him as neatly as if she'd slammed a mental door.

"Look, I'm late for my appointment and your friend is waiting." She stepped away from him. "I don't want to hold you up."

"Let him wait."

"I don't think that would make him very happy." She nodded politely, moved around him, and started to walk away.

"Wait!" he called softly, taking a couple of steps to close the distance between them. "At least tell me your name." He was puzzled by the look of regret that shuttered her expression, as puzzled as he was by the regret that shaded her voice when after a moment she decided to answer him.

"Kelly. Kelly Wylie."

She turned and left the cafeteria, leaving him standing there not understanding what had driven her away but curious to find out. Sliding his own coin into the machine, he waited for his coffee and smiled when it and Kelly's errant quarter hit bottom together. A pleasant omen? Maybe.

"All right," Nick said when he'd joined the other man. "Spill it."

David shook his head. "You really don't know, do you?"

"Know what?"

"Who she is."

"As a matter of fact, she just told me. And unless you're as unperceptive as you are rude, you'll understand when I tell you I'd like to get to know her better."

"What did she say to you?"

"That she blew up the Government Building, man. What do you think? She told me her name. What's the problem?"

"She's bad news. That's the problem. You know that business about Jim?"

It took Nick a moment to make the shift. When he did, his curiosity doubled.

Jim Nolan was the veteran patrolman who had been busted internally just a week ago. Nick recalled thinking Nolan's drug habit might have been mitigated after he'd dutifully gotten the help and counseling he'd been advised to seek. Unfortunately, the unlucky street deal he'd initiated couldn't be. Not even for a stack of medical bills racked up by his convalescing wife.

"What's the connection between Jim and Kelly?" Nick knew he didn't want to hear the answer.

"Jim might have gotten a little slack if it weren't for a negative recommendation from the investigating IA officer. That little lady you think is so cute was the officer. She flipped off the circumstances of Jim's actions and pushed for his termination. You know what kind of shape he's in now. The force was all he knew."

Internal Affairs. Just like most cops, Nick respected the need for IA, but he bore no love for the officers who did the job. Generally, he stayed away from them. Generally, all of the cops outside Internal Affairs did because no one was comfortable for long with the officers whose jobs it was to police the police.

The general assumption was you couldn't trust

them. It was an assumption he had no reason to believe didn't apply to Kelly Wylie. Maybe Jim's situation justified that.

"Stay away from her, Nick. Leave her to her own kind, where she belongs," David said.

"Maybe." Nick was noncommittal. "Now's not the time to discuss it." He got up. "Like you said, Brower's screaming for me."

"Yep. Listen to what I'm saying, man," David called as Nick walked away.

Nick merely raised a hand in acknowledgment before he walked through the double doors and out into the corridor.

So Kelly Wylie was IA. It put a slightly different complexion on things, maybe, but it didn't do much to change the fact that she was a very attractive woman.

Up on the third floor, Nick peered through the frosted pane of the door to the office Sheriff Anton Brower was using. He knocked perfunctorily and without waiting for an answer walked in.

"Nick," Brower greeted him.

The sheriff's blunt features were tight and he failed to offer Nick the barest glimmer of cordiality beyond the terse greeting. Family histories, including a few shared family cookouts during Nick's childhood, took him and Brower a few years back. The unusual abruptness coming from the older man now had Nick recalling what David had said earlier.

"What's up, Anton?"

"Something I absolutely guarantee you you're not going to like. There's been a development on the Cain murder. Come over here, I want you to take a look at this."

Feeling little of the nonchalance he exhibited, Nick took the time to light a cigarette before seating himself across from Brower's desk. The acrid smoke did little for his headache, but it soothed his nerves as it filled his lungs.

"What have you got?"

"One of the boys in forensics found this mixed in with the debris that was collected from the alley." He tossed a thin silver bracelet across his desk.

Nick leaned forward and picked it up. There was nothing spectacular or even notable about it except the fact that the clasp was broken and its weight told him it had maybe cost more than the average vanity piece. But there was something nigglingly familiar about it.

He turned it over. There was an inscription. J. A. SANDY. He'd seen the inscription yesterday morning just before his father had wrapped it to present at the party that evening, the party he'd missed after being delayed on a stakeout.

"What's this supposed to mean?"

Brower leaned back with a heavy sigh and lifted tired eyes to the ceiling. "You do recognize it, don't you." It was a statement, not a question.

"Theo got it down in forensics," he continued. "He remembered this morning where he'd seen it. Said everybody saw your father give it to Joey at that birthday party last night. I had to be certain before I did anything." He turned to face Nick. "If I had any doubts before I showed it to you just now, your reaction just erased them. I don't know what's going on, Nick, but at this point I can't ignore what's in front of my eyes."

The two men were so focused on each other neither turned immediately to acknowledge the person who slipped quietly inside the room.

"I don't give a damn what's in front of your eyes." The calm in Nick's statement would have deceived anyone who didn't know him. "There's a legitimate explanation for this, because sure as hell my brother isn't a killer!"

"Sheriff, you wanted to see me?"

The feminine, level tone drew both men's attention. Brower simply nodded while Nick's brow creased with surprise. He'd no sooner asked himself what she was doing here than, with a sinking feeling, he knew.

"Come in, Kelly," Brower said. "Nick, Sergeant Kelly Wylie, Internal Affairs, County Sheriff's Department. Kelly, Detective Sergeant Nicholas Abella, Sedgwick City Homicide." He turned back to Nick. "She's just relocated from Chicago back to Indiana and left you city guys here to join us over in County."

She walked across the room and held out her hand to Nick.

"Sergeant." Nick's lips were stiff and his tone, even to his own ears, sounded brittle. He couldn't help it. He was off-balance, having first been hit with Brower's news only to be broadsided minutes later by Kelly Wylie's involvement with it.

The hell of it was, at this moment he honestly couldn't decide which upset him more, the fact that his little brother was a prime suspect in the biggest murder to rock this town in years, or the necessity of squelching a half-formed gut attraction toward the woman whose job it was to hunt him down.

"If you two think I'm going to sit here and willingly help you hang my little brother, you're both crazy." He looked from Brower to Kelly, letting his look linger on Kelly. Some inner devil goaded him to say, "And I don't care how pretty the hangman is. Your bait's not working, Anton."

The insult registered with Kelly. "Rest assured, Sergeant, I am very good at my job. Damned good. I don't have to resort to subterfuge to get it done."

"Calm down, sweetheart. I wasn't talking to you." Nick regretted his words instantly. But that devil inside urged him to stand his ground.

"Abella, what the hell is the matter with you!" Brower demanded.

Nick's cool gaze swung to Brower. Brower held it with a hard stare.

As he should have, Nick thought. With her looks and her job, Kelly must run into the kind of bastard he was acting like every day. He knew he should apologize, but he felt cornered and his defenses were running high.

"Oh, don't worry, Sheriff." Kelly's voice was controlled. "I assure you I'm more than capable of taking care of myself."

"Well, then, if you two don't mind, can we please get down to business?" Brower asked.

Nick assessed Kelly a moment longer and she

assessed him right back. That annoyed him even more. He swung his gaze back to Brower and gave his nod of assent. Kelly, he noted, gave the same.

"Thank you," Brower said. "Now. Kelly will be handling this investigation. If you've got any problems with that, Nick, I suggest you get over them in a hurry, because that's the way it's going to be. Do you understand me?"

"Yes, sir," Nick said, slouching low in his chair. He hooked an ankle across his knee, took a steady pull from his cigarette, and proceeded to study its glowing red tip.

"Kelly," Brower continued, "I want you to make this case your first priority. Shift the rest of your caseload accordingly."

"Yes, sir. Has Joey Abella been apprehended yet for questioning?"

"Nobody's heard from him this morning. So I sent two plainclothes officers down to Brown County on the outside chance he left last night to take the vacation he'd scheduled to spend down at his cabin."

Kelly read Brower's telling look. "He's disappeared."

"Bingo."

Nick vaulted from his chair and didn't stop moving until he'd slammed out of the office.

2

"Let him go," Brower said as Kelly started to rise. "When he calms down, we'll be able to talk to him."

Kelly sat back and crossed her legs. "I feel sorry for him. His brother . . . I can imagine what he's going through."

"Yes," Brower said levelly, "I would imagine you can."

Kelly's eyes lifted to his and she read in them a greater degree of awareness than she wanted to see.

"I know your record and I know you're a good cop," Brower said. "And yes, I know about Chicago. A lot of people held you responsible for that, I know that too. But I've been an officer too many years not to understand how it could have happened. Maybe I even put you on this case because it did." He looked at her meaningfully. "But that's all in the past now and I'm not passing judgment."

"Thank you, sir." She knew Brower understood she was thanking him for more than the vote of confidence. A vote of faith went a long way for someone who had once despaired of ever hearing it again. "I won't let you down."

"I know that, Kelly, or I would never have put you on this case. Now, how would you like to proceed?"

Grateful for the man's tact, Kelly let the matter rest and concentrated for the next few minutes on how to best initiate the search for Joey Abella.

She was all business as the meeting concluded. "I'll need records, files, names, and any other preliminary documentation that can be accessed. The sooner I have that, the sooner I can start chasing down leads."

Brower nodded. "Done. But after you've read the files, the first thing I want you to do is talk to Nick. He and Joey are close. He may be your best initial source."

Kelly leaned back in her chair, trying to choose her words carefully. "Considering Detective Abella's hostility, do you really think approaching him right now would be the wisest thing to do?"

Brower clasped his hands on top of his desk. Strong, capable hands, Kelly thought. From what she had seen so far, they suited the man.

"There's something you have to understand, Kelly. Nick is a good cop. I mean a really fine officer. And I'm not just talking about his record. I mean deep down"—Brower tapped his chest—"in here."

"With all due respect, Sheriff, I don't doubt your sincerity—"

"But you can't quite believe it, right? Look, no matter what Nick says in the heat of the moment, you can believe one thing. The man is committed to doing what's right. That kind of attitude was as solid as a rock in his father, and now it's the same with Nick. And that's not just my liking for the man talking. It's my experience of him and respect for him."

Kelly considered. Her instincts told her that Brower was a man whose opinions could be trusted. But Joey was Nick's brother. And hadn't she learned firsthand how familial loyalties could blind, how they could cloud one's judgment about matters like truth and honor?

Her own ideals had been tarnished, and there was no denying that these days she functioned mostly beneath a layer of cynicism. But she was also a sworn officer of the law, and the plain truth was, Brower was her superior. No matter how nicely he had couched it, he had just given her an order.

She pressed back a sigh. She didn't want to deal with Nicholas Abella yet, not until she'd gotten a better handle on this case and a better feel for how to approach him.

The problem was, despite their bad footing now, the awareness they'd shared in the cafeteria had been real. She was very much afraid it had created personal defenses neither of them needed.

About two seconds after Brower had introduced her to Nick, he'd looked as if he had been slapped across the face. She'd bitten back a sigh and must have hidden her own reaction well, because she'd felt the same way.

On the way to Brower's office, she'd replayed

the encounter in the cafeteria and almost convinced herself that the attractive stranger didn't necessarily have to remain off limits. Now the possibilities enhancing that conclusion had been dashed because fate had decreed him to be none other than the brother of the prime murder suspect she had been ordered this morning to bring down.

She sighed again, remembering the exciting sensation of falling into those darkly fringed, whiskey-colored eyes of his. Remembering the way his half smile had lent a certain boyishness to his lean, attractive face. Remembering the way his flirtatious intensity had turned first to puzzlement, then to watchful curiosity, after his friend had intruded upon them.

She looked back up at Brower, thinking ruefully how pointless her concern in the cafeteria seemed now.

The fact that her job had again provoked a colleague's wariness and mistrust toward her didn't matter. The fact that that colleague was the first man in a long time to slip past her usual guard mattered even less.

Because the truth of the situation was, despite their earlier flirtation, she and Nicholas Abella could have nothing in common beyond whatever professional boundaries decreed.

"Kelly?" Brower prompted her.

"I'll need to see those files before I approach Abella."

"Good." He nodded approvingly. "Kelly?"

She paused on her way out.

"You haven't been with my department long, and I know you're taking my word for a lot. Trust me."

Kelly held Brower's gaze. It was too early to know how to respond to that. So she merely nodded and closed the door behind her with a firm click.

"Freshen that up for you, Nick?"

"Thanks, John, I'm fine." Nick contemplated the single bottle of beer he'd been nursing for nearly an hour. For personal reasons he was keeping the number low, as always. But then, it wasn't really the alcohol he sought comfort from.

It was going on seven o'clock and Johnnie's was just beginning to come alive, which translated to ten customers having trickled into the tiny pub, which at capacity held maybe forty. And that was okay with Nick; it kept the atmosphere familiar, low-key. Just like the people in it.

No designer wines or designer puffed pastries stuffed with health-conscious delicacies here. Johnnie's served nothing that couldn't be paired with home fries or comfortably chased with something simple and wet, as icy cold as it was potent.

A jukebox in the corner played a low, steady stream of Top Forty easy listening, which at the moment suited his pensive mood just fine. Gripping the bottle's neck, he lifted the still-cool beer for another swallow and for the second time met the eye of an interested blonde at the end of the bar.

He lowered the bottle, keeping the eye contact

for the moment it took him to consider and reject her interest. It wasn't that she wasn't attractive. And she wasn't flashy, which was a plus. In fact, he got the distinct impression she was fighting her nervousness to flirt with him. He studied her a little closer.

Not a working girl. In his business, you saw them all, including the best. Nothing about this woman's hesitancy was calculated. She was just an ordinary businesswoman winding down after work.

She had the kind of smooth, pale beauty he usually gravitated to, and any other time he'd already have joined her and they'd be having a cozy conversation in a booth. Any other time.

He smiled slightly, offered an almost imperceptible shake of his head, and breathed a sigh tinged with regret when she lowered her own to study her drink with intense concentration. It was strange how that made him feel like a heel.

"Whoa, something's got to be wrong for you to pass up something that lovely."

Recognizing the voice, Nick smiled and turned his head to the freckle-faced black man who had taken the seat on his right. "What're you doing here, Alan? Peggy loosen the leash for good behavior on Thursdays?"

"Eat shit, man." The words were without heat. "I tried you at home." He paused. "Heard you had a talk with brass this afternoon, that it had to do with Cain. Wanna talk?"

Nick studied Alan Parsons, the homicide detective who was also his best friend. How much had he heard?

"Do you?"

Alan looked away from the bar, reached into his shirt pocket, and pulled out a pack of cigarettes. He lit one casually enough, but Nick could tell when he stiffened just the same.

"Now, you know I wouldn't come here to jerk you around, so I'll ignore that dig." The drag Alan took on his cigarette was as slow and measured as his words. "You want me to leave, just say the word."

Nick debated it. He decided maybe he did want the company. "Come on, let's get a booth."

Alan grabbed his beer and followed. When they were settled and he was facing Nick, Alan turned sideways enough to hitch one long leg up on the seat. When Nick was in this kind of mood, Alan never knew if they were in for a long night of talking or drinking, although whenever it was the latter he was the only one who did the real drinking. He decided to get comfortable for whichever way it turned out.

"Word around the precinct is it was a cop who shot Cain. You find out if there's any truth to it?"

"That's the word, buddy. But I don't know that it's true. Neither does Brower."

"But he's not ruling it out?"

Nick looked out over the small space of the pub. Business was picking up. A large number of blue-collars and a respectable number of yuppies were arriving to unwind. Some for the night, others before an evening round of negotiations and power dinners. "No. He's not ruling it out."

Nick took a last sip of his beer and thought of Joey's bracelet. Instantly he rejected its implication while wishing he could make some guess at its relevance. He signaled for another beer. "Brower might have a reason. And that's all I can tell you, Alan."

That was all he was going to tell him, Alan corrected him silently. He, like everybody else, had heard the cop rumor. But he hadn't really given it serious thought until he'd approached McElroy himself only to find the man had suddenly gone stonewall blank. Not just silent as in coy, but blank as in, I-don't-know-what-the-hell-you're-talking-about-and-even-if-I-did-the-last-goddamn-thing-I'd-do-is-talk-about-it.

Now here he was getting the same response from Nick. The difference was, he respected Nick's judgment enough not to push. As far back as the academy, Nick had established a reputation for saying what needed to be said, keeping his mouth shut about things that didn't, and being a pretty fair judge on what constituted the two. For Alan, it had been that sense of fairness, of approaching everything from a plane of balance, that had drawn him to Nick. No doubt the color of his skin had given him a particular sensitivity to the issue. Nevertheless, it was an outlook he and Nick shared.

What had drawn Nick to him was harder to figure, seeing as how they were opposites in more ways than not. Nicholas Abella's dad had been a cop. Alan Parsons's parents had clocked in at an auto plant all their lives. Nick had a sibling he could honestly say he was close to. Alan's only sibling, a sister, was in the state's federal penitentiary. She was serving three to seven for theft.

Nick had a reputation. His success with women was only slightly exaggerated. But Alan was his friend and knew Nick had a real problem linking women and intimate commitment into a joint concept. Alan had his suspicions why, but he wasn't sure. Because there was a point beyond which Nick never opened up, even with him. As for himself, Alan was strictly a one-woman man. The solidity of his marriage and his three children's affection kept him sane in a job whose ugliness tested his sanity every day.

Yet he and Nick were friends. There was no one either could decompress with at the end of a day with more ease, fewer questions. And maybe that last was what kept them close. Even when they disagreed, they understood and respected each other's silence. It frustrated him, but Alan decided to respect Nick's now. He signaled for another drink and in that intuitive way of friends, sensed there was something more.

"So what else is bugging you?"

"I don't know, Dr. Parsons. You tell me."

Alan accepted the sarcasm in Nick's words for what it was, a feint. He thought of the blonde. "How's your love life?"

Nick lifted his eyes to his friend's. "What's your point?"

"Touchy. You could be sitting here sipping beer

with someone a lot cuter than me. So, why aren't you?''

Good question, Nick thought. Had he been even slightly buzzed, he would have dismissed the image of wine-dark hair and brown sloe eyes that kept crowding his memory. "I guess I just prefer my own company tonight."

Alan didn't respond. Nick didn't look like a man who was content. In fact, he looked like a man who was troubled.

"How old are you now, Nick, thirty-four?"

Nick cocked a brow. "As I recall, that was my cake you were shoveling down last week with the rest of the guys."

"Stop bitchin'. I bought you another one, didn't I? Thirty-four. That can be a momentous age for a man. Starts him to thinking about what it'll be like when he hits forty. My mama says it's the first real age when a man starts feeling the weight of things."

"Should I be taking notes?" Nick asked.

"If you need to. She said there are lots of things a man can have and lots of ways he can walk in this world. But God's offered only one thing that lasts."

Nick waited with resignation.

"Aren't you going to ask what?"

"What, and jag your momentum?"

Alan ignored him. "Family. Mama said the love of a good woman, the respect of your children, and the security of a home you can call your own is the only real thing worth striving for in life. All the rest is just for foolin'."

Nick said nothing, knowing what was coming next.

"You ought to get married, man."

"And you ought to give it a rest. Christ, the way you nag, how the hell do we ever find time to talk about anything else?"

"Something to be said about sleeping with a woman you actually want to have a conversation with in the morning."

"They're not dimwits, Alan."

"They're not mother-of-my-children material either. Trouble with you is, women come too easy, so you think you have all the time in the world."

So why couldn't he get one out of his mind who'd told him in plain terms she wasn't impressed? "Meaning?"

Alan got serious. "One day, you're going to find the woman you really give a damn about. And I'll tell you right now, she won't be the one who topples for those dark, Italian looks, or that the-world-can-go-to-hell charm."

"You make me sound like Casanova." This was a topic Nick didn't want to discuss seriously even when his spirits were up.

"Not Casanova," Alan said after a pensive moment. "Just a man who's supremely unaware of the truth behind a great old saying. Pride goeth before the fall, buddy."

"Yeah, well, don't think I don't appreciate your concern. But I'm a big boy, Alan. I've got my life under control, thank you. I know what I need."
What he didn't need was a starry-eyed romantic,

no matter how good a friend, giving him a lecture on life and love.

The truth was, Nick knew all about love. It was a fanciful euphemism for need. And he'd learned early to put that drive in perspective.

Need for accomplishment was the reason you got out of bed in the morning, the reason you busted your ass to do something with your life that wouldn't shame you in the night. Need for self-respect kept you humble, kept you remembering, lest you were tempted, that assholes were a dime a dozen and never mourned for long. Sexual need was purely an aphrodisiac he used as spice to add dimension to a relationship with a woman.

But ultimately, need was something you controlled. Always. As long as you kept that straight, it would never have the chance to control you.

And he'd had enough solemnity for the day. His headache wasn't going to allow him any insight into answers to Joey's puzzle tonight. And all of Alan's talk about hypothetical, unattainable women had inexplicably etched Kelly Wylie's image further into his brain. Which was ridiculous since he didn't even know the woman—correction, the IA investigator. Just for a while, he wanted to relax. So he aimed a bland smile at his friend until Alan cracked and smiled back.

"So, what'll it be, teacher, same song, second verse? Or can we order some food now?" Nick began to chuckle as the other man shook his head.

"Just understand this, Abella. If I didn't know you had some sense beneath that knucklehead exterior, I'd have given up on you long ago." Beyond that, Alan said nothing. He just settled back and finished his beer.

"Here, I've brought you some wine, my dear. I hope you don't mind, I thought you looked thirsty."

"Thank you." Kelly gracefully accepted the fluted glass and studied the pleasant young man her mother had thrown at her the minute she'd walked into the party.

He wasn't bad, really. Attractive, well-spoken, attentive. Almost too attentive. Okay, maybe the word she was avoiding was dull. Predictable. Just like this charity benefit at her mother's home.

She smiled politely at something he'd just said and was glad he didn't seem to expect her to elaborate on whatever point he had been making.

"Paul! There you are. Are you two having a good time?" Kelly turned toward her mother and tried to keep her social smile in place.

That too-airy tone her mother used when she was trying to be subtle didn't hoodwink Kelly one bit. Her mother was maneuvering again. From the affectionate little pat she gave Kelly's chin, one would think she was thirteen rather than thirty, freshly pleated, powdered, and passing inspection at her first cotillion.

"Lovely, Mrs. Wylie. You've done a beautiful job, as usual. I was just telling Kelly about the weekend my brother and I spent up East. Some of the best sailing we've had all summer."

Paul threw an appreciative glance around the room. Kelly read the look and knew he felt perfectly at ease with the party and these beautiful people who were enjoying it. Ten years ago she would have too. But the truth was, for the better part of the evening she'd been striving to mask her impatience with small talk and an expression of polite interest. She feared her fatigue had started to undermine her success.

"Joyce mentioned you two boys had taken off," Ellen Wylie was saying. "Tell me, how is your brother? I hear he's landed a bit of a coup with that Collins acquisition." She laid a delicate hand on the shoulder of a passing waiter and deposited her half-empty glass on a gleaming Sèvres tray.

Paul was making the required response, to which Ellen murmured an absent "Uhm-hmm," Kelly noted. Her mother's attention had already wandered in the direction of a prominent banker, a friend of her deceased husband's. Ellen had been cultivating the man's charitable contributions for years.

"You must persuade Kelly to get away with you and your friends next time," Ellen was saying. "She simply won't listen to me when I tell her she works too hard. You two will excuse me, won't you?" She was already floating away in a trail of blue silk.

If Paul felt at all awkward being abandoned in midstream of what he was saying, he recovered quickly, Kelly observed. But then, he, like her mother, was a social creature, bred to rely on deft flexibility when social occasion demanded it. When he turned his attention back to her, Kelly decided to gently set him straight about the remainder of the evening.

"Paul, I really feel I should apologize for my mother's not so subtly throwing us together. It has to be awkward for you, politely pretending you hadn't noticed?" She took another sip of her drink and felt herself relax a bit when Paul's smile widened to become genuine.

"Oh, I've been consigned to tougher fates. I haven't found her, shall we say, gentle nudging annoying in the least."

"Thank you," she said, accepting the compliment and his penetrating look of interest with quiet hesitancy. He really was a nice man, and he didn't deserve to be led into thinking she was encouraging his interest when all she wanted to do was to get away.

Kelly laid a hand on his arm. "Please don't think I'm rude, but I really would like to get some fresh air. I think I'll step out into the garden for a while."

"Fine. I'll come with you."

"No," Kelly said quickly. "I mean, I'd really like to be alone for a bit."

"Oh," he said after a moment. "All right. I'll be here somewhere when you get back." And Kelly was relieved when his eyes told her he wouldn't push.

Out in the garden, couples were scarce, undoubtedly preferring the air-conditioned comfort inside to the still unseasonably hot August temperatures. Kelly nodded a greeting here and there until she'd made her way down a manicured path to a stone bench at its end. It rested against a low wall of sculptured rock that separated the boundary of the property from the vast reservoir that undulated darkly under the moonlight.

A very romantic setting, Kelly mused. Had she chosen a different path in life, would she be sitting here now, contentedly sharing it with a husband she loved? With a husband who loved her? Would she be savoring the sweet anticipation of returning to her own home in which her children slept?

Once long ago, when existing in a monied, cushioned world had been as natural to her as breathing, she would have answered, unequivocally, *yes*. But that was before she'd taken a real look around and realized the trade-off she had been destined to make.

Had she not overheard that fateful conversation between her father and the father of her fiancé, she would never have paused to question her acceptance of an existence that had already been mapped out for her. She would never have examined the lack of satisfaction to be found in a lifelong round of parties, charity benefits, of becoming a placid society matron, of generally being an adjunct to her husband.

But she had overheard that conversation, and it had changed her life.

It had been here, during her engagement party. She'd been searching for her father to get his last-minute approval on some minute detail about dinner when she overheard voices in the study. Approaching quietly so as not to disturb him and the person he was with, she'd raised her hand to tap on the partially open door when the exchange inside arrested her.

"Since when does love have anything to do with this marriage?" her father said. "He doesn't have to love Kelly, all he has to do is marry her and keep up a damned respectable front after he's done it."

"Yes, Phillip, I know. And the boy is genuinely fond of her. But he told me last night he wants to call it off because he doesn't love her. It's that Marlowe girl. He said despite what I say, despite what you say, he's going to marry her instead."

Stunned at what she was hearing, Kelly had eased the door open a little wider to watch the two inside. The man facing her father was calmly lighting a cigarette. "He also said to tell you the money and the vice presidency you promised him in the company could go hang."

"The hell you say! You tell that snot-nosed little punk he can go hang." Her father had turned angrily from his friend to the sideboard behind him. After he'd poured himself a drink to calm himself, he continued.

"Now you listen to me. You and I both know we're not going to let this merger be jeopardized because your boy's dick is telling him he's in love with somebody else. Kelly's all I've got; Ellen didn't give me any sons to turn the reins over to. And John's the only one of your sons still eligible to marry. This marriage is going to happen.

"So you whip that boy of yours into shape. I don't care how you do it. For God's sake, if it helps, assure him that he *can* have his cake and eat it too. 'Love' outside of marriage is hardly a novel concept. Your boy is going to give me grandchildren and a legacy, our legacy, to carry on.''

"And what about Kelly, Phillip?'' the other man had asked quietly. But Kelly could hear that he had already conceded.

"What about her? If I tell her to be happy, she'll be happy. She does what I tell her to do. Always did, always will. Rest assured, she'll be the best little wife your son could ever hope to have. That is, as long as you convince him he has to be discreet.'' Phillip Wylie finished what was in his glass.

His voice was quite detached when he added, "Kelly's a good girl. She's got spirit and a fire in her I used to think I could groom. Years ago I even started to think it didn't matter that I didn't have a son. But I was wrong. Kelly's soft, too soft to be my successor. The most she can do for me now is to be the mother of the sons who are going to take over our corporation one day.''

Whatever else the two men said faded beneath the weight of Kelly's shock. This couldn't be the father she adored, nearly worshiped, callously disregarding her happiness in the name of cinching some business deal. The hard-voiced stranger in there couldn't be the same man who had cuddled and rocked his baby daughter to sleep when she was sick, who had awakened her on hazy predawn mornings following business trips with hugs and kisses and huge overstuffed toys. Not the man who had still continued to do so with boxes of

candy and flowers when she'd outgrown childhood.

And yet she'd just heard that very man dismiss
her as a business pawn, an obstacle he could push
aside when her needs threatened to conflict with
his own. At that moment something fragile and
innocent died inside Kelly as she wiped away her
tears and backed quietly away from the door.

From that moment on she'd never viewed her
father or the calm, unruffled order of her life in
the same way.

She'd needed to get away to make room for herself to think. Defying her father to break up with
her fiancé had been nothing less than an ordeal.
But strangely, she'd been equipped to deal with
his anger and his subsequent coldness because
she'd already had time to deal with what he really
thought on the subject. And later, her pain was
lessened when she broke the news to the man she
thought she loved and witnessed the guilty relief
he didn't quite manage to hide.

So she'd fled the cocoon in which she'd existed
for twenty years and the parents who had sheltered her in it. Her escape lay in a graduate school
in Chicago. There she'd taken a part-time job, determined to start her independent life by making
herself independent of her parents' money. She'd
also taken her first, uncluttered look at people and
the variations of life around her.

She'd uncovered emotional depths she'd never
fully tapped within herself. And in the process,
she'd discovered a new set of priorities.

Increasingly those priorities had less to do with

repressing the woman within as an expedient way to please others. Increasingly they had more to do with cultivating the rebel within as she took lessons from a multileveled society, blemishes and all, and in the process pleased herself.

In many ways she'd never looked back. But now, ten years later, neither had she fully shaken a quiet disillusionment. In her most private moments she wondered if she was destined to walk through her brave, new life alone.

The truth was, deep down she still wanted the pot of gold at the end of the rainbow. She wanted the vine-covered cottage, the children, that special someone to love. How could all that have seemed so ridiculously attainable a short lifetime ago? A lifetime before she'd discovered that even the most stalwart idols could have feet of clay.

The frightened girl who had run in search of herself all those years ago was a mature woman now, secure in herself and a fulfilling career that gave her purpose. Not long ago she'd even thought she'd found that someone to love. What she'd found instead was that sometimes love alone wasn't enough to make you happy. What she'd found was that along with someone to love, what she needed, perhaps even more, was someone to believe in.

"You're much too beautiful to cloister yourself out here with the oleanders, darling."

Kelly gazed out at the water a moment longer and suppressed a sigh that her moment of solitude had ended. "Hello, Mother." She turned away from the view to face Ellen.

Ellen studied the beautiful, somewhat somber woman before her and wondered for perhaps the thousandth time why she had such trouble understanding her child. She sat down next to her and lifted a hand to gently stroke a wisp of hair from Kelly's brow. "What's wrong?"

Kelly smiled for her mother, wanting to shake her own sudden sadness. "Nothing. I was just taking in this lovely view. Back in Chicago, the beauty here was what I used to remember most."

Ellen said nothing and Kelly fought the urge to drop her eyes from her mother's. Reaching down, she captured both her mother's hands and gave them a light squeeze. They weren't enemies, but neither were they soul mates. How could she begin to explain her restlessness to her mother when she couldn't understand it herself? "Really, Mother. I'm fine."

"At the risk of sounding trite, this is your mother you're talking to, dear."

Kelly sought a topic that was neutral, safe. "I've been given the Cain case." Her words immediately conjured the image of a tall, angry, and much too attractive homicide detective. Immediately she knew she hadn't latched on to a safe topic after all. Or a subject her mother would objectively discuss.

Kelly caught the flash of distaste her mother quickly tried to conceal. Her mother's attitude toward what she did for a living would never cease to be a bone of contention between them. But tonight Kelly didn't have the energy to launch into that same old disagreement. Unfortunately, her mother wasn't so disinclined.

Ellen drew her hands away from her daughter's. "I thought when you moved back here, after —all that trouble—in Chicago, you'd give up that foolishness. Working with riffraff is not what you were raised for. It's not where you belong."

Kelly suppressed a wave of impatience and reminded herself that her mother's snobbery was not her fault. She simply viewed the world from the structured, privileged parameters within which she'd been raised. Her prejudices toward those not ensconced within its confines were the result of unenlightenment, not malice.

"We had this discussion years ago, Mother. I've made my life what I want it to be. I wish you would just accept that."

Impatient herself now, Ellen rose to stand beside the bench. She rested her hands on the wall, as if she were trying to carefully construct what she was going to say. When she turned around and folded her hands behind her, Kelly was calmly waiting.

"Do you think my life is so awful?" Ellen asked quietly.

"Of course not, Mom."

"Do you think these people here are so awful?"

"No."

"Then why did you leave?" Ellen's voice was filled with gentle bewilderment. "If only you'd married John, you could have had a family of your own by now. You could have been happy, darling."

Kelly sighed with an old frustration. She'd never told her mother the truth about John. "I am happy, Mom. I've been telling you that for years. Why do you refuse to believe me?"

Ellen's expression turned solemn, and Kelly knew she was thinking about her husband. The character of Phillip Wylie was one point upon which they shared a mutual, unclouded understanding. "You're my daughter, and I love you," Ellen said. "And I recognize sadness when I see it, Kelly. I know my life hasn't been perfect, but it's all I know. It's all I've had to offer. If you'll let it, it can give you so much."

Kelly took her mother's hands once more, feeling guilty for spurring that justification for who she was. Kelly didn't want her to justify anything; she never had. She just wanted Ellen to realize that way of living, of thinking, wasn't enough for her. Inner contentment, if she were ever to find it, would come from a different direction. Perhaps her mother could never believe that, but at least Kelly could reassure her of the one thing she could believe.

"I love you too, Mom. No matter what, that's always been true. All right?"

Ellen studied her daughter a little longer, then her brow smoothed and she smiled. She squeezed Kelly's hands in return. "All right."

"Come on, then," Kelly said. She stood and wrapped her arm around her mother's shoulders. "Let's go inside."

* * *

Joey's fingers had just touched the box when he heard the click of the front door's lock. The box was too far back on the closet shelf for him to grab it cleanly. Impatiently he turned away and searched for a place to hide. He found it behind the kitchen door, which stood slightly ajar.

It wasn't much as cover, but combined with his gun it was adequate to buy him time to stall his intruder.

He watched as a patrolman stepped inside his apartment and carefully shut the door behind him. Joey kept his breath slow and even as the man made a methodical search of the apartment. It soon became apparent he wasn't making the search Joey expected. He wasn't looking for something, he was looking for someone, or rather, signs of recent inhabitation. Joey could tell by the way the officer inspected the butts in the ashtray, checked the warmth of the television set with his hand, scanned the room for anything out of place, anything that might have been hastily abandoned.

Why wasn't he looking for something more tangible? Joey wondered uneasily. When the obvious solution struck him, a cold sensation spread through his stomach. But the officer's presence effectively pinned him where he was, unable to check it out.

Joey watched the policeman check the living room, dining room, back bedroom, and even the bathroom before he returned to the living room. Joey knew there was nothing to alert the man to his presence, because he had watched the apartment all last night and again this morning before

chancing an entry after the official police search
had ended an hour ago.

The officer stood indecisively in the middle of
the living room. He gazed around once more until
his eyes rested on the kitchen doorway. Slowly he
started to approach, and Joey gripped his gun
tighter. The last thing he wanted to do was to
complicate things, but this was life and death and
he had no choice.

A half dozen more steps and the officer would
be at the kitchen door. Joey tensed, ready for
the confrontation, when a sudden pounding on
the front door made him and the officer jump. The
startled patrolman whirled around to face the
door.

"Joey? Hey, Joey!" More pounding. "You in
there?"

God bless nosy landladies, Joey thought, throwing a grateful look above. He'd never had much
use for Mrs. Thompson's inordinate interest in her
tenants' comings and goings, but right now he
could have kissed her for her timing.

The patrolman shoved his gun back into his holster from where he had half drawn it and strode
toward the door with obvious irritation. His effort
to rein it in before he pulled the door open was
just as apparent.

"Hel—hey, where's Joey? You one of those police who was here earlier?" Joey could hear the
suspicion lacing her voice, that and an unholy
spark of glee. "I thought you all were a group of
his buddies at the time, but . . . is he in some
kind of trouble or something?"

"No, ma'am." The officer was forced to step aside as the old woman pushed her way in. Joey couldn't help being amused by the annoyance that flashed across the officer's face before he dredged up a smile. Mrs. Thompson tended to have that effect on people. "Some of the fellas and I are just trying to pull a birthday gag on him. We planted a little surprise for him in his bedroom." He followed his explanation with a suggestive wink.

The landlady smiled slowly at the officer. His suggestiveness sidetracked her and brightened the gleam in her eye. "You mean"—she lowered her voice to a whisper—"something naughty?"

"Well, ma'am, I guess you might say so, yeah."

"What?" she asked excitedly before quickly retrenching. "I mean, it isn't anything too bad, I hope." She backed up her statement with a stern look of disapproval that would have fooled anybody except her tenants, who knew her. "I don't go along with none of those depraved, kinky things they're doing nowadays, even if you all are policemen."

"Oh, no, ma'am." He placed a hand on her shoulder and turned her to gently usher her toward the door. "We wouldn't do anything like that, it's just a little joke. Nothing Joey can't tell you all about himself." His hand was on the knob and the old woman was standing on the threshold.

"Well," she said reluctantly, "if you say so." She paused a minute, then made to move back inside. "Maybe I'd better have a look myself."

"That's not necessary." Joey detected the strain

in the officer's patience and saw him touch the landlady's arm to hold her back. "I mean, well, you know how it is, boys will be boys. And frankly, ma'am, I just don't want you to be embarrassed."

She was still peering past him when for some reason Joey couldn't figure, she uncharacteristically relented. "Well . . . when's Joey coming back?"

"Uh, probably he won't be able to get away until later this afternoon. Things are pretty hectic. That's why I came over to make sure everything was in place before the other boys brought him home. Now if you don't mind, ma'am, I'll just finish and be gone. You have a nice day now." He started to close the door. Mrs. Thompson stopped him.

"You can do that later. I want you to come help me get my window unstuck." She grabbed his arm and started pulling him out into the hall.

"What!" Joey heard the officer's utter disbelief. He laughed softly. *Way to go, Thompson,* he exclaimed silently at the latest of his landlady's harebrained requests. The woman seemed to think the status of police officers tagged them as everything from public servants to handymen. He'd always thought her assumption a blessed annoyance until now. Again, he could have kissed her.

The last thing he heard her mutter was something about the officer's not wanting a helpless old lady to suffocate in 100-degree weather because of a stupid old window. Joey didn't waste time.

He left his hiding place and was back at the closet in a flash. This time when he located the box, he pulled it forward and tipped it to lift the lid. *Shit*. They'd beaten him to it. The tapes were gone.

He replaced the lid and shoved the empty box back to its space. With those tapes, they'd taken his only alibi, the only evidence he possessed to clear himself of the murder. Without those tapes he was a dead man in more ways than one. The police would be after him for obvious reasons, and those who were his enemies, as he had just seen, were already hunting him.

The longer he stayed in town, the quicker he was dead. He had to get out. But how? He closed the closet door and headed toward his bedroom. His fire escape led to an alley. It would be easier to scan the space between the buildings for a trap than the busy street from the front entrance. Joey made the scan. All clear.

There was no one he could trust, no one he could turn to. Not even Nick, not yet. Until he could figure a plan, Joey needed to protect Nick with his silence. But he needed help now. Who could he . . . a brief smile touched his lips. Of course.

A plan was already half formed as Joey used the escape and ran for his life.

3

Saturday. It was a little after nine and an early-morning sun was at Kelly's back as she cruised into Nicholas Abella's neighborhood. It surprised her.

She'd expected him to live somewhere more urban, functional. Instead a cloudless blue sky lay smoothly over the spacious lawns and shrubs of the houses surrounding her. Here and there joggers paused to wave to older residents watering their flowers or just taking in the clear August air.

Kelly had done some homework, and as she turned her car west on Kimmler Boulevard en route to the subject of her study, she mused again on what she'd learned. That, at least, jibed with her impression of him.

Shortly into his career, he'd earned the distinction of being a "cop's cop." A couple of citations for bravery accompanied a solid record of impressive collars over the past ten years. A majority of those arrests had resulted from following thorough, though somewhat loose, police procedure. When she'd read that, she'd recalled his insolence in Brower's office and had taken it in stride.

In fact, she would have been surprised if any description less than unorthodox had attached itself to the volatile detective's record. She hadn't even needed to read the rest of that record to know that he worked harder and put in longer hours than most of his fellow officers. Nor had she needed to talk to his support staff and fellow cops to know that he was well liked, easily accepted, and respected. Or that for all of that, he was still recognized as an occasional loner.

The quintessential bad-boy lone wolf was Nicholas Abella, it seemed. She knew his type well. In fact, firsthand experience had given her a better understanding than she would have liked.

Nicholas Abella's breed of officer was the sort you wanted backing you up in a gunfight or a dark alley, the sort who'd tolerate a partner because he was smart enough to appreciate the necessity. But even while he understood, an inner defiance would have him wishing like hell he didn't have a partner slowing him down.

Her dilemma was plain. To get anywhere in a hurry with this investigation, she had to gain some insight into Joey Abella's mind. And the most logical way to gain it was with the cooperation of Joey's defensive brother, the good detective Abella. The question was, how was she going to win Nick's trust?

If she'd been a fellow homicide detective, the situation would be infinitely easier. Not his resentment of the situation, but his acceptance of her.

She'd accepted the resentment as part of her job description when she'd taken the promotion

to Internal Affairs. But she couldn't remember a
time when another officer's scorn had stung her
so.

Her initial attraction to any man had never
been so swift and strong. Not even to Jeff. And
she'd married him.

Suddenly she damned this assignment, damned
the disruption to her peace of mind since meeting
Nicholas Abella. Because instinctively she knew
that the hardest thing she would ever have to do
would be to regard Nick not as an attractive man
she would like to get to know but as the adversary
whose trust she'd have to fight to win to get a
professional job done.

So she'd better start now, she thought, turning
a corner with an impatient sigh. It was useless to
indulge in speculative regrets. Besides, she'd had
enough recent upheavals in her life without add-
ing the pros and cons of a romantic entanglement.
Especially with a headstrong cop. Any headstrong
cop.

She'd had that kind of relationship once. It had
been enough to last her a lifetime.

So she directed her thoughts back to the issue at
hand, specifically, trying to figure out how to win
the detective's trust. The problem was, they were
both professionals and this case was too hot for
temperamental indulgence. How tough it would
be to get the detective to concede that point remained to be seen.

The colonial-style apartment complex she
sought slid into view from behind a wide green
privacy hedge. His building was at the north end

of the property. Locating it easily, she glided into an empty space along the drive and headed for Nick's second-floor apartment.

The low, unmistakable sounds of either a radio or a stereo bled faintly through the trim blue-and-white oak door of his apartment. Kelly knocked, then ran a straightening hand down the cream linen of her skirt just as Nick opened up.

Short denim cutoffs accentuated the long symmetry of bare, hair-dusted legs and an expanse of taut, tanned flesh. A faded-out black T-shirt was draped loosely from his wide shoulders. The sleeves and bottom had been sheared off so that now the much-washed fabric flirted with the damp skin of his midriff. Her gaze went past him to the pair of weights lying on the living room carpet.

"Good morning," she offered with an easy smile. She ignored the faint fluttering in her stomach and remembered her resolutions when those intense, disturbing amber eyes of his locked with hers as he lifted a wet can of cola to his lips. He took a long swig, and she watched him drink his fill, lower the can, then continue to clutch it as he leaned his shoulder against the doorway. His message was obvious. She wasn't getting in.

"I thought I made myself clear the other day. Nothing you have to say interests me, lady."

"Believe me, Detective, I know how you feel. If I could just—"

"Lady, you can't have the slightest notion of how I feel. Don't stand there insulting me, pretending you do when you're here to do a job. Cut to the chase. I'm in no mood to indulge you." She looked so cool, so composed, so damned beautiful . . . and his brother's neck was on the line.

Kelly hesitated until she saw the door actually closing in her face. "Abella, if you're so sure your brother is innocent, I can't believe you'd be bull-headed enough to throw away the chance to prove it!" She thought he was going to shut it in her face anyway. Instead, he surprised her by hesitating, then backing away to let her inside.

Light from the French windows, which stood open to admit the mild morning breeze, domi-nated the living room. And while the neutral-tone decor looked neat and lived in, the apartment es-sentially had the look and feel of a bachelor's place. Again she thought of her expectations and the homey reality that was his neighborhood. She was intrigued with how his home embodied a strange symbiosis of the two.

Kelly dropped her purse on the sofa and sat down while Nick went to his CD player to shut it off. Then he surprised her again.

"I owe you an apology. The things I said to you in Brower's office were inexcusable, unprofes-sional as hell." He shrugged. "Sometimes I let my temper get the better of me."

Kelly studied him, trying to gauge his sincerity. He met her scrutiny unblinkingly.

A temper, maybe, she thought. But she very much doubted this man often let anything, least of all a loss of control, get the better of him. "Apol-ogy accepted."

Nick inclined his head and stayed propped

against the breakfast bar, waiting for her to say her piece. With an urgency he refused to examine, he wanted her gone.

It seemed his apology was all that was going to be forthcoming, Kelly realized. Getting anything else out of him was going to be like pulling teeth.

But dammit, she didn't want to pull teeth. She wanted Nick's cooperation. She had to make him understand she wasn't the bad guy he thought she was.

"Nick, I'm not your enemy. I just want to talk."

"Fine. Great weather we're having, isn't it?"

She sighed. "You're determined to make this hard, aren't you?"

"It's already hard, sweetheart. What makes it harder is this let's-be-friends routine you're trying to snow me with. What's the plan? You exhibit the proper amount of sympathy for my being caught between the proverbial rock and hard place until I'm pliant enough to be pumped for what you think is the relevant lowdown on my brother?"

"That's not—"

"Never forgetting, all the while, to reassure me that investigating Joey pains you every bit as much as it pains me, but that you'll bend over backward to see Joey's treated fairly. Because, after all, you're a hell of a lot more compassionate than just the average IA officer doing her damndest to nail another cop." He wanted her out.

She knew what he wanted and she wasn't moving. If she couldn't make him listen now, she never would.

"Contrary to what you think, Detective, you don't know everything. You've told me off very nicely. So maybe now you can manage to take a breath, control your tantrum, and sit down to hear what I have to say?"

Pure obstinance held him still. That and irritation at her damned conciliatory attitude. He didn't want to be reasonable. He wanted to fight.

So when she leaned back against the cushions and crossed her elegant legs as if she had all the time in the world, he lingered against the bar. He took satisfaction from the slight furrow that creased her brow. She reminded him of a watchful kitten, one moment compliant, the next poising to strike.

"Sit down," Kelly said. She refused to let him intimidate her.

Her words were low, challenging. Nick couldn't recall ever having been issued a challenge so audaciously in his own home. He tempered a sudden urge to smile and leisurely finished his cola before doing as she asked.

When he was seated on the love seat opposite her, his arms folded across his chest, Kelly paused, wondering how to begin. His stir of impatience told her. With the unvarnished truth. She'd already learned that nothing less would do with this man.

"Three years ago, I was married. A year ago, my husband died. He was a cop."

Nick's brow arched. Whatever he had been expecting to hear, it hadn't been that.

"I don't have to tell you that every cop who

works the streets lives with the knowledge that on any given day he or she might not make it home alive," Kelly said. "Well, as a cop and as the wife of a cop, I found out fast that living with that apprehension was two times as bad. But I handled it until one night, a week after our first anniversary, Jeff was shot.

"No, he wasn't killed," she said, anticipating Nick's question, "but he was seriously hurt. The irony was, the shooting wasn't the worst. That came after the follow-up investigation revealed Jeff and his partners had been set up."

Surprised again, Nick settled back, feeling some of his tension fade in the wake of genuine interest in what she was saying.

Kelly told him how one of the officers working the sting with Jeff and a team of vice officers had sold them out. She told him how Jeff and the others hadn't been intended to make it through the bust alive, how Jeff was the last of the officers left in the house when everything went wrong.

"By the time he and the others realized what was happening, one of Jeff's men forced his way back inside the house in time to see Jeff take three bullets in the chest."

And Jeff hadn't been the only victim, Nick realized, watching her. Jeff had been the one shot, but the haunted memories shadowing Kelly's eyes told him plainly she had been just as badly wounded.

Her candidness also forced him to admit something else. He'd been a fool.

When she'd walked through his door, he'd

wanted her to be the hard-bitten, insensitive automaton cop just going through the motions. He'd wanted to neutralize too-vivid memories of the woman whose laughter had teased something spontaneous from him, touched vulnerable emotions he'd pushed to the recesses of his heart eons ago. He'd wanted to dismiss the melancholy he'd been helpless to conceal that night from Alan, wanted to convince himself it lay rooted in uncertainty about Joey rather than in some hazy foreboding about her.

Kelly had fallen silent. She sat bathed serenely in the early-morning light, and Nick used the break to really study the details of her appearance.

From her white summer suit to her clear, unblemished skin, to the soft confinement of hair at her nape, she projected an image every inch the professional. And yet shock, anger, and grief were all etched there in her eyes. Only those subtle shadows hinted she was closer to the woman than to the girl a first glance suggested. And perhaps more vulnerable.

"What happened after the shooting?" Nick prompted her quietly.

"Jeff wasn't the same. Afterward he was remote, a little wild, cruel. No one close to him was immune. He deteriorated and I watched. And the fact that I couldn't stop it made me sick." She raised a slender hand to her forehead. "It also made me angry."

Nick watched her fingers knead at lines of tension, and something started to uncoil inside him.

Impulsively he touched her shoulder. His hand stayed when she looked up, startled. "Sit tight," he murmured.

When he returned with a cup of coffee, he pushed it gently into her hands and sat back down. This time he followed an impulse and closed the distance between them.

"Thanks. I—I guess this isn't going to be as easy as I thought."

"Take your time. I'm through snapping for the morning." He smiled, allowing, perhaps foolishly, his softening toward her to linger.

Kelly smiled back. She was grateful for more than his sensitivity and surprised by the strange measure of comfort she took from his expression of it.

"Jeff buried himself deeper in his work," she continued. "I couldn't. At least not in the work I was doing. When I looked at him, remembering the man he used to be, seeing the man he had become, I wanted to do something more. I wanted to prevent other casualties if I could. So I chose Internal Affairs."

"And?"

How had he lulled her into becoming so personal? No, that wasn't accurate. When had she made the unconscious decision to trust this man with the things she was telling him?

What she had intended to be a modulated expression of empathy was fast becoming a catharsis she'd never had. Her head was telling her that allowing this man to be her sounding board was perhaps the most foolhardy thing in the world.

But her intuition and an inexplicable certainty that he had set aside his hostility to give her a fair hearing were assuring her of quite the opposite. She answered his question.

"Jeff started doing drugs."

Jesus, Nick thought.

"The tragedy was, I didn't really face it for a long time, not until it became impossible to shrug off his mood swings. When I confronted him, he of course promised he'd get help. And I guess I felt I owed it to our marriage to give him the chance to try."

"But that wasn't the end of it," Nick guessed.

"No. Although he did go into treatment and slowly beat his addiction. After that, I tried to convince myself things could change—that we could rekindle our feelings toward each other." But she'd been fooling herself.

Dispassionately, Kelly told Nick about Jeff's succession of gifts, each more expensive than the last, until even an offhand attribution to a raise couldn't negate her suspicions. Her questions had invited his heated accusations of ingratitude and mistrust.

"I knew in my heart he was dealing," Kelly told Nick.

Kelly Wylie. *Of course*, Nick thought. Why hadn't he made the connection earlier? He remembered now how the scandal had briefly made national news. To be honest, his opinion of Kelly Wylie's conduct had pretty much coincided with the public's condemnation. But he was acutely aware that he wasn't listening to sound bites now.

He wasn't hearing a newscaster's simplified version of the facts. The woman sitting beside him was flesh and blood and all too human in her fallibilities. But there was still something he wanted to understand.

"Why didn't you confide in a superior? Jeff had a good record. There had to be avenues of help still there for him."

"I've repeatedly analyzed why I didn't," Kelly finally said. The answer she had found was no easier to accept now than it had been then. "In the beginning, I guess it was because I refused to accept that Jeff had betrayed me, had betrayed everyone. Then, by the time I could face that truth, I was ashamed. Ashamed that I had let my emotions blind me to his duplicity, and ashamed that in so doing I had pushed my values and my oath as a sworn officer of the law to a mental back burner.

"Somewhere in there, I justified my silence with the rationalization that I'd confront him before the situation was beyond salvaging. I'd persuade him to get help for what was driving him."

"Obviously that didn't happen."

"No," she said simply. "We fought over something. To this day I can't remember what. The point is, he walked. He didn't come home for three days. On the fourth, his sergeant woke me at four in the morning. Jeff had overdosed in some motel room."

When Nick touched her hand this time, it was ice-cold. But again, she didn't withdraw.

"The manager had gotten suspicious when Jeff's lights stayed on all night."

"Suicide."

"Yes. But that wasn't the end. A postinvestigation flushed out Jeff's supplier and he opened up the proverbial can of worms. For more than a year, Jeff had been stealing confiscated drug money from the department. Naturally, suspicion made its way back to me. Didn't I know he was stealing? How could a dishonest vice cop dupe his own wife? What kind of internal affairs investigator did that make me?

"No real case for collusion could be made against me. Being a slovenly cop was about the only charge that could stick, but it was enough. Afterward my record was ignored, my reputation and credibility destroyed. I stuck it out for more than a year, but I was washed up in Chicago and I knew it."

For a long while Nick sat watching her, his fingers linked with hers. Leveling condemnation would be so easy. But he'd seen too much during his years on the force not to know that variations of her tragedy happened all the time. What was impressing him more was that despite everything she sat here in no way trying to excuse herself.

The woman had guts, and that was hard not to admire. How many people could he name who had the courage to be as candid about their own failings?

But even so, he still felt at odds because he knew what she wanted him to think, wanted him to say. He gently laid her hand aside and got up to pace.

"I know what it had to cost you to tell me all this, and I see what you're trying to do. I'd be a fool not to see the parallel you're drawing between yourself and Jeff and me and Joey. But, Kelly, I just can't believe our situations are the same."

"Don't you see, Nick, that's the trap." Kelly leaned forward, imploring him to understand. "Blind faith. Blinder loyalty. As cops, we can't afford to get so involved that we lose sight of what's the truth and what's wishful thinking."

"All the more reason for a man to follow what's in his heart, what he knows is true," he said. "And I know that Joey's innocence is true. His involvement is a fact I obviously can't deny. But he's no murderer, Kelly. And if no one else is willing to believe that, I have to."

Kelly sat back. She liked his sense of loyalty. But she'd learned long ago the wisdom of tempering her trust in blind faith. "If you're still determined to believe that, to brook no room for discussion, then we're at an impasse."

Nick returned to the sofa. He leaned his back against the armrest and steepled his hands beneath his chin. "Maybe we don't have to be," he said at length.

"I don't see how it can be avoided. You're absolutely certain of your brother's innocence. I'm absolutely certain of the possibility of his guilt."

"And the most expedient key that breaks the deadlock is Joey."

"Precisely," Kelly answered.

For a minute, maybe two, Nick looked thoughtfully out the window. The faint sound of a child's laughter drifted in on the morning breeze. A dog barked. Heavy seconds ticked by. Presently he spoke. "I'll help you track him."

They were the words she wanted to hear, but Kelly didn't trust the ease of Nick's concession.

"On one condition," he added.

Ah, Kelly thought. "What?"

"That you don't turn him in until I've had time to talk to him."

"Nick—"

"Come on," he said aggressively. "What do you expect me to do? Run off with him? How far could we get? I'm not proposing you help me obstruct justice. I'm just asking for a delay before due process is served. I've got a hunch—"

"No."

"Kelly, listen to me. My guess is, Joey's scared and he's running. From what, I can't guess. But for him to dodge the authorities, it must be something powerful. Let me have a shot at getting what it is out of him before you turn him in."

"I can't, Nick."

"You won't."

"All right, I won't."

"Listen, you've read Joey's record. Did it suggest to you anything that would cause him to turn? It's got to be more complicated than anything circumstantial evidence can suggest. Can you think of a better person to get it out of him than me?"

"Perhaps not. But these circumstances are just too hot to play fast and loose with the rules." Her look was pointed.

Nick had to smile. "Right. Okay, I can appreciate that. I'm just asking you to cut a fellow officer some slack, to concede a benefit of the doubt."

Kelly remained silent.

Nick dropped his head in frustration at Kelly's refusal to yield, then he tried again. She'd leveled with him; it was time for him to level with her.

"I wanted to hate you when you walked through that door. The last thing I wanted to do was to help you or anyone else gunning for my brother.

"So I shot off my mouth and—oh, hell, what I'm trying to say is, if you can bend a little to help me, maybe the least I can do is bend a little to help you. But you're still IA, and I'll tell you, the extent of my trust has limits."

"Thanks for that honesty. It makes it easier for me to trust you."

Nick nodded thoughtfully. "Good. Then you can also trust this. This case goes beyond my brother. My gut tells me something deeper is going on here." What happened next was up to her.

The ball was in her court. Kelly wondered if she could afford to take the chance on his being right. It was her turn to get up and pace.

She had read Joey's record. And while it didn't rival his brother's, it was exemplary. But her specialty was looking beyond the exemplary to the aberration, to the pieces that didn't fit. And Nick was right in one respect. It didn't fit that a twenty-nine-year-old cop, the son and brother of cops, would inexplicably throw his career away. Was there a hidden explanation?

Nick could be right. And so could Brower, for that matter. He had suggested that Nick could be key to this case. How much of that suggestion had been instinct and how much had been speculation? Perhaps acceding to Nick's request would buy her the time to find out.

But there was more, if she were honest with herself. She thought of the concern he'd shown as she'd talked, the apology for his bigotry against her just now. The plain truth was, she didn't want to be Nicholas Abella's adversary. And maybe she had misjudged his motives. But did that mean she could really trust him? He was waiting for her answer.

"All right," she said. "I'll give you first shot. But after that, he's mine, Nick."

"That's all I'm asking."

Kelly reached for her purse. "So, you have any fresh ideas where he could be?"

"As a matter of fact, I might. I want to go down to Hell's Acre myself."

"Why? Our men have already hit that area pretty thoroughly."

"What they know of it. I know some things they don't."

"I see," Kelly said slowly. "Well, just know that whatever you do, I'll be sticking to you like glue. And that is not negotiable, Sergeant."

"Somehow I didn't expect it would be, Sergeant."

Kelly's smile was faint. "Fine, then. Let's make that trip later this evening. I've got some things at the station I have to take care of."

"Sure," Nick said after a moment. He wasn't at all certain how easy it was going to be to swallow this collaboration.

Kelly walked back over to where he sat. She offered her hand and Nick gripped it. His fingers were cool and firm. Kelly didn't let go immediately. An awful lot had been exchanged between them this morning. And she wasn't naïve enough to believe it had all been within the realm of business. "Don't play with me, Abella. That's a warning."

Nick weighed the caution for its full worth. "Ditto. I guess for better or worse, we're in this together now."

Kelly nodded slowly. "For better or worse." She released his hand and walked to the front door. "Oh, and by the way—" She kept her back to him, her hand on the knob.

"Yeah?"

"Thanks. For the coffee."

Nick smiled, understanding completely. "You're welcome. For the coffee."

Later that evening as the crimson rays of the dying sun flooded the sky, they sped west of downtown along Marrington Street. Nick squinted against the glare, feeling along the dashboard for his shades. The heat still hovered around 80 degrees, but with Kelly's permission he flicked off the air and they cranked down the windows. It was good feeling the wind rush against his face.

The police search of Joey's place had yielded nothing except for the fact that Joey had indeed bolted. Some clothes were gone along with the emergency cash Nick knew he kept stashed away. He'd left no clues, no trail, nothing for anyone to follow, which was why Nick needed leads from another source.

And he had a good idea who that source might be.

4

Darkness had fallen by the time they drove into the Acre a short time later. Nick slowed his car to a crawl. The seaminess of this four-block radius and of the people who populated it never ceased to fascinate him. More to the point, he was always amazed at how shabbily some people chose to live.

During the last thirty-five years a young subculture of gang members, prostitutes, and drug dealers had been trying to squeeze the old-timers out. A lot of the old ones who stayed could have found a more peaceful existence in some nice retirement community. But stubbornness kept them rooted.

The same gritty determination that had led them to create a thriving billboard representation for all that was baseball and apple pie during his father's time had them refusing to give up their homes a generation later. Suburban flight had long ago rendered inner-city living in this area passé. And though gang skirmishes and signature graffiti intimidated, it would never move them. So a stalemate of animosity existed between the aging neighborhood regulars and the opportunistic young punks they despised.

Kelly noted the easy way Nick maneuvered the streets and the casual way he acknowledged people here and there. She noticed the way their eyes occasionally left him to check her out. "You do come down a here lot, don't you?"

"Enough," he said noncommittally. "In my line, it's fertile ground." He thought of the questions surrounding his brother, the doubts they cast over his family's name, and wondered if her comment entailed more than an offhand observation. "Or was that the point?"

Kelly cast a glance his way. His eyes were firmly on the road, but he'd been prickly ever since they left the station. "Easy, Detective. I wasn't making a snide insinuation." Nick offered a thoroughly unapproachable "hmm," so Kelly turned from him to study the night life around her.

Dereliction and decay bracketed the vagrants and working girls who sporadically dotted the streets. Dead-eyed teenagers loitering casually on street corners watched her and Nick pass before returning to the desultory conversations that engaged them.

Commercial buildings that weren't boarded up were falling down. The weathered-brick tenements Kelly assumed were apartments looked ready to. The only establishments that seemed to be thriving were a sea of dingy convenience stores, neon taverns, and hole-in-the-wall bars that dotted the heart of the area. And over everything hung a dim, dank metallic pall from the smoke-spitting industrial complex flanking the neighborhood.

Against the deepening shadows of evening, the bar Nick sought slid into view on the right. Pulling neatly into its lot, he killed the engine and glanced over at Kelly. She was studying two rough-looking characters who leaned against the entrance.

"Stay close," Nick told her as they started to get out of the car. "This shouldn't take long."

"Good. This is depressing."

"What, you mean this isn't how you cushy IA types visualize the glamour of the streets?"

"Go to hell, Abella."

Nick answered with a slow grin and surreptitiously took another look at what she was wearing. She was on the ball, he'd give her that. No unimaginative paper pusher would have dressed so effectively for a street meet.

She wore leather to complement his denim. The thigh-length leather mini and black heels she wore hugged her as effortlessly as the air of bored cockiness she affected as she walked beside him.

The white chiffon overblouse knotted at her waist was just thin enough, just provocative enough to highlight the black leather vest that rested beneath it. The display of skin it revealed wasn't overabundant, but it was tantalizingly adequate. She'd done something with her hair, too, so that it looked as suggestive and untamed as the shadow that deepened her eyes and the color that glossed her lips. No one inside the bar would look at her twice. Maybe.

Nick gave the two at the door another assessment and took Kelly's hand firmly in his.

"Hey, man," the taller one said as Nick reached out to push open the door. The smell of beer that floated from the bar mingled with the earthier odor clinging to the man. A greasy shag of long blond hair touched the shoulders of the "Lords" T-shirt stretched across his heavy chest. His dark-haired friend, who stood with his hands buried in the pockets of a thin denim jacket, moved a little more into the light from the open door.

"Want some action?"

Nick dropped his hand and turned with Kelly to face the blond. His face was as new to them as theirs were to him. This was their turf; he'd yield to their rules.

"What you got?" Nick rested against the door, crossing one booted ankle over the other. With one smooth tug he brought Kelly close against him. She didn't resist, but the tenseness of her body let him know she was just keeping up appearances. Not for a moment did he assume she was really relying on his protection.

All the same, he couldn't ignore the way the curve of her body fit perfectly against his side. No degree of enlightenment could stop the primal awareness that he was a man and she was a woman and that some things were basic. She had his protection whether she wanted it or not.

The blond reached around to a hip pocket and pulled back a fist he opened at his waist. "Best blow in town, man." His eyes were hard and confident as he watched Nick.

Nick looked down at the square of cellophane, the white powder inside, then back up to the dealer. "How much?" He was struck suddenly by how young the punks were. Neither could be more than twenty or so. What a waste.

The punk named his price and Nick hesitated for a moment, pretending to think it over. Chances were that in the future this kid could clue him in to a whole lot more than how to buy an ounce of instant joy. No need to scare him or his friend off entirely. From the looks of them, the exchange of a little information for cold, hard cash probably wouldn't work any hardship.

"Let's take it, honey." Kelly turned in Nick's arms until every sultry line of her lay pressed flush against him. "You *promised* you'd be good to me tonight."

The cop in Nick applauded her performance, but she'd taken him off guard. For a split second he saw only the woman she portrayed, a sultry kitten, and he smoldered. Then he met her eye and knew he'd been had. The struggle not to laugh was precarious for a second before he remembered the lowlifes were waiting. He turned his attention back to them and ignored Kelly with an ease calculated to maintain their respect.

"Not bad, but I know somebody else who can do better." He turned to push open the door. The blond spoke up.

"What do you want, man? What you looking for?"

Nick and Kelly turned again to face the two. The expressions that had been so accommodating a moment ago were tense now with suspicion and distrust.

"Earl," Nick said. "Is he here?"

"Earl, huh?" the dark one said. Nick didn't miss the reevaluation they both gave him as their eyes drifted over him, over to the sleek lines of his Mazda, then back.

"You seen him?" Nick asked again. With a smooth, unhurried movement, he slid one hand down the front pocket of his jeans. His other arm rested easily around Kelly's waist.

"Yeah, we seen him. But he ain't talking to nobody. The old man's been outranked."

Suddenly the blond was beside him and the dark one was moving in. Before they could take their next breaths, Nick had Kelly pushed behind him and a switchblade out and snapped open. His tone was as glacial as his eyes. "Get the hell out of here!"

The surprised looks on the punks' faces would have been amusing had the situation not been so charged. They glanced uncertainly at each other, then backed off, disappearing around the back of the building. Nick slid his weapon back inside the pocket of his jeans. As he did, he turned in time to see Kelly slip a small semiautomatic pistol back into her waistband beneath her blouse.

The punks' precipitous flight made sudden sense, he thought ruefully. He draped an arm easily across her shoulders just before they walked inside. "You know, Slick . . ." he began.

"Yes?"

He looked down into her wide, guileless eyes

and felt something hot and vibrant squeeze his gut. "I've got a feeling about you."

Kelly slanted a warmly amused look up at him. She was appreciating how well he handled himself. "You know, Abella, it's mutual." They both chuckled softly and walked inside.

He was prepared for it, so his eyes adjusted quickly to the perpetual gloom of the interior. Not that there was much to see. A bar, plain and massive, dominated the tavern. No pretensions here. And no one was looking, not beyond his bottle of beer or his whiskey.

Chipped brown paint lined four bare walls that formed a square already filled nearly to capacity. A popular rap, loud and distorted, was pounding cheerlessly over the half dozen or so men and women hunched along the bar. Maybe twice that number had moved out to the tiny tables scattered around the floor. Nick could tell by the steady rise and fall of a glass here, an unbroken huddle of conversation there, that these regulars were deaf to anything except the deal, the lie, the hustle of the moment.

He had learned long ago that this dive occasionally turned up an excellent source of information. The source he wanted was presently drinking alone at a table wedged into the shadows at the back of the room. He headed that way and slid smoothly onto one of the other chairs at the table. Kelly took the one beside him.

"Hello, Earl."

"You turn up like a bad penny," came the sullen reply. "Who's the chick?"

"A friend. Come on, don't hurt my feelings. Is that the best you can do for an old buddy?" Nick glanced up at the waitress who waited. "Whiskey," he said after Kelly declined. The woman left and he continued. "So how you been?"

"You want to know about that prosecutor gettin' shot, don't you?"

Nick wasn't surprised at Earl's astuteness. His sharpness made him the valuable informer he was. "Well, as a matter of fact, yeah. What can you tell me?"

"I can't tell you nothin'." Earl's eyes were slightly fuzzy, but there was nothing fuzzy about his response.

"Now, don't be in such a hurry, Earl. You don't even know what I'm going to ask," Nick said, watching the old man carefully. "You might know more than you think."

"Listen, Nick," Earl said, "I done a lot for you over the years. Hell, if it wasn't for Sandy, I'd have been dead a long time ago. I ain't never forgot it."

Neither had Nick. Sandy hadn't let him. A man's loyalties, his father used to say, ran deep.

Earl Mack had made his reputation years ago as a narcotics dealer. Once upon a time he had even climbed to the top of the heap. Unfortunately the trade had gotten rougher and so had the players. Gang warfare, automatic weaponry, an expanding baby market, each had disgusted the aging man who had refused to give up his autonomy and his own code of honor. Even if it was chiefly among thieves. Unfortunately not all of those thieves had shared his code.

If twenty years ago an off-duty patrolman named Santino Abella hadn't been cruising past an alley that should have been deserted, Earl Mack would have died with his legend. Luckily, the menace of the patrolman's gun had taken the death out of a pair of thieves' slashing knives. The old man, though seriously wounded, had lived. An alliance had formed. It was, Earl said, a debt of gratitude.

"Listen to me, Nick. I ain't lying. I can't tell you nothin' because I don't know nothin'. Nobody knows nothin'. And I'll tell you somethin' else. Don't nobody wanna know nothin' about anybody crazy enough to kill a prosecutor. Anybody who'd do that's crazy enough to do anything!" Earl tightened a gnarled hand around his glass and took a good, long swallow.

Nick finished his own whiskey. "How much do you want?"

"Are you listenin', man? It ain't about money! I'm bein' straight with you. I don't know who killed Cain. I don't even know what the hell he was doin' down here!"

The old man was telling the truth, Nick thought with frustration. He was also scared. But of what? Whatever it was, he wasn't going to spill it tonight. Nick controlled a surge of impatience.

"You got someplace to go tonight?" Nick asked. Earl's addresses rotated as frequently as his bottles.

"Yeah. I'm okay. But I don't want you comin'

round. Since that shooting, people are getting mighty anxious. Everybody's lookin' cross-eyed at everybody else. I don't need to give nobody no extra cause to start lookin' at me."

"Relax," Nick said. "To anybody who's looking, you're just a businessman, and I'm just a client."

Earl looked swiftly over at Nick.

"Don't even start," Nick said. "You may be officially out of the business, but we both know you keep your hands wet."

Earl's eyes shifted away from Nick's. "Yeah, well. It's only once in a while. Besides, I done come to a decision. I'm gettin' out."

Nick snorted. "You said that ten years ago."

"No. I mean I'm gettin' out of town. It's too hot around here lately. And I'm too old."

Nick looked into the old man's eyes and saw that he was perfectly serious. What was he scared of? "Where would you go?"

"I got a kid brother in Chicago. Been wantin' to see him before it's too late. Ain't no reason now not to do it."

"Well," Nick said after a moment, "you aren't leaving tonight." He pushed back his chair and got up. "Come on. I'll give you a ride home."

"You don't have to," Earl protested. But Nick could see in the old man's eyes that he was relieved to be spared the walk.

"It's not a problem. Besides, anyone interested enough to look twice will think you're making a score. Come on."

The old man was slow rising to his feet. He grimaced at the effort it took to move his stiff joints.

It suddenly occurred to Nick that he must be going on—what? Eighty? Nick dug out a few dollar bills, threw them down on the table, and took Kelly's hand. They followed behind Earl, who was already walking to the door.

The ride to the apartments where Earl was living took less than five minutes. The ancient brick building stood two stories tall and crumbling behind a group of teenagers who idled and smoked around its entrance. Earl reached for the car door and started to get out.

"Wait a minute," Nick said, laying a hand on Earl's arm. He reached his free hand back to his jeans pocket and pulled out some money. Pressing it into the old man's hand, he said, "You've got my number. Day or night."

The informant took the money and shoved it into his hip pocket. Nick watched silently as Earl ambled away.

"How long has he been your informant?" Kelly asked, once they were under way. She shifted sideways so that she could remove one, then the other high-heeled pump.

"Ever since I've been on the force. I guess you could say I inherited him."

"Inherited? How do you mean?"

"When my old man was still active, he looked out for Earl; then, when he couldn't anymore, Earl sort of transferred his loyalties to me. He couldn't survive on the streets alone. So he proposed I continue the arrangement my father started, occasional information in exchange for money."

"But you didn't really get any information to-night. Why the money?"

Nick shrugged.

"You, Nicholas Abella," Kelly said, propping her chin on the fist she rested along the back of her seat, "are a fraud. That go-to-hell exterior is just that, isn't it?"

"You're dreaming," he said dismissively.

"And that old man is twenty dollars richer for a snarl and a lift back to his place."

"I have to keep him primed for whatever might come up, that's all."

"Uh-huh," Kelly said consideringly. But then, the money hadn't really been inconsistent with what she had already seen of Nick.

He'd shoved aside his hostility that morning to console her when she needed it, though she hadn't asked for it. He'd risked blatant insubordination not only to Sheriff Brower but to this investigation to fight for his brother's innocence when every indication was that his brother didn't need that fight.

And now, he'd made a broken-down wino a few dollars richer just because the man needed the money and had been too proud to ask. Though she suspected he'd deny it until the day he couldn't draw breath, Nicholas Abella was a very kind man. No, kind was too benign. The word she wanted was . . . honorable. He possessed an old-fashioned honor and an unaffected humility that would rarely allow him to admit it.

She found that vastly appealing. She found him

vastly appealing, she admitted reluctantly. "Don't worry," she said. "I won't let it get out."

"Let what get out?" he asked, pulling inside the precinct parking garage.

"Never mind," she answered with a private smile.

He waited until they were out of the car and he'd walked her to the glass entrance doors. "Don't think you can peg me so easily, sweetheart."

Kelly paused with her hand against the doors. "Oh, I wouldn't," she was quick to insist.

Nick scowled. "Look, don't think just because I'm cooperating with you that makes us buddies."

"I would never presume." Kelly was smiling.

Nick wanted to be irritated. But he found himself smiling too as he watched her salute, then disappear down the corridor. "Smart-ass," he muttered.

He was still smiling as he walked back to his car.

Later that night an anxious call was placed from a graffiti-marked phone booth two blocks from Earl's apartment building.

"It's me."

"What do you have?" asked the calm voice on the other end of the receiver.

"Abella and the woman have been trawling down in the Acre."

A soft laugh. "Yeah, well, it's his kid brother's ass on the line. Did you expect any less?"

"I didn't expect him to have a heart-to-heart

with Earl. Word on the streets is that Earl's still got big ears. A perpetual live wire. I don't like it."

Scorpio hesitated. "That old man's a booze head," he said carefully. "He's been out of real commission for years. Common knowledge."

"Common knowledge or not, he's still kicking, and that makes him worth consideration in my book."

"Well, even if he is," Scorpio pointed out, "he wasn't around last night. No one was. Nothing in that alley can be traced. Besides, the kid lost his bracelet."

"Yeah, it was a lucky break, all right. But don't be too quick to gloat. I did some checking on Kelly Wylie."

"And?"

"And she ain't no dummy, man. Her record is impressive, to say the least. Two commendations following her input on a couple of task force investigations. Another handful of citations and up until that trouble with her husband not a little speculation about her being eyed for a major brass promotion."

After a minute of silence, Scorpio said, "I see. Well, it looks like we're going to have two birds to watch in addition to Joey."

"I'll get someone to take care of it."

"No. I'll take care of it myself for the time being. Any luck tracing the kid yet?"

"No. But don't worry. We've got everything covered. There's no way he's getting out of here without our knowing about it."

"Okay. Good." Scorpio expelled a hard breath.

"Dammit, we can't afford to let this thing blow up! Not now when we're so close. Joey Abella is a complication we simply cannot afford. He has to be silenced. Do you hear me? *Silenced!*"

"Don't worry. He will be. I know it was your call, but I never trusted that kid. I told you I had a feeling about him."

"Yes, well, maybe I should have listened to you, but the temptation was too big. Who better to join us than the brother of Nicholas Abella. First Joey, then . . . Nicholas might have been our ally. Now, I'm afraid he's been forced to become our enemy."

"And Kelly Wylie?"

"If we're very careful, that situation can be controlled. If it can't, she's expendable."

"Understood."

"Sleep well, my friend," Scorpio said. "We've got a lot to do over the next few days."

Two receivers clicked securely in their cradles. Two minds shared simultaneous thoughts. The last players were in place, the battle lines firmly drawn.

The door to the interrogation room opened and Kelly looked up. She beckoned Nick inside, then turned her attention back to the officer sitting in front of her.

"So you say to the best of your knowledge Prosecutor Cain never ventured into Hell's Acre. It was your duty as well as his other two bodyguards' to alternately protect him at any given time, day or night, and all you can come up with is

'to the best of my knowledge.' You're telling me
that between you, David Robbins, and Joey
Abella, the three of you had trouble keeping tabs
on your charge?'' Kelly watched John Butler bris-
tle. ''Or was it just you on the day he got shot?''
She wanted his anger. Anger was an invaluable
ally in getting the truth.

''I don't have anything to apologize for,'' Butler
snapped. ''I did my job. I guarded that man from
the time he got to his office until the time he left at
five that evening.''

''Yet you're sitting here telling me that you can't
even remember something as simple as if he went
out for lunch that day?'' Kelly insisted mildly.

Kelly saw Nick walk over to the far corner,
nursing a steaming mug, and quietly take a seat
by the wall. He looked well rested and his gaze
was as sharp as she'd come to expect. He
wouldn't miss the faint lines of fatigue around her
eyes. She wondered if he would see beyond them
to the rush of excitement she felt at his presence.

''That was almost a week ago—how can you expect me to remember something as trivial as
where Peter ate lunch?'' Butler demanded.

''During the time you've been sitting here, your
memory has been extraordinarily accurate about
the details of what happened that day, Officer.''

Butler's eyes dropped from hers.

Kelly's voice turned to velvet steel. ''You're lying
—about the thoroughness of your protection that
day and about your ability to execute your job.
What else are you lying about? For all you know,
Cain could have taken off anywhere—certainly

even Hell's Acre—whenever he wanted to, and you wouldn't have known."

"It wasn't like that," Butler ground out, his neck staining red.

"Then what was it like? Start telling me the truth, Butler!"

Butler's face was stony, his voice low. "I went to take a frigging leak, for God's sake. When I got back he was gone. I—"

"Did he often give you the slip?" Kelly asked, latching on to the admission.

"No! Look, sometimes the man just wanted to take a breather, you know? I mean, Christ, he was human."

Kelly pinned him with a steady look, let him squirm a little. "One more thing. Were you aware of any friction between Cain and Joey Abella?"

Butler shot a discomfited glance Nick's way. "No. All of us got on well with the prosecutor. Hell, I don't know anybody who didn't." He hesitated. "And for the record, I think the reason for this whole investigation is ridiculous. Of all the people in this town, why would Cain's killer be a cop? I mean, Peter Cain was one of us. He was on our side. It just doesn't make sense."

Kelly uncrossed her legs and got up from the table. She walked over by the door and leaned against the wall.

"That's right, Officer. This investigation is necessary precisely for that reason. What happened doesn't make sense. Murder never makes sense. Can you think of anything at all that struck you as unusual or suspicious about Cain's behavior that afternoon?"

"No. I told you I can't."

"All right. Fine." Kelly's voice was weary. "That's all. If you do think of anything, I want to know about it. I may want to talk to you again later. Oh, and by the way," she added.

"What?"

"The next time we have a little chat, you can bring your attorney along."

Even a rookie couldn't mistake what she was telling him. He got up to leave. Before he did, he turned back to Nick, who was regarding him steadily. "I . . . I just want you to know that none of the guys believes Joey's guilty in any of this for a minute. If there's anything we can do . . ." He cast a defiant look at Kelly. "Anytime."

Nick nodded. "Thanks, John."

Butler grunted softly and left the room.

"So," Nick said. "That concludes it?"

Kelly turned from the door. "I talked to Robbins earlier," she answered. "Three bodyguards, two interrogations, two alibis, and one missing. Butler's story checks out. After he got off duty, he went to his six-year-old's school play. He went home afterward, and at approximately the time Peter Cain was getting shot, Butler was threatening the teenage kids next door with arrest unless they toned their party down. So with no witnesses, no insight into motive, and no leads, we are essentially back at square one."

Nick got up and walked over to where Kelly was

standing. He laid a gentle hand on her wrist. She was tough, but Saturday's revelations still lingered in his memory. He was catching on to her, beginning to see past the veneer she presented to her fragility.

Kelly looked up and smiled gratefully as he offered her a sip of his coffee. Her lips touched the rim, picking up the slight moisture from his, and she curled a hand around his larger one to steady the mug for a deeper sip. He didn't seem to regret the spontaneity of her gesture. She was glad. "Mmm, that's good, thanks," she said, taking a second sip.

Her heart stumbled when he lowered the mug from her mouth and raised a long finger to lift a single drop of moisture from her upper lip. She wasn't trying to be provocative when impulse compelled her to trace the path of his finger with the tip of her tongue. But she knew her action had that effect when Nick went still and tracked the movement with his gaze.

The atmosphere between them turned charged. Without warning they were both suspended, caught in a flare of sensual awareness.

"Correct me if I'm wrong," Nick said slowly, "but Joey's still the chief bad guy in all of this, isn't he?" Even to his own ears the rumble of his voice sounded hoarse, faintly aroused.

Kelly took a slow breath and stepped away. "Yes. At this point, he's the only one who makes sense."

Nick gave his pulse a moment to slow, then answered her with words he hadn't intended to say. "You look tired."

"So would you be if you'd spent nearly seventy-two hours straight chasing down cold leads and questioning colder suspects, crackpot witnesses, and sundry other clueless associates and personnel of the late, great Peter Cain." She fought the craziest impulse to step into his arms. Their eyes locked and she fought the crazier certainty that he would welcome her.

"Part of the job, Sergeant," Nick chided her absently.

"And I'm not complaining, Detective. I'm just frustrated. Murders can be well planned, even flawlessly executed. But they're never neat. This one is too neat, and that bothers me."

He murmured some noncommittal response and let his eyes touch each feature of her face. He felt as if before this moment he had never truly seen her.

Kelly drew in a softly labored breath. Dear God, why couldn't she be indifferent to this man? The phone on the desk rang.

"Wylie," Kelly said inaudibly into the receiver. Clearing her throat, she tried again. "Who? Okay, Sheila, thanks. Put him through."

She risked a glance at Nick. Her concentration faltered when his golden gaze met hers and shuttered with lingering traces of something banked yet searing. "Yes, this is Kelly Wylie. Can I help you?"

"I can help you," the gravel-rough voice answered.

"Who is this?" Kelly dragged her eyes away and looked at her watch.

"You the detective on the Peter Cain case?"

The questions were pulling her back, though she was willing to bet money she was giving answers to a crackpot. "One of them." Her voice was clipped. "Can I help you?" she repeated.

"I saw the whole thing."

"Oh yeah? And what did you see?" She relaxed her hip against the table.

"I saw Cain get shot, then I saw the guy running away."

The pen Kelly had been doodling with went still. The hairs on the back of her neck prickled. She looked up at Nick, who had crossed over to her side.

"Whatsa matter, lady, don't you listen so good? I said I saw Cain buy it, then I saw the guy running away."

"Let me understand you. You're saying that you eyewitnessed the murder of Prosecutor Peter Cain?"

An impatient sigh burst over the wire. "What do I gotta do, spell it out for you? Yeah, I saw the whole thing, and I saw who did it. You wanna talk, or what?"

"What's your name?"

"Hey, uh-uh. I ain't giving you nothing until you tell me that I won't be going to all this trouble without something to show for it."

"Where are you?"

"It'll cost you."

"Listen, fella, you called me. If I hang up now,

I'm no worse off than before you started wasting my time. Now, where are you?'' There was silence at the end of the line. Kelly's heart thudded as she looked up at Nick.

"You some tough broad, huh?" the caller finally responded. "Okay. I'm at the Regency Arms, two-twenty-two West Mitchell. Room seventeen." Kelly wrote down the address. "And bring lotsa cash, lady." There was a scratchy laugh before the line went dead.

Kelly slowly replaced the receiver. "There was nothing in the papers about details of the crime," Kelly thought aloud. "I have a hunch, Nick, that this guy could be on the level. It might be a break."

Nick wasn't about to disagree when Joey's exoneration could be sitting mere blocks away. Besides, he'd watched her closely as she'd listened to the receiver. She was too experienced a cop to tense like that if her sixth sense wasn't telling her it was warranted.

"Let's go," he said, taking her arm.

5

The apartment was in a decrepit old brick building in the seedier part of town. It was a common kind of building invisible to the dozens of downtrodden locals who passed it every day, the kind of building their more affluent counterparts called a disgrace and "embarrassment to the city." Kelly knew that to the poor drudges who called it home, it was a haven in the winter and a dry roof in the summer.

She also knew before they stepped inside to expect the dingy, peeling walls of its drab, olive-green lobby, the stench of old whiskey, unwashed bodies, and indelible grime. She wasn't disappointed.

Room 17 was on the second floor. Nick raised his hand to knock on the gunmetal-gray door, and Kelly's eyes fell briefly to the shoulder holster housing his 9mm semiautomatic pistol. A few seconds passed. There was no answer. Nick hammered on the door this time.

"Is anybody in there!" They heard a faint scraping inside followed by a muted cry.

Nick's weapon was out and cocked before the

sound died. He motioned for Kelly to stand back, then gave the door a hard kick with the flat of his foot. The old, rusted hinges gave easily.

Nick ducked into the room and dropped into a defensive crouch, keeping his back to the outer wall. His eyes did a practiced scan of the room. Kelly knelt down beside him, her own weapon drawn.

The room appeared to be empty, everything within still, except for the dingy white curtain on the room's single far window. A breeze fluttered it in and out of the open sash. Beyond the window, they heard muffled metallic clanging.

Nick raced across the room and leaned over the windowsill. The twisting steps of the rickety fire escape below were empty. Whoever had fled was gone. He muttered an expletive as he holstered his pistol.

"Nick!" Kelly called. "Take a look at this."

Nick turned from the window and walked over to the room's far corner, where Kelly stood looking down on the bed. There lay, he presumed, the occupant of the room. He was very old. And he was very dead. He'd been stabbed.

Kelly was already on the phone calling for a unit. Nick examined the body. The old man lay flat on his back, his face haggard and gray, his clothes stained with dirt and something else Nick couldn't identify. He might have been taking an afternoon nap were it not for the bright red stain spread across his sunken chest.

"Anything?" Kelly asked.

"The bed is relatively neat. Doesn't look like he gave whoever it was much of a struggle."

How much of a struggle could this pitiful old man have put up, Kelly thought with disgust? She walked over to the sagging, splintered bureau on the wall facing the bed. There was a small collection of personal items gathered there, a sad little epitaph to a life brutally ended.

A black plastic rattail comb rested on a stained doily of indiscernible color. A cigarette lighter lay open-lidded beside a crushed, nearly empty pack of Lucky Strikes. A minuscule hand mirror lay faceup beside the cigarettes, its glass surface only marginally clearer than the mirror resting atop the bureau. There was a note lying half on, half off the edge of the bureau. Kelly took a tissue from her purse and picked it up.

Printed in a slightly wavering scrawl were the words "Jack, I owe you ten bucks." Written beneath, in a tiny, very precise script, were the words "Ha Ha, fat chance." That made Kelly smile. Then her eyes fell on the item that had lain beneath the note. It was a scarred, brown-leather billfold. Using the tissue, she rummaged gingerly around its sparse contents until her fingers encountered a square of stiff, flat plastic. She pulled it out. It was a driver's license.

"Jackson Cabot."

"What?" Nick said, moving over to her side. He leaned in close to peer over Kelly's shoulder and breathed in the light, floral scent she favored.

"His name was Jackson Cabot. And this driver's license expired in 1982."

"Jackson Cabot, Jackson Cabot," Nick murmured, his eyes narrowed in concentration. "Jackie. I knew I'd heard that name before. My God, it's old Jackie Cabot."

"Who was he?"

"In my father's day, he was just about the biggest snitch this town had. According to cop lore, he eyewitnessed more crimes, informed on more scams, and had an arrest record longer than any street snitch before or since. He was called the Flying Dutchman because he always turned up at the least likely place at the least likely time."

"Well, he was sure at the wrong place at the wrong time this time," Kelly said.

"That old man had a thousand enemies," Nick continued. "So why is my head telling me that his murder and that call he made to you are hardly a coincidence?"

"For the same reason I'm telling myself the same thing. If they were," Kelly said, "it would be too neat. Besides, I don't believe in coincidences, at least not until all my other possibilities have been exhausted."

Just then the heavy tread of footsteps thundered up the steps outside the door and up the hallway. A team of forensic officers, two uniformed patrolmen, the coroner, and another homicide detective and his partner entered the room.

"What have we got here, you two?"

"Hello, Tony," Kelly said.

"Hi, yourself, sweet stuff," Tony Martin answered. Nick shot Tony a look.

"Well, if it isn't Abella the Great. Didn't even

notice it was you standing there, man," Tony teased.

"Then it's just as well you're here to see the corpse, isn't it?"

Tony laughed. "Who is it?"

"The Flying Dutchman. Jackie Cabot."

"The Dutchman? Get out of here! He disappeared ten years ago. Word was that he had crawled off somewhere and died. Any ideas?" Tony asked as they all moved over to the bed. The forensic specialists were busy snapping photos and collecting any pieces of evidence they could find.

Kelly and Nick exchanged looks.

"Not really," Kelly said. "I understand the man had a lot of enemies, any one of whom had ample motive to do him in."

"So why are the two of you here?" Tony asked.

"He was back up to his old tricks," Nick answered.

"He called the precinct about an hour ago," Kelly said. "Claimed he witnessed the Cain murder."

"Heavy," Tony said. "So then, you're thinking that whoever murdered him did it to keep him from talking?"

"It's possible," Kelly said. *More like probable*, she thought.

Talk of the suspicion surrounding Joey had made its way around the precinct. Kelly knew the moment Tony jumped to the easy assumption when his eyes met Nick's and skittered away.

"Well," Tony said. "We've got everything under

control here. If we find anything interesting, I'll let you guys know."

Nick's voice was whisper soft. "You got something to say, Tony, say it." The other men in the room paused in what they were doing and turned uneasily toward the two detectives. The aggression behind Nick's words was palpable. Kelly didn't debate whether or not to intervene. She moved.

Catching Nick's arm, she started toward the door. "Okay, Tony. We'll get out of your way." The muscles beneath her fingers had tensed to granite. She was profoundly grateful when after a moment's hesitation Nick stopped resisting her and followed along.

She'd averted trouble, but she was impatient herself with Tony's lack of finesse and with the embarrassment reflected in the averted looks of the other officers.

"They were clumsy but they didn't mean any harm," she said to him when they were headed back to the station. "They just didn't know what to say. Surely you can understand."

"Understanding it, as you put it, and accepting it are two different things. It's not your brother everyone has already mentally tried and convicted." No, he thought, wincing inwardly just as he said it. She'd been the one mentally tried and convicted. "Sorry."

"It's okay."

It's okay. Nick heard a wealth of suppressed hurt in those simple words. The strength of his urge to comfort her astounded him.

This woman had been through a hell of accusation and condemnation, and she'd survived. Though she'd internalized her pain, it was still there. And despite a perfect opportunity a moment ago, she expected no quarter of his sympathy.

He glanced at her. Her profile was turned toward the window, her expression self-possessed, controlled. He knew as surely as the sun rose she'd never solicit pity from him or anyone else. Her problems were her own; so were their solutions. He wondered what had made her so fiercely self-reliant. He guessed it somehow went beyond a tarnished career and a bad marriage.

They drove on in silence and Nick used it to focus his concentration back on the road and give himself a mental shake. His trouble was he'd been everybody's caretaker for too long. First his mother, then his father, and now Joey. He'd been soothing hurts for so long, he was beginning to imagine them where they didn't exist. Kelly Wylie was a strong lady. She had put her life back on track. The best thing he could do for both of them was to fight this crazy compulsion to get involved.

They were two cops, two professionals. Nothing more.

"About what happened back there, thanks," he said.

"For what?"

"For the support. You didn't have to."

"I meant it," she said simply. Kelly looked out at the thickening crowds who bustled along the outskirts of the business district they were reentering. "I can hear you thinking. What's it about?"

He wasn't about to tell her that particular truth, so he moved on to another one. "It just rankles like hell to have all this damning suspicion hanging over Joey. Especially now when the public is just waiting to pillory any cop remotely suspected of wrongdoing."

"Well, no one's going to pillory Joey unjustly if I can help it. We're still living in a country where you're innocent until proven guilty."

"Yeah. But you know as well as I do that too many determinations of guilt and innocence are made way outside legal arenas."

Kelly wondered if he knew how hard he was gripping the steering wheel. She looked away from him, fearing she would allow her hand to cover his if she didn't. She wanted to ease his anxiety, calm his frustrations.

Dammit, she thought. She wanted to stem these protective feelings extending to the man beyond the cop. She didn't want to be touched by the gentleness in him. From the beginning she'd sensed it, and she'd been frightened of her response to it. She also worried it could undermine her objective investigation of this case.

Was that happening already? Nick was a proud man, and she knew that the taint on his family's name touched a very sensitive chord. She'd uncovered some things about his family, about his father, she wouldn't have hesitated to toss at him for a reaction a week ago. Today she hesitated.

Instead, she wanted to soothe him. "I'll do everything I can to get to the truth of this case," she told him. "If Joey's innocent, Nick, I won't spare anything or anyone to prove it."

If. That one little word was enough to reinforce his determination to resist his attraction to her. She was who she was, and he was who he was. All of the fanciful wishing in the world wasn't going to change that. And dammit, he didn't want it to change, he reminded himself.

They had pulled into the station's underground parking garage and Kelly listened to Nick kill the engine. She looked over at him, saw the determined set of his jaw, and felt strangely uncertain of what to do, what to say. She was starting to get out when she heard Nick say, "Wait."

She paused, her hand on the door handle. She wouldn't look at him.

"I . . ."

Kelly kept her head averted, seeing and not seeing the lot beyond the window. She dropped her hand to her lap. "I've got to go," she whispered.

Yes, go, Nick's inner voice responded. But in the next moment he couldn't concentrate on what that voice was telling him because the scent of her, the softness of her, the beauty of her were making things all confused in his head. Heavy-laden moments ticked by. Then Nick sighed heavily. "Dammit, I know."

A patrol car careened past them toward the exit. Its squealing tires effectively severed the spell within the car. Slowly, Kelly groped again for the handle.

"I'll keep you updated." She frowned at the

breathlessness in her voice, at her hand that fumbled once before releasing the latch.

Nick slung one arm across the back of the seat and watched her walk away. A sinking feeling of inevitability settled over him, and he hated it.

When he got to the squad room, he had a visitor. At a glance, Nick took in the slightly unkempt hair, the clothes that looked rumpled despite the effort that had been made to coordinate them, the frowning mouth set firm with displeasure beneath eyes that looked faintly bleary. The overall appearance was all too familiar, and it embarrassed Nick.

"Hello, Sandy."

"Why didn't you tell me, boy?"

"Come on, I'll buy you some coffee."

"Not until you answer me." Santino Abella's voice rose, and the other detectives in the suddenly very quiet room looked away uncomfortably.

Nick laid a heavy hand on his father's shoulder and urged him to his feet. The elder Abella stumbled, which unfortunately didn't surprise Nick. He concentrated on hustling him out of the office before he made a scene.

He tried again. "Come on, Sandy."

"Come on, Sandy, come on, Sandy," Sandy mimicked. "I guess you think I've been drinking too much. That's what you always say. That's what my perfect son always says!"

His words were steady, but not for a second was Nick fooled. He abandoned the finesse, pulled the

older man to his feet, and ushered him out into
the hallway. "How did you get here?"

"I took a cab."

"Well, you can take another one back. Why
didn't I tell you, you ask? Precisely because I
wanted to avoid this. And for your information, I
came to the house to tell you, but you were so
goddammed drunk, you were out cold. What was
the point?"

They were nearly at the precinct exit doors.

"Look at you, standing there condemning me."
The old man's voice was bitter. "Your life is so
easy. If you'd had to live through what I had to
live through, you wouldn't be the big man. You've
had everything!" he spit out. "How do you think it
felt to show up here to have lunch with you, only
to have one of the guys tell me how sorry he was
about Joey? Do you think that was easy, having to
be told by an outsider that my little boy is being
tracked as a killer!"

"Keep your voice down," Nick growled. He released Sandy's arm to shove a quarter in the pay
phone on the wall.

"Nick, wait." Sandy laid a restraining hand
over his son's wrist. "Don't send me away." His
eyes pleaded now, and his voice became apolo-
getic. "Of course he's not a killer. I never believed
it for a minute. You know that. It was just a shock
—don't be mad, Nicky. Please. Don't be mad."

Nick dropped his hand from the coin slot and
hung his head at Sandy's defeated tone. A familiar
fury engulfed him as anger and pity for this man
who was his father warred for the upper hand.

"Please, son, don't send me away. I know I shouldn't have caused a scene back there. I know I'm an embarrassment to you. Hell, I'm an embarrassment to myself."

Nick's gut twisted. Why did his father's self-pity still reduce him to the confused, angry boy he had been during those early days after his mother had walked out? "Don't say that, Pop," he mumbled automatically.

"Why not? It's true. I know I've been no great shakes as a father. But I'd at least hoped that now that you were a man, you might give me a second chance to be your friend."

Nick's hand clenched around the phone's cable. No, Sandy hadn't been any great shakes as a father. Nick's earliest memories of him were of distance and preoccupation. When he was home from the job, that was. And when he was, he'd found more comfort at the bottom of a glass than in the company of his wife and two sons.

Even so, he had always been there materially if not emotionally. And despite the fact that Nick and Joey had practically had to raise themselves after their mother left, there had been some good times to offset the bad. Occasionally there still were.

Maybe it was because despite Sandy's shortcomings he hadn't been the one to cut out on his children, leaving nothing of himself behind but a one-page lie saying he'd be back after he got his "head together." Whatever he was, Sandy was still his father, and for that Nick owed him something.

"Come on," he said, "I'll take you home."

Pulling up in front of the white-brick one-story house he'd lived in for seventeen years conjured up a thousand memories for Nick. He had taught Joey how to toss a football behind the fenced-in enclosure of the backyard. He and Joey had ridden their bikes along every inch of these streets. What the neighbors hadn't known, of course, was that "those Abella boys" had often preferred being in the streets to being trapped inside their own home, unwilling spectators to their parents' bitter arguments and later to their father's drunken depressions.

Sandy opened his door and Nick unfolded his arms from the steering wheel to do the same. A glance at his watch showed him it was going on three.

He followed Sandy into the house, noticing that everything was still relatively neat from Mrs. Randolf's last regular Friday visit. Nick had provided for the cleaning service two years ago when it became obvious that Sandy had lost interest in cleaning up after himself. Mrs. Randolf had been a godsend. She did her work faithfully and never said a judgmental word when she emptied the beer bottles along with the ashtrays.

"There's some leftover pot roast, I think, in the refrigerator. Randolf brought it with her." Sandy looked at his son, then away. He didn't seem to know what to do with himself.

"That's fine, Pop. I'll heat it up. Why don't you turn on the television and relax."

"Yeah, yeah, okay," Sandy said, rubbing his hands along his arms. "I'll do that."

Nick returned with two sandwiches, and Sandy turned away from the game show he was watching to accept his. He thanked Nick awkwardly and Nick shrugged it off just as awkwardly. Every bite was more tasteless than the last to Nick as they ate in silence, mutually consenting to let the game show do their talking for them. Finally they finished and Nick stacked Sandy's plate with his own. He started for the kitchen.

"Nick?" Sandy looked deep into Nick's eyes, his focus as clear as he could make it. "I'm glad you came home with me, son." His hands clutched the sofa cushions beside him. "I—I know I don't say it often enough, but, well, I didn't mean that other stuff. I'm proud of you. You're a good son."

A rush of ambivalent feelings washed over Nick. He couldn't think of a thing to say.

Sandy Abella cleared his throat. "Your mother would be proud of you too if she were here." He looked sightlessly off into the distance.

Nick's throat closed. He fought against a hurt he told himself had healed over long ago. At any rate, he'd forced himself long ago to stop wanting to care. "Why don't you just sit back and relax, Pop. I'll be back in a minute." He went to the kitchen.

When he returned to the living room minutes later, Sandy lay curled up on the sofa fast asleep. Nick went into his father's bedroom and pulled a lightweight afghan off the foot of the bed. As he knelt beside his father to tuck it in, Sandy shifted.

Nestled against his chest and still lying within the crook of his arm was a bottle.

His face expressionless, Nick finished tucking the cover around his father. Taking one last look around the room, he walked out.

Eight P.M. Kelly snapped off her desk lamp and raised her arms in a wide stretch. Most of the paperwork she'd been trying to get caught up on was nearly finished, and she was hungry. Maybe she'd grab a hamburger on the way home. That was about the only thing she had the energy left to eat.

"And I thought I was a workaholic."

Kelly looked up from her desk. Ruthlessly she quelled her pleasure at seeing him. "Nick. Why are you still here? I thought you would have been long gone."

"I was, but I started feeling guilty about the stack on my desk, so I came back about three hours ago."

Kelly closed her drawer and gathered up her purse and suit jacket. "So, did you get what you wanted accomplished?"

"Enough. You?"

"Enough," she replied, wondering if she was imagining the melancholy in his voice.

He smiled. She smiled.

"Look," Nick said; his voice was reluctant. "I'm sure you're pretty bushed, and I know I am. But I'm hungry. You wanna grab something?"

Kelly hesitated. He looked so tired. His jacket was slung over one shoulder, and the sleeves of his white shirt were rolled up to his forearms.

He'd loosened his tie, and as she looked at how the knot rested low at his throat, she noticed that the shadow that had just been a hint along his jaw when she'd last seen him was much darker.

He looked incredibly approachable, appealing. Sexy.

"No. I mean, thanks," Kelly said, moving past him, "but I'm really tired. I think I'll just go home."

Nick laid a hand on her shoulder, staying her. "And fix what at this hour? A bologna sandwich? Peanut butter and jelly?" She looked down, so he knew he was right. "You're about to swoon, Wylie. Come on. It's no big deal."

Liar, Kelly thought, taking a thoughtful step back to lean against her desk. He stood against the door, partially wrapped in shadow while his golden eyes watched her steadily, assessingly.

Nick was edgy tonight, restless. And as she crossed her arms, debating, Kelly realized she was restless too. Had been since they'd returned to the precinct this afternoon. She lowered her eyes and idly followed the direction of a crack marring the tile beneath her feet.

If she decided to be alone with him, she would be making a big mistake. At this moment, she could still walk away from the seduction of him that made her forget everything except the fact that she was a woman and he was a man.

And it was a seduction. The question was, why? Was it the dramatic way his dark, good looks were sharpened by that overlay of tough masculinity? Unlikely. She'd withstood that kind of attraction plenty of times from plenty of other men, especially cops. Was it that softness she'd glimpsed at times when she least expected it? Maybe. And maybe it was the fact her life had been devoid of softness for too long.

"We'd be making a mistake, Nick," she said.

Nick didn't pretend to misunderstand her. "We can handle it."

Kelly still hesitated until a flash of impatience made her think, yes, dammit, they could. And on the heels of that rose a greater impatience at herself and her self-imposed restraints that had allowed her to fall into the habit of eating alone, of being alone.

She lifted her eyes. "Let's go."

A moment passed. Then Nick said levelly, "Where to?"

"Hey, I said yes. Any other thought tonight is beyond me." She almost backed out when the recklessness in his smile took her breath away.

He found himself taking her to a little restaurant that was a favorite of his. Owned and run by a genial couple, it specialized in the exotic combination of African-and-Italian cuisine. At that hour of the night, the crowd was still thick enough to cocoon him and Kelly within their own cozy niche at their table.

"How's your food?" he asked with a knowing grin as Kelly's eyes widened with pleasure at the bite she was tasting.

"Wonderful. Is everything here this good?"

"Yep. That's why it's just about my favorite restaurant. Sally's the only one who's ever even come close to my mama's cooking."

Kelly arched a brow. "Your mother must be jealous."

Nick took another bite of his lasagna. "It's a moot point. She walked when I was twelve."

Kelly's pause as she lifted her wineglass was slight. "I'm sorry. That had to be rough."

Nick looked up and shrugged. "It wasn't cata-strophic. Joey and Pop and I, we coped well enough in the end."

Kelly knew Sandy Abella's history. She could only speculate on how his alcoholism coincided with his wife's desertion and the unexpected re-sponsibility of raising two young boys alone.

"I never saw my mother lift a hand in the kitchen," Kelly said easily. "To this day, I have no idea whether she can cook or not."

"Ah," Nick said, smiling once more, "so you were born with a silver spoon in your mouth."

Kelly made a face. "Not a silver spoon, exactly. But I guess most would have called my family comfortably well-off."

"So what does your dad do?"

"He was in investment banking morning, noon, and night. I hardly ever saw him, so I didn't really get to know him until just before he died."

"I'm sorry."

"Thanks. It wasn't sudden. He had cancer. It was the only thing that could slow him down enough to smell the roses, and by the time he did, forging missed relationships was too late."

"What about your mother, how did she cope?"

"Same way as when he was living. Clubs, charities, board meetings. I was swept along. But as you see, her attempts to assimilate me failed. I'm afraid I disappointed her horribly when I deviated from the social fold."

Finished, Nick sat back in his chair and sipped his wine. He hadn't missed the forced indifference that had crept into her voice. "In light of your background, why law enforcement?"

Kelly smiled, taking a sip of her wine. "At the risk of sounding like a bad cliché, I wanted to do something *meaningful* with my life. My eyes weren't completely shut while I rode that social merry-go-round. I learned there were a lot of people out there who needed around-the-clock help more desperately than they needed benevolent words and holiday care packages." She gazed thoughtfully beyond Nick.

Nick caught their hostess's eye and signaled for coffee. At this moment Kelly looked every inch the socialite she eschewed. Smoothly polished and coolly lovely, she was enthralling him with another side of herself, a relaxed, introspective one he found much too appealing. "If your mother can't appreciate the woman you are," he said softly, "her shortsightedness is her loss."

That brought Kelly's attention back to Nick, and she flushed a little at the frank approval in his eyes.

"Thanks," she murmured.

"You're welcome," he returned just as softly.

A short while later Kelly finished the last bite of her apple cobbler. "I don't know when I last had a good, to-hell-with-the-calories, down-home meal."

"Sally and Leo will be glad to hear it. The restaurant was written up in *Circle* magazine last month. Business has boomed ever since."

Just then, Sally approached their table with the check. "Would you all like some more coffee? Or tea?" she asked softly, looking down at Kelly's empty cup.

"Thank you, Sally, none for me. If I have another drop of anything, I'll burst."

Sally laughed with pleasure. "How 'bout you, Nick? I don't care what they say, you're still a growing boy."

"I certainly will be if I eat anything more. Thanks, Sally, but no. Dinner was delicious, as usual."

"Glad you two enjoyed it. You make him bring you back, Kelly, okay?"

"Promise," Kelly said politely, watching the plump little woman walk away. She looked over at Nick and read in his eyes what she was thinking. They shouldn't do this again. The thought brought a heaviness with it.

"Well," she said, "it's my bedtime." Nick's silent study of her made her a little self-conscious until he seemed to sense it and lowered his eyes to tap out the cigarette he had been smoking.

"Ditto," he said, walking around the table to pull Kelly's chair back for her.

He walked her to her car. "I'll follow you home. And I don't want to hear any arguments from you.

I'm too tired to defend any attacks on my macho pride." She caught a wicked flash of dimples.

"And I'm too tired to launch any," she replied. "Thanks again for the dinner, Nick. It was nice." And it really had been, she thought. She climbed into her car and waited for him to get into his before she pulled away and headed home.

The drive to her condo took no more than fifteen minutes, and as Kelly pulled into her driveway, she was surprised to see Nick pull up behind her and cut his engine. Closing her car door, she stood beside her car watching him get out and walk up to her.

"Did you forget something?" she asked.

"Nope. I was just taught that seeing a lady home also included seeing her to her door." He reached down and took advantage of her surprise to gently pry her key from her hand. Kelly trailed him to her door.

He turned the key in the lock and handed it back to her.

She turned to him. "Well," she said again, "good night." She started to go inside but was stalled by Nick's hands against her shoulders.

She didn't know whether to blame her fatigue, the lateness of the hour, or her satisfied state after a good meal, but with the first touch of his lips, thoughts of resistance seeped from her consciousness as easily as the sigh she emitted seeped across his lips.

She felt Nick reach behind her to push her door open wide enough to allow them to step inside. The front door closed against his back. When she realized how deftly he had maneuvered her, Kelly broke the kiss.

"Stop, Nick. We have to stop."

He spared her a second's glance before letting his eyes shutter. Dropping his mouth back to hers, he pulled lightly at her lower lip and began to nibble. "Why do we have to stop?" he breathed.

"Because . . . because . . ." Kelly couldn't think beyond the tiny little curls of pleasure that were tickling her stomach with each tug of his teeth. Abandoning the tease, he took her lips fully and Kelly slowly looped her arms around his neck.

She smelled like crushed rose petals, he thought dizzily, like crushed rose petals on a misty spring day. And she felt twice as soft. He'd promised himself all through dinner that he wouldn't touch her. But all during the ride to her house, he kept remembering the way the softness of her mouth had beckoned with every bite of food she'd taken.

He kept remembering how soft and kissable her lovely face had looked with most of the makeup melted away, with her deep brown eyes slightly heavy with fatigue. He'd kept imagining how soft the lushness of her hair would feel against his palms. But in all his imaginings, he'd not been prepared for the seductive reality.

He wanted her. Now, this minute. He wanted to feel the velvet of her skin against him, wanted to lose himself in the softness of her petal-fresh scent. Wanted to absorb more of the peace she gave him.

They had to stop, Kelly thought. Even as she

lowered her arms from around his neck to push him away, his tongue coaxed its way into her mouth and snuggled against hers until, lazily, it began to stroke up and down. Kelly groaned and her head fell back against her shoulder. The hands that rested at his chest were grasped in a soft, unyielding grip and dragged down until she felt them pressed into the backs of his thighs. And then his palms were at the backs of hers, and she was being pulled flush into the heat of his desire.

The realization of where they were rapidly heading gave her strength. "No, Nick," she said, pulling her lips away from his.

Her firm tone broke through the haze of his passion, and Nick released her. He took a hesitant step back.

"We're both adults."

"Yes," she admitted. "We are. And we both know what we want. But we can't because it would be wrong. You know the fact that you're my colleague is reason enough." She didn't need to go beyond that.

Of course he knew, Nick thought, giving himself a mental shake. And now that there was some distance between them, he also knew that he had been on the verge of throwing aside all of the warnings he had given himself about becoming involved with her. He'd had his share of involvements with women, but he could honestly say that until this moment he had never lost his head with one. That he had now disturbed him.

"Yes, of course you're right," he said. She looked, he thought, as confused as he felt. All the more reason for him to leave. Fast. He walked to the door. "It won't happen again," he said quietly just before closing it.

Kelly listened to him drive away. She'd been right to call a halt to things. And he'd complied correctly by leaving. So why did she feel as though something wonderful had been nipped in the bud before it could even start?

6

Maybe if she ignored it, it would stop. Ten seconds later, the phone rang again and Kelly groaned in earnest. She groped for the receiver, only to lie there in confusion when the dial tone droned steadily in her ear. The next strident peal told her why. It was the doorbell.

She dislodged the pile of gray hair slumped across her feet and checked the bedside clock. Six thirty A.M.

Kelly swept her legs over the side of the bed and inched her toes along the carpet until she located her slippers. Gino bounded from the bed, gave a bone-shivering morning stretch, and loped barking for the front door. His enthusiasm had Kelly only slightly more awake by the time she got to the door and peeked beyond the chain out onto the porch. Her yawn stopped in mid-progress.

"What are you doing here!" she asked, startled. For a hazy moment, she wasn't sure if Nick was real or a vibrant continuation of her dream. She nudged Gino away from her knee where he was pressing, trying to get his large, shaggy head through the crack to see who had disturbed the peace.

"I'm bearing gifts," he said, raising a wax-coated bag to Kelly's eye level.

One whiff of the heavenly aroma of fresh doughnuts convinced her he was real, and she closed the door long enough to remove the chain and let him in. "You'd better—" Gino beat her to the punch. His forelegs were already against Nick's chest, and his cold black nose, the only visible feature on his face, was rooting hungrily against the bag. Nick was staggering against his ninety-pound weight. "Give me the sack," Kelly finished weakly.

"Your killer attack dog, I presume?" He pushed unsuccessfully at the canine wall that had besieged him.

"I'm sorry," Kelly told him. "Gino can be a little overwhelming if you're not expecting him. Come on, sweetie," she said, pulling gently at the scruff of the bearded collie's neck, "let the poor man move. If you're nice, maybe he'll even give you one." Her plea did the trick. Gino took a step back and sat on his haunches, his tail wagging furiously. One bright blue eye was exposed when a long hank of white hair fell to one side of his expectant face.

"Catch!" Nick said, holding a warm doughnut high in the air before giving it a toss. "Attaboy." He chuckled as Gino caught it like a pro and trotted off to the cool tiles of the kitchen floor to eat it. "Where was he last night?"

"At my neighbor's, Mrs. Jablonski's," Kelly replied absently. "Look, don't think I'm rude or anything, but was I expecting you?"

Nick walked over to where she stood and pressed the sack into her hands. "We're taking a trip to Nashville." At Kelly's dubious look, he added with a grin, "Indiana, sweetheart. Brown County. There's someone down there we should talk to. Come on, wipe the sleep out of your eye, Wylie. I like my partners alert and functioning. Where's the coffee?"

Feeling as if a whirlwind had swept into her midst, Kelly shook her head slightly and turned to see that Nick was already in the kitchen going through cabinets.

"Second on the right," she told him.

"Gotcha," he answered, pulling the canister from the shelf and deftly loading the coffeemaker on the counter. "Why don't you go ahead and shower. I'll have this done by the time you're through."

Kelly stood in the middle of the floor and opened her mouth, thinking there was something she ought to be objecting to. But since Nick seemed to have everything in hand—including another doughnut for Gino—she couldn't think of what it was.

Nick watched her disappear down the hallway off the living room and knew he'd never seen anything lovelier in his life. When she'd opened the door, the only thing that had caught him off guard more than the ton of fur she called a dog was the sight of her greeting him, still fuzzy with sleep, in an oversize, sleep-rumpled nightshirt. With her face scrubbed bare of makeup and that mane of sleep-mussed hair clashing adorably with the hot pink of her cotton sleepwear, she'd looked about eighteen.

He'd debated long and hard this morning on whether or not to come over. Last night had shown them just how explosive the attraction between them could be. The heat of that kiss had scorched them both, and he'd meant what he'd said when he told her it wouldn't happen again.

But he'd also known that his attraction for her was more than just sexual. Physically she turned him on. But there was a solidity about her, a calmness that soothed him as well.

The simple truth was, when he'd awakened this morning, his first thought had been of how much he wanted to see her. The second was that the idea of sharing breakfast with her seemed a whole lot more appealing than the prospect of grabbing something in the precinct cafeteria and eating it alone. His feelings for Kelly were complex, dangerous, given the situation, but for all that, undeniably real. He poured two mugs of coffee and sat at her kitchen table to wait.

Kelly gave her hair a final stroke of the brush, then reached for her perfume bottle. Her actions were controlled. Her turbulent emotions were not.

After Nick had left last night, she hadn't been sure how she'd feel when she saw him this morning. Now she knew. Glad. Excited. And a little frightened, because she'd lain awake long into the night thinking about what that kiss meant. Nicholas Abella was a dangerous man.

Along with the shadows, she'd glimpsed a sensitivity inside him he tried to hide and a thoughtfulness he couldn't. Friendly admiration for those qualities she could understand, but personal attraction beyond them to the man was something she told herself she didn't want, especially now that her life was beginning to lose its complications.

Because the plain, cold fact was, Nicholas Abella was a renegade, and she'd already loved a renegade once. The thrill would ultimately outweigh the commitment with a man like him, and the fallout would decimate anyone in its wake.

She set the perfume down and lifted her eyes to her reflection. She could handle Nick. She could cope with the threat he presented to her safe, self-contained life. If nothing else, past experience had taught her she could cope with anything that threatened her peace of mind. She tucked a stray strand of hair into the smooth French knot at her nape, gave her suit a final check, and headed out to rejoin the detective who waited for her.

"Another minute and it would have gotten cold," Nick said casually, gesturing to her coffee.

Kelly seated herself. "Then I would have had to get another one, wouldn't I?" she said tartly.

He considered the thrust, gave an easy nod of his head, and decided for the moment to decline the parry. "Eat up, there's plenty." He gestured to the plate he had organized.

Kelly selected one dripping with strawberry jelly. "So who is it we're going to see?"

Nick watched her bite into the pastry and re-membered the feel of those smooth, white teeth against his tongue. "A friend. His name is Jean Le Beau. He owns a little crafts shop in Nashville. Next to me, Jean is the person Joey is closest to. He may know something."

Kelly leaned forward to stroke Gino, who had padded over to her side. She knew there was a strain between the father and sons, and though she'd come across Le Beau's name in her re-search, she knew him only as a piece of type on a sheet of paper. Blood was supposed to be thicker than water, but apparently it wasn't in this case. Interesting. "Does he know we're coming?"

"No, I'd rather surprise him." And then, as if he'd just realized what Kelly hadn't asked, he glanced at her suspiciously. "Jean's like a second father to us. Or am I telling you something you don't know?"

"No, not exactly," she conceded. "In a situation as serious as this, though, why would Joey go to Jean before his real father? Or you?"

"Ah, now she resorts to getting it from the horse's mouth."

"Just fill me in," she said patiently.

He did twenty minutes later after they deposited Gino next door and left the outskirts of Sedgwick. Nick took a sharp curve at a smooth clip that would have concerned her had someone less com-petent been driving.

"He and my father were best pals. Jean was

originally from Louisiana, but they met when they served in Korea together. After the war, Jean didn't have any immediate family, so he moved here and he and my father stayed close."

"But you're Joey's brother. I still want to know why him and not you." At his silence, Kelly turned away from the window and the view of the rich, green southern Indiana hillside they were climbing. Nick's face was closed. "For better or worse," she murmured softly. "Remember?"

Yes, he remembered. But that didn't make it easy letting her into his personal corners. He'd guarded them for too long.

"Not long after the war, my father married. Three years later I came along and five years after that Joey was born. Somewhere in between, things started to go sour for my folks. Joey and I were usually caught in the middle of their arguments. Jean turned up time after time to step into the breach."

"How?" Kelly asked.

"By trying to play peacemaker between my father and mother. And when that didn't work, by taking me and Joey out to a movie, or a ball game, or anything until things settled down at the house. He didn't have a family of his own, so he had lots of time for us."

"Why did they fight?"

Nick expected the familiar defensiveness. Instead, he felt a strange relief. He'd shared some of this with Alan, but even with him he'd been reluctant to take it further.

"Old story. Stresses of the job on top of the

stress of two people realizing that maybe they'd married too quickly. You're a cop. My mother was a civilian. You know what that means. She wanted all of my father, and all was something he couldn't give. He couldn't just come home and shed the streets like he shed his overcoat. She couldn't understand or accept that, so they drifted apart. You've seen it a hundred times before."

Unfortunately, she had. Some of her own memories were still raw, she realized, thinking of Jeff. She'd understood his allegiance to his job. But as his wife and the woman who'd married him, she hadn't really been able to accept either. Finally she could face that and the old guilt about blaming him for making her share him with his job.

"My father began to drink," Nick continued. "Not a lot at first, and never on the job. But when he did, he drank steadily and alone. Eventually, he pushed my mother out."

And his children, Kelly guessed.

"Not long after that, he started throwing out accusations about Jean and my mother."

Jeff had grown pretty good at throwing around unfounded accusations himself in their final days together, Kelly remembered.

"Naturally, he and Jean argued bitterly," Nick said. "And those arguments just aggravated an already explosive situation until it wasn't long after that Jean removed himself from it. He moved down to Nashville."

"But he didn't drop out of your lives?"

"No. He didn't drop out." Kelly could fill in the gaps.

Soon after Sandy Abella had begun to drink in earnest, the effects had spilled over onto his job. Enough so that his lieutenant reluctantly pulled him off the street. Enough so that eventually, his chief pulled him off the force.

So, in a surrogate way, Jean Le Beau had stepped in and taken over with the boys where Sandy Abella left off. It was conceivable then that Joey might have confided in him if not in his brother. Assuming, of course, that he chose to confide in anyone.

The morning was still young, but already the summer heat had started to climb outside the air-conditioned confines of the car. Nick wasn't inclined toward any more conversation, and Kelly wasn't inclined to push anymore for the moment.

Duncan County gave way to Morgan County and Morgan County gave way to Monroe. Fifteen minutes later they crossed the border into Brown County. Despite the fact that it was a weekday, they still had to slow down considerably to contend with the traffic crowding the tourist town of Nashville. Kelly settled back, prepared to enjoy the sights and sounds around her.

Nick weaved his way in and out of the two-lane traffic like a pro, and Kelly knew that he had been here many times before. They drove a little farther south until the milling crowds were as thick as the cars and neither faction seemed particularly inclined to move beyond a crawl.

Mothers held tight to baby strollers and toddlers who strained against their grasps, seemingly ready to take off in a hundred different directions.

Occasional mom-and-pop gas stations were dotted amid artisans' shops that boasted names like The Quilted Bee and Tea and Sympathy. Polaroids and Nikons clicked all around, and strolling pedestrians lounged at wooden picnic tables scattered strategically around the area.

Kelly had enjoyed browsing through folksy areas like this back in Chicago when she had the time, and she was enjoying the sights of this one now. She liked the carnival atmosphere immensely.

"You should see it in autumn," Nick commented. "The colors then are absolutely spectacular, really something to see."

Unbidden, yet suddenly as clear as a picture, he could visualize her as the loveliest part of it all. He could hear the crackle of the fire that would lick the weathered brick of the fireplace dominating his family's cabin a few miles east of here. He could see the gold, flickering beauty the flames would cast across Kelly's fine-boned features as she sat in his arms on the floor against the sofa.

"I could show it to you."

She didn't answer.

"Nothing to say?"

"What were you expecting?" Kelly replied carefully.

"Actually, something in the affirmative would be nice."

"Nick, you know—"

"I know what I'm feeling; I know that no woman who doesn't feel the same could melt in my arms as completely as you do."

"We hardly know each other. We've shared one kiss." She didn't want to hear this. "You're feeling vulnerable and I'm a convenient shoulder to lean on. Can't you see? You're going through the fire, and nothing's more seductive than gravitating toward one who's already survived it. How real can these feelings be?"

"Apparently real enough for you to be putting up one hell of a defense against them. No," he added when she started to say more, "you've had your say. Now let me have mine.

"Number one, we're both old enough to know the difference between good old-fashioned lust and mature attraction. Number two, I'm not asking you to sleep with me. I'm merely suggesting that we get to know each other better—without the hypocrisy of pretending it's only allowed within the boundaries of this case, or on some misbegotten basis of misery-loves-company.

"And number three, that wasn't a kiss, lady. It was a revelation. Neither of us would have been able to stop if the only thing at risk had been scratching an itch." He took a deep breath and expelled it just as deeply. "I know you had a raw deal with your marriage. But there comes a time for everyone, Kelly, no matter how wounded, to either move beyond their fear or stay trapped in false security forever."

Absolute silence greeted his outburst. He hadn't meant to be so unrelenting, but her calm disavowal of what was between them made him angry. The truth, though greatly exaggerated, in what she'd said about his vulnerability hadn't helped. But only because that vulnerability provided a start. What was happening between them went much deeper than that.

"No woman has ever made me feel the things you make me feel," he added, resenting fiercely the need that was making him say it. Resenting the fact that for the first time since he'd been a child, he was helpless against it.

No woman had even briefly made him imagine sharing the things he was beginning to conceive of sharing with her. Maybe he could have expressed what he had with a little more polish, but he had wanted to jar a reaction out of her that would let him know she was sharing a little of his emotional imbalance. Curious at her continued silence, he glanced over to see how she'd taken it.

"Oh, baby, don't." A silent tear rolled down her averted cheek. "Don't."

Hell, he'd wanted a reaction, but the last thing he'd wanted was to make her cry. He caught the moisture from her cheek with the back of his fingers.

"Leave me alone," Kelly whispered, pushing his hand away. She didn't have the strength to do it again when he cupped her jaw. She heard him damn the traffic and soon she knew why as he searched for an opening through which to pull over onto a shoulder. Even when he found it, a surprisingly grassy knoll, and shut off the engine to pull her into his arms, she tried to protest. But he wouldn't let her, and she gave in to the soft, muffled sobs that shook her.

Nick could only imagine what a curious spectacle a parked car, a man inside, and a weeping woman in his arms presented to bypassers, but he didn't care. The only thing he cared about was soothing Kelly through what he suspected was going to be a full-fledged crying jag.

"Kelly?" he prompted her softly. She burrowed deeper. "Honey, come on." It was no use. So he held her and tried to soothe the distress his reckless words had caused. Eventually her trembling abated, and Nick gently held her away to assess the damage. When she refused to look at him while she rummaged in her purse for a tissue to dry her eyes, he realized she was embarrassed. He let instinct guide him to the delicate solution.

"That'll teach you to mess with me, won't it, Wylie?" he teased, placing a soft kiss on her brow. "If you can't take the heat . . ."

Gradually, Kelly gathered the courage to look at him. Her breath caught at the utter tenderness that filled his eyes as he began a leisurely inspection of her face.

"You can stop looking for lingering aftereffects, Abella," she sniffed. "In case you hadn't noticed, they're all cried out."

That was better, he thought. He could tell by the way she moved stiffly out of his arms that she was still uncomfortable, but at least she'd come back swinging.

Never, not even at the height of the scandal, had Kelly lost control like that. Rationally, she knew Nick's words had triggered a long-suppressed delayed reaction. Still, she'd never felt so exposed in her life. Nor so sheltered afterward by a touch.

That was why she searched for words to thank him now for teasing her when he might have hesitated, for purging what solemn commiseration couldn't have touched. Everything that occurred to her to say seemed inane until, miraculously, she saw understanding waiting there in his smile. Tremulously, she smiled back, prolonging the tender communication until, slowly, Nick's eyes changed. They ceased to smile, then so did hers as they were caught and held by the glitter in his that compelled like hot, smoldering gold.

"Listen to me," Nick said softly, "and just think about this. We can't know what the future will bring. There are obstacles in our way, obstacles that may, when tomorrow's done, change what you'll mean to me and what I'll mean to you. But there's one thing that won't change. We can't be indifferent to each other, Kelly, and we can't ever pretend that we are."

"I know that, Nick. It frightens me."

Yeah, it frightened him too. "I have a proposal. Until we can sort out what we do or don't want to be to each another, can't we at least be friends?"

"Of course we can," she said simply. "I'm just afraid that the real question will be, can we end up that way?"

Nick let the weight of her doubts settle over him, then he leaned forward and started the ignition. "Well, I guess we'll just have to wait for the answer to that one too."

Minutes later he found a parking space on a nearby residential street and squeezed between two smaller cars.

"Come on, let's walk," he said, resting his hand at her waist.

Trying to give their emotions time to settle, Nick began to point out the sights, commenting on the history of a café here, a stone commemorating a landmark there. They entered a flagstone court-yard where casual spectators had paused to listen to a bearded guitarist who sat perched on the stone rim of a water fountain. His hat rested less than a foot from him, impossible to miss.

Kelly glanced up at Nick and saw him following the direction of her gaze. They shared a smile, then returned their attention to the singer, con-tent to stand there awhile and listen. Content, for now, to let the emotions churning inside them just be.

A sandy-haired mustached man of medium height situated himself beside a heavyset woman who stood two feet behind Nick and Kelly. The man's elbow accidentally nudged the woman and he smiled down with a ready, pleasant apology. Ignoring her coy little simper, he concentrated on Kelly and Nick, his quarry.

Nick leaned down to speak softly in Kelly's ear. "Jean's shop is right up there," he said, gesturing to a steep wooden staircase behind them. His gaze passed over the man who watched them.

Kelly leaned into him when he took her arm. The stairs wound up into a shop fashioned in the style of a log cabin. They entered beneath a sharply pitched shingled roof, and Kelly was im-mediately assailed with the aroma of sandalwood, scented candles, and fresh, raw pine. Sounds from the crowd outside melted faintly through the thin screen door. They amplified briefly, then became muted once more when the door swung open behind her to admit more customers.

Woven baskets filled with colorful balls of scented soap rested beneath a huge bay window on the far right wall. Arranged in the middle of the shop were the main attractions, row upon row of quaint little animal wood carvings. Some Kelly recognized as quite skillfully crafted hunting decoys. She reached out and ran her hand over the painted feathers of a couple of the more impressive wild duck and mallard replicas and turned to Nick with a delighted smile.

"Jean's specialty. His family is Cajun, and the skill has been passed down from generation to generation."

"I'm impressed," Kelly said, nodding. "Do you see him?" she added, looking around the shop.

"No," Nick replied. "But I do see Sue over there. She's been Jean's right hand here for about seven years now."

Kelly took a closer look at the slim blonde perched casually behind the cash register off in the distance. As she did, Sue looked up and spotted them, her eyes resting on Nick with delight. She laid her book down on the counter as Kelly and Nick approached.

"Nick! Long time no see. How have you been?"

"Too long, sugar. I'm doing just fine. Sue, this is Kelly Wylie, a colleague of mine. Kelly, Susan Reynolds. She and her husband live in town."

"Hello," Kelly said politely. She caught the inquisitive look Sue gave Nick after a nodded greeting to her and wondered if Mrs. Reynolds's feelings toward Nick were proprietary or protective.

"I'm looking for Jean," Nick said. "Is he around?"

"As a matter of fact, he isn't," Sue said. "He took off for the cabin yesterday. I know," she added at Nick's look, "he caught us all off guard."

"Did he say why he was leaving this soon in the season?" Nick asked.

"Not really, he—will that be all, sir? Excuse me, you two." Sue turned with a practiced smile to ring up a waiting customer's sale.

Nick took advantage of the break to fill Kelly in. "Jean owns a bait-and-tackle shop down in Louisiana. It's not far from a cabin he inherited from a distant relative in southeast bayou country four years ago. He's been stabilizing the store here, preparing it for turnover to Sue and her husband so that he can live down in Louisiana full-time."

"But he lives at his Louisiana home part of the time every year?"

Nick nodded. "Usually he never leaves for there until around the first part of October, and he stays the winter." He turned back to Sue as she finished with her customer. "So what did he say about leaving?"

"Only that some pressing business came up and that he couldn't wait around."

"Did he say when he was coming back?"

"As a matter of fact, no. He asked me to stand by." She frowned. "I'm surprised he didn't tell you all this himself, Nick."

"Oh, he probably tried to," Nick said easily. "I haven't been exactly easy to reach lately."

"Yeah," Sue said. "We were all pretty shocked down here about that prosecutor getting murdered. Are you all any closer to finding out who did it?"

"Not yet, but we're working on it. Listen, I'm going to try to get in touch with Jean myself, but if you hear anything before the week's out, let me know, will you?"

"Sure thing," Sue agreed. "Hey, is anything the matter? I mean, is Jean in trouble or something?" Again her troubled eyes drifted over to Kelly.

"No. Nothing for you to worry about, honey. I just wanted to talk. Take care."

"Bye, Nick, Ms. Wylie," Sue said as Kelly and Nick turned to leave. "And don't be a stranger for so long next time, Nick!" she called after them.

Nick raised a hand in farewell and ushered Kelly out the door.

The sandy-haired man at the end of the counter neatly replaced the magazine he had been leafing through.

"Can I help you?" Sue asked politely.

"Thank you, no, just looking." He smiled pleasantly. "You have a lovely shop here. Is it yours?" He allowed her to give him the answer he already had.

"No, it belongs to a Cajun gentleman who makes his home here part of the year. We have some lovely things. Feel free to browse around."

"Actually, I'm meeting someone for lunch shortly. But I'll certainly come back when I have more time." His eyes casually shifted to the bay window, where he saw Nicholas and the woman stroll out of the courtyard. He ambled unhurriedly toward the door.

"Have a nice day," Sue called at his back. He didn't move like a man in a hurry, she thought, reaching for her book.

"Sue seems like a nice woman," Kelly said casually back in the car.

"Yes, she's very sweet."

"Is she always that glad to see you?"

Pleasantly suspicious, Nick glanced her way, then back at the road. "Wrong tree, sweetheart. You're barking up the wrong tree. She and her husband"—he stressed the latter—"are very good friends." The back of his hand smoothed over her throat with a stroking caress.

Feeling slightly warm and very foolish, Kelly said, "I'm sorry. I shouldn't have . . ."

"Hey," Nick interrupted softly, "don't spoil it. I'm glad you wanted to know, okay?"

Kelly's hand joined his briefly as she turned to look at him. "Okay."

He barely caught her smile before it and her hand were gone.

After that, the ride back home was uneventful. She looked over at Nick once, but his brow was creased and he seemed to be deep in thought. She lapsed back to her own thoughts until an hour later they arrived at the precinct.

When they were rounding the car, Kelly said, "Nick, I never thanked you for the doughnuts this morning." She hesitated. "If you wanted to do it again sometime I wouldn't mind."

Nick shoved his hands into his pockets and stood there watching her, loving the shyness that shaded the invitation.

"Lady," he answered, "I can't think of anything I'd like better."

As their deal was sealed, John Butler approached the Continental Air ticket counter. He flashed his badge to the eager young man behind the counter and five minutes later left to search for a pay phone along the concourse. He punched in the number and waited. Thirty minutes had passed since Scorpio had called with instructions.

"Yes?" Dull street sounds of laughter and song bled faintly through the background along with Scorpio's question.

"Le Beau left, all right, but the kid wasn't with him, just some other old man," Butler said.

Scorpio chuckled. "Oh, my friend, Joey obviously guessed the authorities would be watching all the major transportation points. He knew he couldn't get out alone, so he went to Le Beau for help."

"So what now? Are you going down there?"

"In good time."

"What makes you think Joey won't contact Nick?"

"Joey thinks he's out of reach. There's no immediate reason for him to enlighten his brother now that he thinks he's bought himself time and distance to untangle things on his own. The brothers are very close. Joey wouldn't give Nick knowledge that might jeopardize his life."

"Well, I hope you're right." Butler had a bad feeling about this, but Scorpio had never guided them wrong. "What do you want me to do?"

"Aside from keeping an eye on things, nothing. I'll be in touch."

Nick was heading out the kitchen door when his phone rang. He was impatient to be with Kelly, but a short debate had him grabbing the receiver.

"Hello?"

"Nick."

"Jesus, Joey!"

"Yeah, man."

"Where the hell are you?"

"At Jean's. I didn't do it, Nick."

"Then why aren't you here explaining that to the police?"

"Ah, Nicky, it's complicated. I can't. Not yet. If I could, I would. But I can't."

"You're not making any sense, brother. Everybody's looking to bust your ass from here to Kalamazoo. We've got to talk."

"You know where I am. But I want you to come alone. Alone! Do you understand? I can't explain what's going on over a phone and I can't stay on the line much longer. Will you come?"

"Dammit, yes, you know I will, but you've got to give me more."

"It's bigger than Cain, Nick. Just remember that and watch your back. It's bigger than Cain."

Nick listened to Joey cut the connection. The dial tone buzzed steadily in his ear. It was seven A.M.

Thirty minutes later Kelly punched line one on her office console and picked up her phone. Nick had called telling her to meet him at the precinct. She hadn't questioned the urgency in his voice; she'd just gotten here, but Nick still hadn't shown up.

"I want you to come to my office now," Brower ordered gruffly.

When Kelly arrived at his office, his secretary motioned her in and she was surprised to see Nick leaning against the corner window, smoking. His eyes softened briefly as he nodded and Kelly sat down and waited.

"Joey's contacted Nick," Brower announced without preliminaries.

"My God," Kelly said. "When?"

"This morning," Nick answered from behind her. Kelly turned in her chair to look at him. "I've already told the sheriff about our trip down to Brown County. It's like we guessed. Joey's in Louisiana with Jean."

"What else did he tell you?"

"Nothing. Except that he wants to talk to me alone." Nick pushed away from the wall and took the other chair beside Brower's desk.

"That's not all he told Nick," Brower put in. "Tell her the rest."

Nick took the time to stub out his cigarette and cross his ankles. "He said this thing, whatever that means, is bigger than we think. And he told me to watch my back."

Kelly felt a coldness seep over her. "What the hell's he talking about? A conspiracy?"

Neither man spoke. Then Brower looked at her while Nick looked down at his crushed cigarette. Brower finally answered.

"I'm afraid that's what it sounds like—as crazy as I'd like to believe it is. Dammit!" he said, bringing his fist down on the scatter of papers on his desk. "I wish I could dismiss it as a trick, but I can't. I've heard and seen crazier things than what Joey's implying."

Kelly's voice was firm. "Well, then. We know where he is. He has to be brought in for questioning."

"There's just one problem," Nick said calmly. "He obviously doesn't want to make contact with the police. Not even you, Anton. That suggests to me that we should proceed with this thing with an inordinate amount of caution and do what he wants. I'm going down there to talk to him."

"Now just hold on," Brower began.

"I think he's right, Sheriff," Kelly said.

"*You* think he's right?"

"I've done my homework, and whatever else Joey Abella may be, he's no fool. His record is spotless. If he's chosen to go into hiding from the police, to jeopardize a perfectly good career, there's got to be a darn good reason. If he's chosen Nick to hear that reason, I don't see that we have a choice other than to give him what he wants."

"Besides," Nick added, "if he's onto a conspiracy of some kind, the department can't afford to ignore what he has to say. And I'm telling you now, you'll only push him away if you give the Louisiana authorities the word to go in after him."

Brower looked from one to the other, then got up to walk over to his window. He stood there for maybe five minutes thinking, his hands clasped behind his back.

"If I let you do this, Nick, Kelly goes with you."

"Yes, sir."

"And I tell the police chief what's going on."

"No," Kelly said.

Brower turned. "What did you say, Sergeant?"

"I said, and I mean it respectfully sir, no. Given Joey's warning, I'd like to keep this thing between the three of us for the time being. Give us a week. If Joey can't be persuaded to come in, we'll take this higher." She felt Nick's eyes on her, but she kept hers fixed on Brower.

Brower's were just as steady. "I don't need to remind you, Sergeant, that you can't afford a screwup."

"And I'm sure I don't need to point out that if Joey's telling the truth and headquarters blows this, everyone will suffer."

Damned if she wasn't playing poker, Nick thought with admiration. A smile quirked his lips, and he transferred his gaze back to Anton, waiting to see what he would do.

"If you two are wrong . . ." Brower warned.

"A week," Kelly insisted. "If he's lying, we'll have him and he won't escape."

Brower walked back over to his desk, took his seat, and glared at her over his hands he propped under his chin. "Four days. No more, do you understand?"

The concession was more than she'd expected. "Perfectly," Kelly answered.

"Yes, sir," Nick added.

"Get out of here," Brower said to them both. "You two leave tomorrow."

"That took a lot of guts," Nick said out in the corridor. "You know what's riding on the line."

"I meant what I said in there. If Joey's innocent, we owe it to this department and to this city to play by his rules."

With a quick smile, Nick gave Kelly's shoulder an encouraging squeeze. "Pack for maximum heat," he said. "And forget the sandals. Bring sneakers or canvas shoes, maybe a pair of boots. We're going to bayou country."

"Fine," Kelly said. "I'll call you later to confirm the flight and the story we'll be using to cover our absence."

"I'll be waiting."

She turned to leave.

"Kelly?" he called impulsively.

"Yes?" she said, turning her head to look at him over her shoulder.

"Keep the faith, sweetheart. This is going to work, I can feel it."

She nodded solemnly.

Nick watched her disappear down the corridor before he turned in the opposite direction. The fading tap of her heels echoed in his ears.

7

The heat hit them with a soft blast outside New Orleans International Airport.

"Boy, you weren't kidding when you said maximum heat, were you?"

"August is the worst. The rest of the time, the temperature just hovers around, oh, a cool seventy-five . . . eighty-five . . . ninety . . ."

"Ha, ha, very funny," Kelly said.

Nick laughed. "Buck up, Wylie, you're going to need more stamina than that in the swamplands."

"I can't wait."

Nick smiled to himself as they got inside the rental car he had just leased. "It's about a thirty-, forty-five-minute drive. Do you want to stop somewhere to get something to eat first?"

"No, I'm fine. Besides, I confess I'm curious to see where you're taking me. Feed me when we get there."

"Good enough. I hope you like your food spicy." Nick threw the car into gear, left the airport, and headed east on Interstate 10.

Ten minutes into the drive, they entered Orleans Parish, and a few minutes after that Nick began veering off onto a series of narrow state roads along either side of which Kelly caught increasingly frequent glimpses of mossy waters.

Tall green cypress trees with knobby, grayish trunks towered like sentinels on either side of them. Kelly smiled at the dramatic abundance of live moss hanging like huge spiderwebs, linking tree to tree. The sight conjured up all sorts of romantic images of the Deep South, New Orleans in particular, that Kelly had absorbed from countless films, photographs, and books. But as they finally turned down a narrow dirt road farther to the east, nothing prepared her for the wild reality of the bayou.

She was so caught up in the view around her that she was startled after a while to see that Nick appeared to be driving them directly into the swamp that surrounded them. At her exclamation, he chuckled indulgently.

"I know. It struck me that way too at first. Trust me, we won't fall in."

"I'm holding you to that," Kelly murmured as she peered intently into the distance, where it appeared for all the world that the road indeed ran out. Nick slowed to a crawl and she was looking around, still skeptical, when they turned onto a gravel drive scarcely wide enough to accommodate the car and a prayer.

Nick followed the drive for about fifty yards until, abruptly, they emerged before a tiny bait-and-tackle shop sitting perched on short wooden stilts at the far end of a circular drive. They were the only customers.

"Jean's?" Kelly asked.

"Yeah."

Kelly climbed out of the car, grateful for her sensible shoes when tiny bits of shell and rock bit into her soles.

Taking everything in with a comprehensive glance, she wondered what it was about dramatic natural surroundings that made ordinary mortals feel so insignificant. Her urban eye was fascinated by the way fallen logs seemed to tangle haphazardly with the long, marshy grasses at the bases of the ever-present cypress surrounding this peninsula.

She walked beside Nick, imagining she could hear the cicadas breathing between each wave of shimmering chirps somewhere out there amid the gently lapping bayou waters. A frog watched her curiously from its perch not three feet away, and birds darted from tree limb to tree limb. Curtains of moss migrated from tree to tree until they formed a dense, dappled green canvas above their heads.

All in all, Kelly decided, everything—the flowers, the wildlife, even the insects—looked larger than life in a lush, verdant, almost surreal sort of way. It was all a little intimidating, but she also found it extremely beautiful.

She was about to comment on it when something light and airy touched her bare shoulder. She turned her head expecting to find a drifting leaf or maybe a piece of floating moss and almost shrieked when she came eye to eye with a dragonfly the size of a B-52.

"Oh, my God!" she gasped disgustedly as she barreled into Nick's side, trying to get away from the huge, ugly insect. She brushed furiously at her shoulder.

Caught off guard by the collision, Nick stumbled slightly under her weight and peered over her head to see what was the matter. Wide, gossamer wings beat unconcernedly off into the distance, and he laughed at Kelly's look of indignation. She turned that look on him and he drew back in mock horror, as if certain she would swat him next.

"It isn't funny." Her heart was still pounding.

"That's because you couldn't see your face— city girl," he taunted.

"Damned straight." Her lips curved slightly, and without a second thought she took Nick's arm and leaned into his shoulder. Nick ruffled her hair as they climbed the wooden steps.

The squeak of the rusty hinges brought a jeans-clad bear of a man out from a back room where Kelly traced the muted sounds of *Wheel of Fortune*.

"Nicky!" His greeting was as effusive as the smile that split his heavily jowled face. Jean Le Beau stepped around the low glass counter to enfold Nick in a bone-crushing hug.

"Jean, you old devil." Nick's voice was muffled against the blue cotton covering Jean's massive shoulders. "Still just as shy as ever, I see."

Jean seemed to find that heartily amusing and gave a shout of laughter.

Kelly admired the way Nick didn't flinch when

the stub of a foul-smelling cigar clenched between his friend's stained teeth swooped dangerously close to his ear.

"Jean never changes, my friend." He leaned back, eyeing Nick fondly. "And you're still just as good-looking and insolent as ever." The two men exchanged wide smiles and Kelly smiled too, appreciating the easy affection between them. Gradually Nick's expression sobered.

"Joey," he said simply.

Jean's gaze swung around to Kelly, who had settled herself against a wall lined with tackle boxes, lines, and reels. His gaze turned speculative, and Kelly thought the Cajun inflection in his accent thickened.

"And who is this very pretty lady you so rudely neglect to introduce me to?"

"This is Kelly Wylie, a colleague of mine. Kelly, this old rascal is Jean Le Beau, owner and proprietor of this humble establishment, which, he'll be happy to tell you, is the only connection with civilization for miles around."

"It's a pleasure," Kelly said softly as she stepped forward to clasp his outstretched hand.

Jean studied her intently, and she grew a little uncomfortable beneath the somber inspection until Jean smiled, breaking the tension.

Not relinquishing her hand, the giant said to Nick, "Your colleague, hmm? Nevertheless, you have a very good eye, my friend." To Kelly he said, "So you wish to know where Joey is too, pretty mademoiselle?"

"We understood," she glanced at Nick, "that he was here."

Jean released her hand and walked back around his display counter. "He was. I tried to get him to stay until Nick arrived, but he wouldn't. He left early this morning for Olmston," he said, naming the little town twenty miles east. He looked from one to the other. "He," Jean said with slight emphasis, "wouldn't give me an explanation either. But it has to do with the police, *non*?"

"Did he say where in Olmston?" Nick asked intently, for the moment ignoring the answer to Jean's question.

Jean's eyes narrowed. "No," he said carefully. "He said only that there were things to be done before he returned here. And from your tone, I think that had better be soon, *non*?" He folded his massive arms across his broad chest and regarded them steadily.

"We need your help, Mr. Le Beau." Kelly moved to Nick's side.

Jean dragged on the foul cigar, exhaled, then with quiet precision spoke around it.

"How?"

"What has he told you?" Nick countered.

"Only that he was being sought out by enemies who would hunt him down unless he left Sedgwick. Nothing before we came here, nothing after. I wanted to call you before we left, but Joey insisted that I not. He insisted that he wasn't going to involve me any more than he had to—as if I weren't already involved."

"It's Cain's murder. Circumstantial evidence points to Joey, and we can't find him to refute it."

"*Mon Dieu!*" Jean burst out. "That is completely ridiculous!"

"We were hoping to find him here so that he could tell us exactly what was going on," Kelly said. "Instead, he's run again."

Jean studied her shrewdly. "You do not think he is innocent of this crime, *oui*?"

Kelly hesitated. "Honestly, I don't know."

Jean reached beneath the counter, drew out another cigar, and lit it. "He said he would return here when he could. When this will be, I don't know."

"We came prepared to wait," Nick said.

"What has Sandy to say about all of this?"

"He doesn't know the details. No one knows why Kelly and I are here except you and our county sheriff. It needs to stay that way."

Jean nodded. "I understand. And these enemies who seek Joseph? Will they not know where he has gone?"

Nick sighed. "Maybe. I hope not."

"But we can't be sure," Kelly said. "Mr. Le Beau," she added thoughtfully, "our time is limited, and maybe Joey's is as well, more than he thinks. Now, he's sure to be lying low, out of the mainstream of things. Do you know anyone in Olmston who might know where to look for someone who doesn't want to be found?"

Jean considered it for a moment. "Michel," he answered. "An even more distant cousin than the one who left me the cabin here. But he is a Le Beau. He will help. What do you want him to do?"

It warmed Kelly to realize that Nick had accepted her control of the situation and that Jean was trusting his lead. "We have to keep things as circumspect as possible. Can you take us to him, convince him that we need to be in on the search?"

"Of course." His answer encompassed Nick. "If this is what you wish."

"It is," Nick agreed.

Jean looked from one to the other, assessing, drawing his own conclusions. "Then it shall be so. Tomorrow. In the meantime, you two will need someplace to stay. My home is humble, but of course it is yours for as long as you need it."

Nick smiled. *"Merci, mon père."*

"In fact," Jean continued, "we will all let go of these troubles a little tonight. I am hosting a celebration, and you two will join my guests."

"A celebration of what?" Nick asked curiously.

"Why, of my return, of course!"

Kelly found herself laughing along with the two men. She liked this bluff, transplanted Cajun. It wasn't hard to imagine his affection and good humor as a stabilizing force in the young lives of Nick and Joey.

"Here," Jean said, digging a key from his pocket and handing it to Nick. "You know where everything is, and the refrigerator is stocked. Make yourselves at home, and I will join you in a few hours."

"Again, Jean, our thanks. Ready?" Nick asked, turning to Kelly.

"Sure, let's go."

"We'll see you later," Nick called over his shoulder.

"As you say, my friend. As you say."

Nick circled the car around the lot, and Kelly caught a glimpse of Jean standing behind the mesh of the screen, his arms crossed over the bulk of his stomach, his eyes thoughtful.

Nick pulled back out onto the dirt road, but instead of going back the way they had come, he headed in the opposite direction past the store until Kelly spotted what looked like a lean-to sitting adjacent to a carport, which was presently empty. They drew closer, and she shook her head ruefully. A couple of skiffs bobbed placidly against a clapboard dock.

"The only way to get to Jean's cabin is by boat."

"That's right, sugar. I'm afraid that compared to what you're used to we'll be roughing it a little. Are you up to it?" he asked, pulling smoothly into one of the carport spaces.

"Oh, I'm tougher than I look, Abella. Don't doubt it."

Nick turned to her within the close, shadowed confines of the car and weighed her words. He thought about the way she had nudged Brower into the confrontation that had put them here and the deft way she'd just won over Jean. "Oh, I don't, honey," he said. "I don't."

* * *

Later, the soft rumble of the motor hummed at Kelly's back as the skiff glided across the gently undulating water. The glare of the sun had forced them both to put on sunglasses, and for the last fifteen minutes or so she had been sitting propped against the front seat watching everything around her with an encompassing gaze. When they rounded a bend and glided past a succession of stilted cabins and houseboats, Kelly asked about them.

"This," Nick said, gesturing to the bayou community around them, "is typical. There are several swampland communities like it scattered all across the bayous of southeast Louisiana. This particular community, like many of them, is heavily Cajun. It's the country Jean's people originally hail from."

"Why did he leave it?" she asked, fascinated to see women here and there hanging out laundry, children laughing and playing, a couple of old men sitting on the bank of their property fishing, their avid gazes returning Kelly's. She was observing all of their normal activities of daily living, transplanted to a world of gently lapping waters and green moss.

"Well, like I told you before, he left initially to go to war. After that, what held him up north, besides his lack of close family here, was the chance for better work. As long as I can remember, though, he's always talked of wanting to come back." Nick smiled. "To live and die among his roots, he says. I guess he's finally made it."

"You sound as if you envy him."

Nick thought about that a moment. He envied Jean's solid sense of family, of closeness of clan. "Maybe I do a little. Since he's been shuttling between Indiana and Louisiana, he's seemed more connected somehow, more . . . I don't know, in tune with himself, I guess. He's a man at ease in his skin. I admire that."

"And you?" she asked.

Nick looked down from his contemplation of the sky, down the length of the boat. "You're asking a lot of questions."

"Because I want to know, Nick."

"Why?"

Kelly turned to look at him. He was leaning back against his seat looking long, lean, and boneless. Involuntarily she swallowed, hit again by the sheer sexiness of the man. "Because I . . . I want to understand you." *Because every time I'm with you*, she added silently, *I feel less and less like a cop and more and more like a woman.*

"Oh, yes. We agreed to be friends."

Though his words were curt, there was no mockery in them. Kelly ignored the thudding of her heart. "Yes."

One corner of his mouth turned up, diffusing the somber image the dark glasses created shading his eyes. He held out his hand and Kelly reached over to take it.

"You wondered once if we could end up being friends," he reminded her. "Now I'm wondering the same thing, but in a slightly different way, I suspect."

"What do you mean?" Kelly asked, succumbing

to the pull of his voice and the dark penetration of his shaded eyes.

His hand tightened and the tug she felt was almost imperceptible. Almost, not quite.

"You know what I mean," he murmured. "Right now I'm not feeling friendly, Kelly. And you know I'm not talking about animosity; quite the opposite."

"Please, Nick, we agreed."

"We agreed to see where our feelings would take us, and I'm trying to be honest. I'm trying to be your friend or your buddy or pal, or whatever it is you want. But you have to know that I'm very close to wanting something more."

Kelly looked down at their hands, but she didn't let go.

Nick sighed. "Don't let it distress you, sweetheart, I just want you to know where I stand."

"I do," she murmured. And she did. She was standing there too. "But what about when this investigation is over? This case with Joey is only one part of what I do, Nick. You respect my job, but you don't like it, and it's too close to who I am and who you are to separate it out of our lives."

"Let me handle my own feelings, okay?"

"And what about mine?" she went on. "I don't know if I want to open myself up to the fear and the uncertainty of caring for a cop again." *Or living with the loneliness of being shut out of a part of your life that only your job can fill,* she could have added.

He didn't relinquish his hold, though he seriously considered her words. There was truth in them that would have to be reconciled. But there was also a void in his life he was beginning to discover Kelly had the power to fill. "At least, tell me one thing?"

"What?"

"If things were different, if there was no case standing between us, if I were just a man and you were just a woman, would this fight still be so hard?"

"Don't make me answer that," she pleaded.

Nick sounded a little sad, a little grim. "You just did."

Kelly pulled her hand away and he let her. She turned back toward the front of the boat.

For the rest of the ride down the bayou, they said little. Both were preoccupied with reevaluating their relationship. Thoughts drifted back to a late-night supper and a forbidden kiss. Hearts remembered a storm of quiet tears one sunny summer morning, the shared aftermath of tender solace, the intimacy exchanged as one took what the other had to give. Both were wondering how to cope with barriers that were irreparably rending.

Time passed smoothly, as gently as the undulation of the calm bayou waters beneath them.

"Is that it?" Kelly asked presently, peering at a partially secluded cabin just easing into view along the distant right bank.

"Yes. We should reach it in another five minutes or so."

Kelly tilted her shades up. The cabin, she saw, was a long, one-story, rambling structure set high on stilts just like all of the other houses she had seen along the bayou. They were almost upon the private jetty designed to house the boat when Nick started to gather up their things.

He cut the motor and let the boat glide to the dock. Kelly sat where she was, helping control the rocking motion of the skiff while Nick moored it to one of the wooden stilts supporting the structure.

With few words and an economy of motion, he helped her out and they started up the path to the cabin. Kelly dropped her bag inside and turned in a slow circle. She didn't know what she had expected, but whatever it was, it hadn't been nearly as comfortable looking as the reality.

The decor was unmistakably masculine and designed for comfort. A long, high-backed brown-and-moss-green sofa faced a huge fireplace of natural brick. Both dominated the room. A brown, high-backed armchair flanked the sofa on the right, a brass magazine rack separating the two. There were two midsize windows on either side of the front door that faced the bayou they had just traveled.

Kelly headed toward the right exit of the living room to the kitchen Nick had indicated before he went back to the boat for the rest of their bags. From what she could see, the cabin was built in a classic shotgun construction typical throughout the South.

She wandered into the kitchen and was checking out something interesting looking in a refrig-

erated deep Dutch oven when she heard Nick
bumping back into the living room.

"Need any help in there?" she called.

"Nah, I got it under control. How 'bout you?"

"Ditto," she called back.

"Come on out here for a minute, then. I'll show
you where you're bunking."

Kelly finished setting a six-pack of cola back in
the refrigerator, then walked around the corner
into the living room.

Nick, she saw, had already conceded to the
heat. He had replaced the wilting khaki he'd been
wearing with a very thin, very white, tank T-shirt.
It displayed beautifully the sculpted musculature
of his chest and his hard, flat stomach where the
shirt tucked low into his jeans. She was suddenly
very conscious of her own wilted state and longed
to bathe and change into something cool and
short.

Nick had her bag in hand. "Come on, I'll give
you the quick tour."

The cabin contained, if not all the creature com-
forts, at least all the necessities of daily living. In
addition to the living room and kitchen, there was
a tiny bathroom and one bedroom in which Nick
deposited her bags.

"Jean will take the sofa in the living room and
I'll take the daybed on the deck." The deck he
referred to was a screened-in porch off the back.
It overlooked a lovely view of the winding water-
ways east of the house. The only item that gave
Kelly pause was an ancient-looking washing machine that actually had a roller attachment.

"Does Jean really use that thing?" Kelly asked with a bemused smile.

Nick looked it up and down very seriously before replying, "He does, and God bless him. Personally, I never come here without an ample supply of my BVDs." His dimple kicked up.

Kelly laughed.

"Why don't you go ahead and change while I put some lunch together."

"Give me ten minutes and I'll help you."

"Nah, I got it. You just settle in."

Kelly gratefully took advantage of the distance he was offering her.

When Nick heard her enter the kitchen later, he turned around holding the tomato he was slicing for the salad. "You look great," he said automatically as his eyes moved appreciatively over her thick ponytail, past her yellow cotton blouse and shorts, on down to the long, silky smoothness of her bare, tanned legs. In a skirt those legs had been tantalizing. In shorts they were devastating.

"You want me to finish that?"

"Finish what?"

Kelly cursed her blush at Nick's arrested look and gestured toward the vegetable bowl.

Nick frowned quickly, cleared his throat, and turned back toward the sink. "No, no," he said. "You just sit down and start on the gumbo there." He nodded to the warm Dutch oven he'd set in the middle of the table. "I'll have this finished in a minute."

Well, well, she thought with a faint smile. She'd wondered how he would look with that unruffle-

able cool ruffled. Now she knew. Flustered. And
adorable. A few minutes later he brought the bowl
to the table and joined her.

"This salad is delicious," she said, tasting a bite.
"Somehow I have a hard time picturing you being
domestic enough to cook."

"I usually don't," he agreed. "I usually grab it
on the run. You should feel privileged."

"I really could have helped, you know."

"Now don't go snatching back your compliment. Another apology for not helping and I'll
start thinking you lied about my cooking just to
spare my feelings."

Kelly looked up at him. Despite his light tone,
she was only half certain that he wasn't serious.
Not about the cooking but about something
deeper. Was he regretting revealing his vulnerability back in the boat? Surely he knew there was
no need to. Then, as if sensing her question, Nick
looked up from beneath his lashes with a slow
smile and a wink.

Reassured that she had overreacted to his
mood, she finished her meal.

Long after the midmorning sun deepened to
gold and cast a shimmering patina across the
bayou, Kelly sat curled up on the sofa, sifting
through some personnel files she had brought
with her. Nick had gone out to the deck to make it
more suitable for habitation. So now the house
was quiet, except for the occasional knocking
from Nick's hammer, and her concentration
could function at its maximum.

She revised her notes of the assorted alibis each

of Cain's staff and bodyguards had given her during the course of the investigation. All had been corroborated and seemed solid. But there was something about Butler that bothered her. On paper, there was no reason to distrust him. But she did. A gut feeling. Which was probably why her eye returned to a detail she hadn't pondered though she'd noticed.

Butler, Joey, and Robbins, all three of Cain's bodyguards, had served for three years in the same army division prior to joining the force. She knew that the bodyguards of public officials frequently came from military backgrounds; frequently they were selected for it because of the discipline military training required.

There was little reason for the coincidence to strike her as odd, but given these unusual circumstances, it did. Could there be an angle here she had overlooked? She made a mental note to follow up.

She was still going over notes when she heard singing. Raising her head to listen a little, she realized it was coming from Nick. His low baritone provided a pleasant counterpoint to his hammering, and if she wasn't mistaken, he was being accompanied by Randy Travis. The song they were sharing was heartfelt and soulful.

Kelly chuckled and leaned her head against the back of the sofa. Who would have guessed Nick could sing? Come to think of it, who would have thought she'd be sitting here in a cabin, not twenty feet from him in the middle of a bayou, listening to him sing? And liking it. There was, she thought with a sigh, entirely too much about Nicholas Abella she had grown to like.

Nick. No matter how she tried to shake his effect on her, it wouldn't be shaken. Respect for the officer had come through professional observation almost from the start. Respect for the man had come following the concessions he had made with parts of himself she knew he held sacred. His privacy and emotional solitude. During this investigation, she had uncovered personal areas inside him she suspected few, with the exception of the handful closest to him, were aware of. And he had smoothly invaded private areas of hers. She sighed again. Where would it all lead to in the end?

Nick's sizzling curse interrupted the distant melody. From the other room something clattered heavily to the floor and Kelly was up like a shot heading for the deck. She got to the threshold of the porch, and it took her only a moment to see what had happened. She sighed, relieved.

Nick was sitting cross-legged on the floor, the discarded hammer beside him. The thumb that he nursed was discoloring already. She knelt by his side.

"Let me see." She pried the fingers of his good hand away to get a better look at the thumb. She turned it carefully this way and that, inspecting it. "I don't think you've broken it, you've just bloodied it a little. What were you doing?"

"Trying to nail back this"—his adjective was more profane than the first—"board that's coming loose at the base of the wall and the netting."

He didn't mention that he had been doing all right until Randy's wailing about a particularly warm and winsome woman and the image of sloe eyes, endless legs, and titian hair had crowded his concentration.

"Well, I think ice will take care of the swelling, but we'd better clean the cut first. Does Jean keep anything?"

"There's a medicine chest in the bathroom," Nick said through gritted teeth.

"Well, come on. Let's see."

First-aid supplies were one provision Jean was low on. Plenty of bandages, Merthiolate, and Band-Aids, but no peroxide. That didn't daunt Kelly.

"You, my friend, just happen to be in luck. Come on," she said, tugging at his wrist.

She pulled Nick behind her until they stood inside her room. Leaving him at the door, she rummaged around in her duffel bag on the bed and pulled out a small leather case. In an instant, she had it unzipped and was holding a pint-size bottle of peroxide and some cotton balls.

"What were you," Nick's expression was sardonic, "a Girl Scout?"

"And aren't you glad of it," Kelly answered with a saucy smirk. Pouring some of the disinfectant on the cotton, she walked back over to the doorway where he stood and reached out to take his hand. He was nursing his thumb again. "Come on, big man," she said, replacing his hand with her own. "This won't hurt a bit." She blotted the wound until she was satisfied that it was clean. "There," she said. "Looks like the bleeding has stopped already. I'd forget a Band-Aid and let the air get to it if I were you. Okay?"

"Sure," he murmured.

Still holding his hand, Kelly looked up at his tone and read in his eyes an echo of her own recent thoughts. Slowly she released his hand. Just as slowly he reached out and took hers back.

"Just once, I promise . . ." His breath was a whisper. "Just this once . . ." And then his breath was mingling with hers as his lips touched and took hers in a kiss aching with tenderness and restraint.

Cool air touched the dewy moisture of her mouth, and Kelly blinked, feeling him drifting away from her, his promise intact.

She didn't even realize she'd uttered his name until his grip on her arms tightened. "Come here," she heard him whisper. His hard, muscled arm was a gentle band around her back as he pulled her into his embrace. She barely drew breath before his lips took hers in a sweetly devouring kiss.

His hands slowly traced down the slope of her back, molding the fabric of her shirt to skin that was growing heated with passion. When he angled his body slightly to the left, Kelly was dimly aware of being pulled along with him. When she felt herself tilted forward to fall onto the tough length of him, she realized that he had braced his back against the knotted wood of the wall. Spreading his legs slightly, he urged her pliant body into even closer contact.

The movement summoned a spark of awareness that urged Kelly to pull her mouth from his in an attempt to slow things down. But Nick was lost, and Kelly almost dissolved on the spot when his lips, deprived of the softness of hers, caressed the warm, fragrant skin of her neck.

He nuzzled sweetly and she felt the tip of his tongue reach out to trace delicate little patterns just beneath her chin, down over her throat, until gradually, like a slow roll of heat lightning, their desire was a living thing. Kelly knew it had overwhelmed Nick too when he drew back, panting softly, drawing in shallow little breaths of air.

She knew she should stop this while he still had the power to, while they both did, but the words got lodged somewhere in her heart. He was dragging her emotions too close to the surface, exerting a control over them that at this moment surpassed her own.

"I want you." Nick's voice was a groan, a plea for fulfillment only she could give. "I'm trying, honey, but I can't stop wanting you." His stroking hands dropped to her hips to draw her close until her soft gasp let him know she understood the force of his arousal.

Kelly was being sucked into a blinding vortex where all that existed was the fire of Nick's kiss and the rhythmic demand of his body against hers. The feel of his hand probing the zipper of her shorts penetrated her awareness at the same moment the throbbing of a boat engine penetrated the silence.

Nick raised his head and peered with dazed

eyes past the room's curtained window. Jean hoisted himself out of the boat and Nick cursed soundly, though he didn't know whom he cursed —the old man for his inopportune timing or himself for his loss of control.

Nick's hands dropped from her and Kelly looked down at her feet, trying to catch her breath. Silently she praised Jean's arrival.

"Nick! Kelly!" Jean's voice boomed from the living room. "Have you two left me already?"

"No," Kelly called weakly. She tried again, forcing strength into her voice. "Nick cut his finger; we were tending to it." Unable to face either Nick or herself right now, she kept her eyes downcast while she tried to get around him to the door. Nick gripped her wrist.

"We've got to talk, Kelly."

"Not now," she said, tugging against his grip. Nick refused to let go.

"Later. Tonight," he said. "I mean it. We talk about this later tonight." She looked up then and saw by the steadiness in his eyes that he was letting her go for now, but he was hardly letting her escape.

8

The party was in full swing, and Kelly grew more tense as the laughing and dancing around her grew less inhibited.

She was sitting on the top step of the cabin porch, sipping lemonade, her back propped against the railing. A rowdy, foot-stomping duel of accordions was being waged by none other than the two elderly Cajun fishermen who had observed her and Nick's progress up the bayou earlier that day. Jean's bash was swinging into its fifth hour.

Kelly's gaze drifted across the yard until it settled on Nick, who sat at one of the many food-laden tables she'd help set up hours ago.

After they had gone out into the living room to greet Jean, there had been little time for dwelling on the emotions that had erupted between them. Jean needed help with his last-minute preparations, and so the afternoon had passed with Kelly and Nick acting polite toward each other with as few words as possible. Each had been too acutely aware of the other to relax completely. And if

Jean's occasional looks meant anything, the tension between them hadn't gone unnoticed.

Now Nick sat tipped back on the legs of his chair, a beer in his hand and an easy smile on his lips as he chatted with Dora Lynn Bundy, a trim and attractive middle-aged widow Jean had introduced as his "special friend." And if her stylishly short brunette hair and her lovely, unlined coffee complexion made her look closer to forty than to the fifty she was as of today, it shouldn't have raised undue concern. But right now it did for Kelly, and it had everything to do with her heightened senses toward the man she watched.

"She is an attractive woman, is she not?"

Kelly jumped a little, startled to see that Jean had materialized out of nowhere. He eased his bulk down beside her.

"Yes, she is."

"A wonderful conversationalist. It's one of the things I like best about her."

Kelly noticed how the smooth expanse of the woman's throat was exposed as she threw back her head to laugh at something Nick had said. "Yes, she does appear to communicate wonderfully well." She was so engrossed in the exchange at the table, she missed Jean's smile.

Jean looked out at his guests, who were waltzing now to a lilting ballad drifting from someone's fiddle. "Do you want to talk about it?"

"There's nothing to talk about," Kelly murmured, dropping her head. All of a sudden she was feeling very melancholy and Jean's sensitivity was making it acute.

Kelly's head was bowed, so she missed the way Nick's gaze idly wandered, seeking her out for maybe the hundredth time since the party had begun. She missed it. But Jean didn't. And when Nick's searching eyes located Kelly, then shifted to Jean, she also missed the silent communication between the men, and the way the old man's smile mocked the challenge in Nick's.

"Well, if you have nothing to talk about," Jean said quietly, "I would like to say something to you, if I may." When Kelly didn't answer, he continued. "When Nicholas was a very small boy, things were not . . . easy . . . at home for him. He learned at a very early age to pull things within himself. An advantage for the detective, no doubt. But for the man, perhaps it has not always been so good."

Kelly looked into his clear, gray eyes. "Why are you telling me this?"

Jean shrugged. "Because I love him," he said simply. He took another puff of his cigar. "I am not blind, *chérie*. This afternoon, something was going on when I came home. And whatever it was, I would guess that it is very strong between you. Even if you do not care to talk about it, *oui*?"

Kelly sighed. The old man saw too much. "Even so, that doesn't mean that Nick and I have the luxury of forgetting that we're involved under circumstances that require a loyalty that outweighs an attraction. We can't afford to nurture these feelings we have for each other."

Jean laughed softly. "Ah, Kelly, how it amuses me to hear the foolishness of the young. If we could all have the luxury of choosing how we feel, of choosing who we care for and who we don't, we would all be much happier human beings rather than poor ordinary mortals, *non*?"

He had her and he knew it, Kelly saw by the gentle glint in his eye. She smiled a little, though "Perhaps" was all she said.

"Well," Jean said, stretching both legs out before him, "this party grows long. And I am an old man who needs his rest. I should end things soon, I think." He paused, looking across the yard. Kelly turned, and her heart quickened. Nick was coming directly toward them and his eyes were all for her.

"A piece of sage wisdom, *ma chérie*, and then I will shut up. Life is much too transitory and complicated as it is. Don't complicate the things that are simple." He smiled. "Remember that."

Nick stopped at the foot of the steps and nodded to Jean. Then he looked down at Kelly. "Dance?" he asked softly, his light eyes unfathomable.

Kelly hesitated and looked out into the starry August night. Some silent communiqué must have transferred itself to Jean's guests, because the fiddler who played was joined by another. "In honor of the night," one of them said, "we'll play a special Cajun tune. Perfect for lovers or for the romantics in our midst."

Kelly looked back at Nick and heard Jean's words. He was a wise old man, she thought. On a night like this, nothing should be so complicated that she couldn't reach out to grasp one thing that was not.

"All right," she heard herself saying. She placed her hand in Nick's and let him pull her exactly where she wanted to be at that moment.

The music ebbed and flowed around them. They were not the only couple who danced, but Kelly closed her eyes and pretended that they were and that the darkness cocooned them from the complications of yesterday and the worries of tomorrow.

"You two were awfully intense over there," Nick murmured in her ear. Kelly felt the softness of her hair tickle her skin under the delicate puff of his breath.

"He's a very special man, your Jean. And he loves you very much. You're lucky to have him."

"Yes. But right now, I'm more interested in you. No, don't stiffen up, we've passed the point of pretending."

"I know." Kelly pulled back a little to look into his eyes. Her hands stayed looped around his neck, her fingers sifting gently through the dark silk at his nape. "Nothing's happened between us yet that we can't walk away from, Nick, and I'm not sure that I want it to."

He searched her eyes for a moment. "Neither am I. But I don't think that's the issue here. I think we're dealing with something that may have been taken out of our hands."

She dropped her eyes and laid her head back against his shoulder. "No. I won't accept that. It's never out of our hands. We always have a choice."

Nick said nothing to that, choosing for a while to let the crooning rhythm of the music move him.

He savored the pleasure of having her near him, thigh to thigh, cheek to cheek, as she wordlessly followed his lead. He was finding it difficult to think that he couldn't have this pleasure, again and again, after this night and this magical moment had passed. He had no name for what he felt for her. He only knew these past few days how good she had made him feel.

"I don't want to let you go, Kelly."

And she knew he wasn't speaking of the dance. Her arms tightened around him. "I know," she whispered. "I don't want to let you go either." She felt his arms tighten around her waist, and she told herself that for tonight it was all right. For tonight she would be content.

Then eventually, as it had to, the dance ended. Slowly, Kelly and Nick came apart. The guests were drifting away, arms entwined, loved ones held close, willing victims under the spell of the night.

Still riding the impulse of the spell, loath to break the easiness of their mood, Nick reached out and took Kelly's hand. Just as easily, she accepted it. Their steps to the cabin were slow, thoughtful. No one remained in the yard now but them. Jean had gone inside and the windows were dark.

Finally Kelly spoke. "Let's just sit with this for a while, okay?"

Nick brushed her soft cheek with the rough tips of his fingers and let his eyes wander over the perfection of her face. "We can try. Slow and easy, it'll give us both time to think. But, Kelly," he warned her, "no way will I pretend to go back to where we were before now." Then, giving the hand clasped in his a little pull, he tugged her close against him and dipped his head.

Kelly barely closed her eyes before the kiss was done. "What did that mean?" she breathed.

"Good night. And that I'll be thinking about you."

She smiled. "Yep," she said softly, "I do like you, Abella." She stepped up the porch steps, leaving him standing below to watch her. Unable to help herself, she turned for one last look. The last image she carried with her into the house was of the silvery wash of moonglow caressing the dimple in his cheek.

Olmston was like a million other sleepy little southern towns in the morning. Kelly found it strange to think that the grocer sweeping his walk with desultory concentration, or the two elderly ladies taking a morning stroll, or even the light traffic that flowed unhurriedly around them could be the hiding place for a man shadowed in murder and intrigue.

Jean parked in front of the rendezvous point he had set up with his cousin, a small corner diner at the end of the town's main street. Michel Le Beau, he'd told them on the way over, owned and managed the local tavern that served as the watering hole for a steady portion of Olmston's male population. Hardly anything new, including comings and goings, went on in town without word of it traveling back to the tavern and Michel.

Kelly ran her hand across the already damp tendrils of hair she had braided to combat the heat and fell in step beside Nick as they followed Jean inside.

She watched Jean's gaze sift through the half dozen patrons who sat eating leisurely breakfasts, drinking coffee, or just reading newspapers, until it lighted on a darkly clad figure hunched at a booth in the back. His back was to them as he leaned over farther to sip from a coffee cup. He looked up casually when she, Nick, and Jean slid into the booth with him.

"Cousin," Jean said, nodding to the man. He made short introductions, then he pulled out a snapshot and tossed it across the table. It slid to rest beside Michel's coffee.

"Briefly." Michel's accented voice was terse. He raised his coffee, took a last sip, then pushed his cup away. "He was in my place briefly yesterday afternoon asking questions."

"About what?" Kelly asked, leaning forward.

Michel gave her a thorough inspection, more assessing than personal. "You mean about whom, mademoiselle. He was asking about a man."

"Cousin," Jean said, leaning forward, "this is a favor, remember? You're not getting paid to dole out bits and pieces."

Michel took the old man's measure and that of the silent, hard-eyed young one who sat beside him. Shrugging as if to say it was worth a try, he answered, *"Bon.* The man is an accountant here, Andrew Malone."

The name rang some distant bell for Nick, but he couldn't bring it into focus. "Did he say why?"

"No, and I didn't think there was a need to ask. Andy hardly leads a cloak-and-dagger existence, although"—he swept them all with a baleful glance—"I am beginning to think I've been missing something all these years, *non?*"

"How do we find Andrew Malone?" Anticipation lent urgency to Kelly's inquiry.

Michel hedged. "Jean, I said I'd give you and your friends here information, but I'm not getting myself dragged into something dangerous when it's not my problem. I have Kathy to think of."

Jean smiled with reassurance. "Your little one is safe and so are you. This is strictly a search, not a hunting expedition."

Michel looked at them all, and what he saw in their eyes seemed to satisfy him. He nodded solemnly and told them how to get to Malone's house on the outskirts of town.

"One last thing," Jean said as he and Kelly and Nick got up to leave. "These two are family. If they need anything or ask for anything I can't give, treat them as one of our own, yes?"

Michel's gray eyes held Jean's and glittered in perfect understanding. *"Oui, cousin, d'accord."*

Kelly shivered a little at the intensity between the two men, but it wasn't with fear. A solemn request for protection had been asked for and received with nothing stronger than familial ties to prompt the giving. They were a protective clan, these men whose lives she had been thrust into. They took very seriously the responsibility of protecting their own, and with Michel's promise, Kelly knew that in some indefinable way she had been accepted as one of them.

The drive to Malone's house took less than twenty minutes, and the first thing that was apparent to them was that his property was deserted. And not just deserted, Kelly thought, peering into the thinly curtained windows flanking the front while Nick and Jean knocked from the porch. It looked abandoned. The property was well kept, the yard neatly tended, and though she didn't inspect it, Kelly could see a small garage off to the side that presently sheltered a car. Beyond the garage, as well as around the parameters of the small yard in back and the two-lane asphalt road in front, the land turned wild green and lush again.

"No luck?" she said, joining the two men back in front.

"No one seems to be home, if that's what you mean," Nick answered, "but on occasion, sweetheart, I make my own luck." He pulled something from his jeans pocket, gave it a twist, and knelt until he was at eye level with the doorknob. As he fiddled with the lock, Jean chuckled at Kelly's apprehensive look around them.

"The nearest neighbor is miles away, and we're too far out for anyone to just happen by before we hear them, *chérie*." Jean threw a massive arm around Kelly's slim shoulders and gave her a squeeze. "Besides, you see? Before you can blink, it is done."

Nick rose, reached beneath his cotton sweatshirt for his gun, and opened the door. He instructed the others to wait while he made the preliminary check. The one-story house was small, so they didn't wait for long before he called them inside.

The house was simple: white walls, a light sofa and two armchairs, a television in the corner, a coffee table holding an ashtray that needed emptying, and a small dining room set adorning a minuscule dining area in the back. Permeating it all was still, humid air that was heavy and stale with old cigarette smoke. Obviously, Kelly guessed, for a day or two at least, Malone hadn't been here. She wondered if Joey had. And if Malone was even now on his way back.

Jean came inside from out back and Nick wandered into the living room off an adjacent hallway. "Anything?" Kelly asked. "Everything looks pretty normal in here."

"Ditto," Jean answered, and Nick agreed. "Although," Jean added, "his clothes and other personal belongings are still here. Maybe he's just left temporarily."

Feeling distinctly claustrophobic, Kelly marched over to the windows and threw them open. Warm, sweet air wafted gently through the room, making the trio's methodical search for clues through desk drawers, cabinets, and any other nooks and crannies they could ferret out bearable. An hour later Malone's absence was still as big a mystery as it had been when they started.

"Where the hell is he?" Nick said, flinging himself down on the sofa in frustration. Kelly took an armchair and Jean the other.

"More importantly, is he with Joey?" Kelly mused. "And who are they to each other?"

Again, that niggling something tickled at the back of Nick's memory, but he couldn't grasp it, which abetted his frustration.

"Michel said nothing about him disappearing," Kelly said, "and I'm assuming from what he told us that Malone's hardly the type to take a mysterious skip without serious provocation."

"None of which discounts the fact that Joey still might turn up." Nick tapped a contemplative tattoo on the arm of the sofa. "We don't really know if he's looking for Malone or something here in this house, in his possession. If it's the latter, I want to be here if or when Joey turns up."

"So do I," Kelly said. She got up and crossed over to the window. "A day's wait won't hurt. If no one shows up tonight, he may in the morning." Taking a step back, she rested her derriere against the sill.

"You may be wasting your time, you know." Jean steepled his hands below his chin.

"Not really," Kelly said. "We know there's something here Joey wants. Either he's been here and gotten it, or he's coming here to get it. So I'd guess whatever his move, he's not going to take much more than a day to make it. He knows Nick's expecting him back at the cabin, so he's not going to waste time deciding on a course of action."

"Then if you two are staying here, you won't

need me. I'm going back to the shop," Jean said, coming to his feet. "If Joey turns up before you return, I will be there. And by the way," he turned his attention to Nick, "I checked the car in the garage. It runs. You may just have to be a little creative to get it started." A devilish smile relaxed his face.

Nick got up to walk him to the door. "Well, old man, if you taught Joey and me anything, it was how to be 'creative' when the occasion necessitated it." He gave him an affectionate slap on the back. "No more than two days, I promise. Then we'll be back."

"*Oui.* Take care of yourself"—Jean turned his eyes toward the window—"and your own." Then he was gone.

"Nothing gets by him, does it?" Kelly asked with amusement.

"Not since the day I've known him," Nick said. "But then, what's going on between us isn't exactly obscure, is it?"

The answer to his question was too obvious to evade, so Kelly let it pass without comment. "Why do you suppose Malone chooses to live out here in the back of beyond? His being unmarried with no family, having a job in the city, I'd think an apartment would be more convenient for him."

"Oh, I don't know," Nick said, coming over to join her at the window. "Solitude has its advantages."

"Like keeping people at a distance, you mean?" Kelly scooted over a little to make room for him.

"Not exactly," Nick said thoughtfully. "At least,

not all the time. No, I meant more like having a retreat where you know you can go and not have to put up with all the crap in the world. Although"—he chuckled—"sometimes that does amount to the same thing."

"Oh, I don't know. Sometimes the best way to alleviate all that crap, as you put it, is to be with people, people you love and care about, and who love and care about you."

"You speaking from personal experience?"

Kelly turned her head to study him. Behind the lighthearted curiosity in his gaze, she saw a very real pensiveness there too. "Maybe. Once upon a time."

The shadows were back in her eyes, and he knew she had gone back to the dark time in her life. "Who's here for you now, Kelly?" Maybe he didn't have the right to ask, but it was important for him to know.

The question was personal, Kelly thought, but coming from him it didn't sting.

"Jeff used to be, in the beginning. In fact, when we married, he was just about the only one. Most of my friends in my circle—God, that sounds so pretentious now, 'in my circle'—none of them knew how to understand what I did. And while my mother was outraged, my father was just distantly amused. Jeff was my haven, maybe in retrospect because he was the first one in my life who was willing to see me as I really was, deep down inside. In those early days he helped me believe it was all right to rebel, to reach out for the life I wanted, and I guess I'll always be grateful to him for that."

Nick was jealous. Not of the man whose self-absorption had destroyed his marriage and taken his life, but of the man who had been lucky enough to make Kelly his, free and unfettered. The sadness in her eyes told him she had to have loved Jeff very, very much at one time. Nick had never known that kind of love, and sitting here beside her now while she reminisced made him feel the lack, made him feel lonely.

"It's not nearly as dismal as I'm making it sound," she said with a slight shake of her head, as if to throw off the gloom her memories had roused. "I have some good friends in Chicago I still correspond with, and my mother and I seem to have made a sort of peace. But I guess most importantly, I've learned to get on with my life, and that's translated into learning not to shut people out. There are too many out there who are willing to care if you'll let them."

"That must be a hard equilibrium to maintain on the force."

Kelly sighed. "I can't deny it, and sometimes the hostility hurts. But it comes with the nature of the job, and I knew what I was getting into when I accepted it. I just keep having to remember not to get so wrapped up in the resentment that I lose my perspective about the people outside the precinct."

Nick was impressed by the dedication that kept her doing what she did, impressed again by the fact that the lady had guts.

"I, on the other hand," he said, "consider most of those guys at the precinct my family. At first, I became a cop because my father was, and it just seemed the thing to do." He wondered if he could even admit the rest, say aloud what he'd never admitted to another soul, not even to himself. Her calm regard and the quiet warmth shining from those depthless brown eyes gave him the reassurance and his answer. "I guess the reason I decided to became a cop was to earn my father's approval."

Quite without thought, Kelly reached over to smooth back a lock of hair that had fallen across his brow. She could guess why that had been so hard for him to say. "Have you tried to get him to get help for his alcoholism?"

Nick pressed down on his anger, but it wouldn't be quelled. "Once, when I was just out of college." His voice was stark as he thrust himself away from the window. "He informed me, in plain terms, that he didn't have any problem except for nagging kids and a nagging wife he wished would either disappear, go to hell, or leave him alone. Then he told me to mind my own damned business."

Kelly winced at the degree of bitterness suffusing Nick's every word, every move. "But you're older now, Nick; surely you realize that was his disease talking."

"Was it his disease that kept him alienated from us even before he started to drink? And I already know the stats on cops and their dysfunctional families. The problem is, I've seen too many that have survived not to suspect that if Sandy had tried a little harder, maybe his could have had a better shot of pulling through too."

With a restless movement he left her side and moved across the room.

Kelly ached for the pain he still lived with. But she also knew that there were too many years of bitterness and hurt to be washed away by any soothing words she might say, too many damaged emotions that Nick and his father were going to have to come to terms with themselves. Even so, the disillusionment in his eyes saddened her because she suspected much of it stemmed from a lifelong habit of not letting himself fully trust anyone. Was the little boy in him still afraid that caring would meet with rejection, love with disappointment?

Not questioning the impulse, Kelly pushed away from the sill and walked across the room to where Nick stood beside a built-in bookcase. One hand gripped the edge of it while he rested his chin on his bent forearm, staring unseeingly off toward the dining room. His other hand was clenched on his hip.

With unobtrusive ease, Kelly offered Nick solace. Sliding her arms around his waist, she rested her soft cheek against his rigid back. Even when she felt him tense, she held on.

Surprise held him immobile for an instant before he turned in her arms and returned the embrace. The soft, flowery fragrance of her hair, the sweet, delicate woman scent that was unmistakably her own, her kindhearted serenity flowed all around him, over him, through him until he felt a measure of peace, until its comfort was splendid.

"Kelly, Kelly, Kelly . . ." he whispered, rocking her gently back and forth. Holding her away a little, he placed a butterfly kiss on her brow, then her nose, then her mouth, where his lips touched, tasted, then merged. Her arms crept to his shoulders, then linked behind his neck as she shifted her head, changing the angle and pressure of the kiss.

The communion of their kisses was sweet, but Nick was surprised when the tenor of them remained strangely unsexual. Kelly seemed content just to touch him, hold him, while for Nick, the desire her touch always inspired was overruled by a deeper tranquillity she was effortlessly giving.

Breaking the kiss, Kelly brought her hands to his face, where she caressed the firm line of his lips, then the hollows of his cheeks, until finally she stroked the black silk of his brows. "You asked me a moment ago who was there for me," she said, soft as a whisper. "I was wondering the same for you. Now I know. Now I think we both know."

Nick's heart missed a beat at the utter sincerity that deepened her voice, the pure emotion that shone from her eyes. For the first time in his life he was utterly speechless. Dipping his head, he let his lips touch and caress the delicate pulse point at one of her slender wrists.

Kelly felt overwhelmed. She was no more prepared for the feelings that were shaking her than was the vulnerable man before her. A lingering barrier had just been crossed by both of them, and the realization left her reeling. Nothing, *nothing* had ever touched her heart as this man was touching it now.

Minutes, maybe hours passed as they stood enmeshed in each other's embrace, both trying to find a way to regain emotional ground, both afraid to face the moment when they could. Gradually, Kelly made the first attempt. Her breath was warmly muffled against his chest.

"Hey?" Her voice was a whisper.

"What?" His was no stronger.

"One of us is going to have to break this up to go into town."

"What for?"

"Food."

Nick raised his head, and Kelly smiled at his puzzled look.

"Provisions. I checked when we got here, Detective. The cupboard is bare. We've got to buy sustenance if we want to eat."

Nick pulled her close for one more kiss, then he stepped away from her. A large part of him hated letting her go, but another part of him was grateful for the temporary distance.

"I'll go," he told her. "One of us ought to stay here. Besides"—he checked the clip in his gun— "I'll feel better knowing you're safe and sound right here."

"Didn't anyone ever tell you, Abella," she teased, "no place is safe anymore?"

He thought of the minutes that had just passed,

of the self-discoveries he had just made, of the awareness they had stumbled into together.

"Damned if you aren't right, Wylie." Damned if she wasn't.

9

They weren't in a cabin in southern Indiana, and
the golden light gilding her features was not ema-
nating from a toasty fire. Instead, she sat bathed
in the amber glow of the living room lamp, its soft
illumination highlighting every stroke of the
brush through her hair, and she'd never been
more beautiful to Nick, not even in his fantasy.

Supper was long since finished and the shadows of the soft summer night outside the house
were deep, and Nick had long ago snapped off the
floor lamp over his shoulder, tired of pretending
to read while the woman before him absorbed his
every thought. So now he sat in the shadows,
watching her lean against the sofa, wanting to be
the one touching her, stroking her.

Kelly started when a warm hand covered her
own and the brush she was holding was gently
pried away. Her breath suspended until she heard
the whisper of denim settling against the fabric of
the sofa, until she felt the slow stroking against
her scalp resume.

Nick's other hand anchored at her shoulder, his
warm thumb sliding beneath the neck of her

T-shirt to probe the bare skin of her collarbone in lazy tandem with the brush. He shifted above her and Kelly shifted against the floor until her back was flat against the sofa, her shoulders ensconced within the denim vee he made for her with his legs. Her hands were clasped loosely in her lap like a prim little schoolgirl's, and each pull was so measured, so steady, that Kelly nearly purred.

"I used to watch my mother do this." Nick's voice was hushed with remembrance. "She'd wait until she thought both Joey and I were asleep, then she'd go out into the living room, or on the front porch in summer, and she'd sit brushing her hair, waiting for him to come home."

His hand moved from her shoulder, slid along the back of her neck and up beneath the weight of her hair until the heavy strands were lifted, then released. To her own eyes, the fall of it that settled over her shoulder, the strands of it that kissed her cheek, looked like a shower of drifting red gold. Then she felt the weight of his hand again, the probe of his thumb once more.

"But I wasn't asleep. Most times I was standing back in the room where she couldn't see me, watching her brood as she sat alone, watching her wait for him . . . watching her cry for him." His voice drifted off to nothing, but the stroking continued.

"Nick . . ." She had no words to ease this hurt of his. It was too old, its wounds buried too deeply inside. But he needed her, and a lonely part of herself she'd locked away for too long needed to give. "Nick," she said again, this time turning in his arms.

He hadn't meant to let her see, hadn't touched her with the intention of revealing his inner scars. But that gentle, nurturing essence of hers was disarming him again, and before he realized it, he was pulling her up and into his arms.

Her breath caught and then escaped on a ragged sigh as Nick settled her full length upon him. His lips nuzzled and teased the corners of her mouth, the curve of her jaw, before he took her lips fully and slowly transformed the kiss into a wet, erotic exchange.

Kelly moaned softly as she let herself be pulled into the kiss, into the man who was holding her, the man who was caressing her as if he'd never let her go.

Joey, Cain, the conflicts in their lives were pushed to the back of her reality. At this moment, Nick was her reality. To find a refuge they could share was her desire. To make him aware of her affections beyond her apprehensions was her need. And then the feel of his hands pressing her into his demanding desire convinced her that the wonder of what they did to each other was fast becoming her anchor.

"Sweetheart . . ." His voice was husky and gruff. "If you don't want this, tell me now."

Kelly levered herself away from him partially, her hands bracing her weight against the cushions beneath his head. Brown eyes locked with gold. Breaths mingled. Hearts pounded.

"Don't stop," she said.

As if in slow motion, she felt herself being turned, felt his weight shifting, until her back was against the cushions and he was muttering something hot, urgent, and sexual in her ear. Her legs moved restlessly against his, and her back arched when his questing hands sought and captured the fullness of her breasts. Her nipples grew hard beneath the circular caress of his fingers, harder when her shirt was discarded and his marauding mouth suckled in their place.

Kelly's breathy little moan opened Nick's eyes and he raised his head to watch the passion his ministrations had evoked. A rosy flush bathed her elegant cheekbones. The disarray of her hair and the delicate curve of her mouth were pure sensual abandon. Idly soothing the fluttering pulse at her throat, letting his hand roam lower to soothe the cooling moisture on her skin, Nick lowered his mouth to hers once more, teased the seam of her lips with his tongue, then stroked deeply when her lips parted to give him access.

Kelly was on fire, but she didn't want to burn alone. Dragging her kneading hands down along the strong line of his back, down to the taut muscles of his hips, she urged him to move up until her slender fingers could slide between them. With heart-stopping precision she closed a gentle fist around the heated fullness of him and began a slow massage. She was rewarded when his mouth wrenched from hers with an agonized groan.

Shaking with need, Nick still managed to speak, "Not yet, honey," then he was gently pushing her hands away. Dragging them up, he anchored them above her head and held them with a gentle fist while his other hand returned with unerring accuracy to the heat of her desire. The warmth of her nearly scorched him, but he was intent on his resolve. With torturous deliberation he lowered her zipper.

"I want . . ." Kelly mouthed.

"Shhh, I know what you want." He wanted it too. He wanted her to have it all. Her panties were a lacy barrier that offered no resistance when his seeking fingers slipped beneath them and sank into the creamy wetness of her.

Even as her hips began a helpless, undulating dance to his experienced touch, Kelly tried to summon the strength to beg him to stop. She tried to tell him that she wanted it to be together, that she wanted to experience the ultimate pleasure wrapped around the warmth of his body. But the seconds passed and her long-starved need held her silent. Then she couldn't speak because that pleasure was too close. Then suddenly consciousness dimmed and nothing mattered as the deep, throbbing pulsations drove every other thought from her mind except riding the hot wave of release that was carrying her away.

Nick watched her ride it, gloried in the frantic beating of her heart, buried his head beside hers to nuzzle that ultrasoft spot where neck met shoulder. But even as he kissed her, even as his fingers drew every last drop of ecstasy from her, her unconscious words lodged a nugget of fear in his heart. *"Love me, I need you."*

How easily he could dismiss her plea as a mindless utterance in the throes of fulfillment. Their passions were running high. But Kelly wasn't a woman to take sex lightly.

"What's wrong?" she asked, confusion clouding her eyes. Her breathing was slowing and the hands he had released were moving down his body to ease the part of him that still pressed hard against her.

"Nothing." He couldn't keep the tension from his voice and he hated the way it transformed her confusion to contrition.

"Let me help you, then," she whispered, reaching for him again. "I was selfish to—"

"Dammit, no, you weren't." His voice was urgent and he gently but firmly moved her hands. "You were giving and beautiful."

"Then why are you angry?"

He sighed. An uncertain tremor had entered her voice.

"I'm not angry, sweetheart. Honest," he said, placing a kiss on her forehead. He tightened his arms around her. "I wanted you to feel good and you did, didn't you?"

"Yes, but—"

"Then that's all that matters. I wanted you to come and it was lovely. I don't need more than that for now."

How could he expect her to believe him when his own body was calling him a liar? "Just let me hold you," he said, willing her not to ask any more questions. "Having you in my arms makes me happy, all right?"

She turned her back to him and pulled her shirt

back on. Then, lying back against his chest, she let him hold her as he had asked. She was very quiet. Nick knew that she was far from satisfied, and the stiffness in her body led him to suspect that maybe she was finding fault with herself. He sighed again. If that was the case, he was a bastard to let her. But how could he explain to her something he didn't understand himself?

He thought he'd understood what it would mean to be with her. He thought he'd be satisfied with the uncomplicated surcease she offered with her loving embrace. What he hadn't foreseen was standing at the brink of relinquishing a part of himself that he was afraid to let go. And merging with her would have entailed just that. Which was why, at the end, he'd been afraid.

He didn't love her, or at least, he wasn't prepared to call what he felt for her love. He'd grown up witnessing firsthand how a person's pride and hope and spirit could be stripped in the name of love. He had made sure it had never happened to him. The problem was, he'd felt a lot safer when he'd believed it never could.

Long after Kelly's breathing had grown regular, long after he had left her once to switch off the lamp and fetch a light sheet to cover them, he lay back on the sofa, holding her in his arms. Sleep was a long time coming.

The phone jarred Nick awake and he reached automatically for it. "Yeah." His voice was scratchy with sleep.

"Ah, I see you were ready for my call this morning, Andrew. Somehow after the last time we spoke I didn't think that would be the case."

Completely awake now, Nick pressed the receiver tighter to his ear while Kelly disengaged herself from his arms to sit up. Nick waited to hear what the mysterious caller had to say to who he thought was Andrew Malone.

"Cat got your tongue, Andrew? You're usually more vocal than this."

The caller was deliberately keeping his voice low and whispery, no doubt as an intimidation tactic. Still, an inflection here and there had Nick wondering if the voice was completely alien to him.

"Well, no matter," the caller said. "I'll be there to see you soon enough, and we'll have plenty to talk about for old times' sake, won't we?"

Menacing was a melodramatic word, but it was honestly the only one Nick could apply to the laugh that preceded the click of the disconnected line.

"Who was it?" Kelly asked, watching him closely.

"A man."

"What did he want?"

"To intimidate the hell out of Andrew Malone, and by the looks of things around here, I guess he's done just that."

Kelly rubbed her hands along her arms. "I don't know, Nick. I'm not having good vibes about this whole situation. Something tells me there are angles working here that this case is only a part of."

"Yeah." Nick sat up beside her. "You could be

right." He gazed around the room, not liking the way the light of dawn was muting everything in an artificial glow. "I think it might be a good idea to get back to the cabin. Something tells me Malone isn't coming back anytime soon, and I've got a feeling Joey knows it."

"What else do you have a feeling about?"

He smiled without humor and ran a hand along the back of his neck. "That obvious, huh? I don't know, Kelly. Something just doesn't feel right, you know?"

She knew it was usually a good idea to trust a cop's instincts about danger. "Let's get our stuff together and get out of here." As she rose, Nick reached out and caught her hand.

"Are you okay about last night?" he asked.

She'd asked herself the same thing when she'd awakened deep in the night to the sound of the cicadas outside and his gentle breathing at her back. At first she'd vacillated between irritation and regret because she didn't for a moment believe their aborted lovemaking was as easily explained away as Nick would have her believe.

So she'd replayed what had happened and wound up assuring herself that up to the point where he'd withdrawn, Nick had been with her every step of the way. And then afterward, not for a minute had he wanted her to believe his withdrawal was her fault. Which meant he must have had his own reasons for pulling back.

What she regretted was that he'd felt he couldn't share them with her. "Yes, I'm fine." She smiled, squeezed his hand, and left to freshen up before they left.

Nick sat back against the cushions, watching her go. She was finer than she knew. He wasn't at all sure he deserved her lack of recrimination.

They left Andrew's car in back of Michel's place. Michel, who gave them a lift back to Jean's, promised he'd have someone return it to Malone's house later that day.

To their disappointment, Jean wasn't around when they arrived. His truck was gone and a sign indicating he would be back in a while had been posted in the window. Rather than waiting, Kelly and Nick took one of the skiffs back to the cabin and set about the business of settling back in.

Back at the shop, Jean hauled some stock he'd just collected from a neighboring fisherman's place up the steps to his door. Propped in the window beneath his sign was a note. He read it and smiled, eager to hear what Nick and Kelly had to report. And eager to see what interesting new things had developed between them. He'd hoped to see the day when Nick would finally find himself a good woman.

Jean spent the day rearranging shelves and had started tidying the front of the shop when the sound of a car engine brought his head up from the glass of the display case he was polishing. A sandy-haired man entered the store and approached the case with an unhurried gait and an easy smile. Some sixth sense told Jean not to trust either.

"Can I help you, monsieur?" he asked unsmilingly.

"Nice shop you got here," the man answered. "Kind of off the beaten track, isn't it?"

Jean didn't bother to confirm the obvious. "You were looking for something, monsieur?"

"As a matter of fact, yes. A friend of mine. Joey Abella. You know him?"

Definitely on his guard, Jean evened his tone to conceal his suspicions.

"Yes, I know him."

The man nodded agreeably. "Yes, he told me about you, Jim? John? No—Jean. Right?"

"Jean Le Beau."

The man snapped his fingers. "Yes, that's right. Le Beau. I knew it was something French." He smiled engagingly and chuckled. "Joey said you were Cajun. I should have remembered that."

Jean's impassive regard didn't alter.

"As a matter of fact, Jean, Joey said that you'd be the one who could tell me how to get to that place out here where he stays when he's on vacation. I'm taking him up on a standing invitation, only he doesn't know it. Thought I'd kind of surprise him if he's down here, know what I mean?"

"Hmm," Jean grunted. It was possible that this man wasn't connected with the police or the nameless enemies Joseph had spoken of. And if that was so, he could innocently have just bumbled down here for the reasons he stated, knowing nothing about the inopportune nature of the time.

"Told me he'd give me a bayou tour that wasn't even on the tourist maps if I ever got brave enough to take him up on it, and since I'm on vacation for a week or so, here I am." The stranger smiled again, this time bracing one arm against the glass countertop.

"If that is so, monsieur," Jean said thoughtfully, "why did he not tell you himself how to get to his place?"

The man shrugged. "Well, to tell the truth, I don't think he ever really believed I'd take him up on it. That's why I can't wait to see his face when I show up on his doorstep and he sees that I'm not quite the chicken he thinks I am. If you're worried about all of this not being on the up-and-up, you can relax. I mean, I wouldn't have known to ask you if it wasn't, would I?"

Jean put the dustrag down and busied himself rearranging a display of fishing flies beneath the glass of the counter while he debated. Who was this man? Not for a minute did Jean believe he was a friend of Joseph's. For one thing, he was lying about being on vacation. His manner was easy enough, but his eyes gave him away. They were too restless, too tense, too predatory, as if his mind was already cooking up a contingency plan in case Jean didn't come through with the information he sought.

No, this was a bad man. A man whom perhaps Nick should be alerted about, since he was looking for his brother.

"I could tell you how to get to his cabin, monsieur, but the truth is, I haven't seen Joseph in months."

The man's smile faltered slightly and his eyes narrowed with something before he masked his expression with a look of disappointment.

"Well, I was sure that he said he was going to vacation down here right around now, get in some fishing. You sure you couldn't have just missed his arrival?"

"I am in this shop all day long. If anyone comes or goes, I see. So I would know if Joey had been here. He has not. Therefore, there would be no point in your taking the trouble to find his cabin, would there?"

"But he told me those were his plans," the man muttered as he ducked his head in feigned frustration.

"Obviously he's changed his plans, *oui*?"

Cajun bastard. He'd heard they were a clannish bunch, and this one wasn't going to give an inch, the man saw disgustedly. "Well, damn." He was careful to lace his voice with just the right amount of regret. "I wish I'd known before I detoured all the way down here from New Orleans. Tell you what, though, thanks for your help." He started to move toward the door. "I'm sure gonna give him hell when I get back home, you can bet on that!"

The man was holding the screened door open and about to step through when he heard Le Beau ask, "If he shows up, who should I say was looking for him?"

The man paused on the stoop and then turned slowly to face Le Beau. For a span of seconds, he kept his face perfectly blank, matching the Cajun stare for unblinking stare. Then he permitted himself a smile and forced his body to relax. "Oh, just forget it. I'll tell him myself when I see him. Besides, I'm due to leave tomorrow and I'll miss him anyway." He nodded and let the door swack behind him as he stepped lightly down the wooden steps.

Jean waited to hear the man start his car. When he did, he turned to go into the back room. Pushing aside a clutter of newspapers and a cigar box from which the tips of old, yellowed invoices protruded, he picked up the receiver of his desk phone and dialed Nick.

"Hello?"

"Nicky, you may have trouble, my friend."

There was a brief pause at the other end of the line.

"Explain," came the curt response.

"A stranger was here looking for Joseph. He called himself a friend, but he was no friend. He was a bad man, *mon ami*."

"Did you get a name?"

"What?" Jean had missed the question. He thought he heard something out in the shop.

"I said, did you get a name? A name?"

"No, I . . . a moment, don't hang up." Laying the receiver down quietly, Jean slid open his desk drawer and extracted a long, deadly-looking bowie knife. Easing the drawer shut, he moved toward the doorway, his ears alert for the merest sound. At the threshold, he paused. From one corner of the store to the other, his eyes scanned. He saw nothing, but that wasn't good enough. He had to check the aisles.

Slowly he moved out into the room until he reached the first aisle. Every sense alert for danger, he made his way through it, then the next and the next. Holding the weapon tightly in a fighter's grip, he stepped around the corner of the last aisle, ready to use the knife if necessary.

It was empty. Relaxing the tension in his shoulders, he dropped his arm—then he gasped in surprise and pain. His hand reached uselessly around his neck to grope at the top of his shoulders.

Even as he sank to his knees, he felt the razor-sharp blade plunge again. Black anger rose up inside him, yet the animal snarl he pushed past frozen lips was the only epithet he had strength to hurl.

It made no impression whatsoever on the sandy-haired assassin who hovered above him.

"Nick, what's wrong?" Kelly asked from the sofa. She had heard the tension in Nick's voice when he answered the phone. Her immediate thought had been of Joey. Now the expression on Nick's face had her laying aside the folder in her hand as she came to her feet.

"I don't know. It's Jean. He says someone's nosing around about Joey. Now he's put me on hold."

Kelly didn't like the worried tone in his voice at all. She frowned and crossed over to Nick.

"Hello? Hello!" he demanded into the silent receiver.

Frightened now, Kelly laid a hand on his shoulder.

Nick glanced down at Kelly and shook his head at her expectant look when Jean's line clicked. With an awful feeling in his gut, he replaced the phone on the hook.

"Nick," Kelly whispered, "what's wrong?"

Nick spared her only a second's glance before his mouth tightened. Kelly crossed her arms, absently rubbing the goose bumps that were rising.

"He's in trouble. I'm going out there." Even while he said it, he was pulling his pistol out of a drawer. He snapped a full clip into place with a deft movement. "Call the police and have them meet me there."

Kelly wasted no time with further questions. She dialed the Orleans Parish sheriff. It was as she hung up that she saw Nick already striding toward the door.

"Wait, I'm going with you."

Nick turned on his heel to face her. He gave her a look of exasperation. "The hell you are. I don't know what's happening out there. It could be messy." When the look on her face failed to waver, he added emotively, "Kelly, I don't want you hurt!"

Kelly's voice was just as implacable as her expression, her voice as unyielding.

"In case you've forgotten, Detective, you're not the only police officer standing here. What if you need backup before the cavalry arrives? Or hadn't you thought of that, cowboy?"

The struggle between his acceptance of her logic and his very macho need to protect was as thrilling as it was fascinating to watch. Had Kelly not been so intent on making him react rationally, she would have appreciated the full weight of his words. But as it was, all she could think was that if he wanted to fight her on this, she would give him a fight he wouldn't forget. She was grappling with some very protective emotions of her own.

Finally, with a growl, Nick conceded, his professionalism winning out.

In a flash Kelly retrieved her own semiautomatic from her purse. She checked the ammunition, nodded her readiness, and sailed out of the door Nick held open for her.

This trip back up the waterway bore no resemblance to the first, Kelly reflected grimly. For one thing, the sun had gone in shortly after noon and now the sky was overcast. Whereas everything that first time had been bathed in a picturesque, sunny glow, everything now appeared to have been thrown into sharp, slate-gray relief. This image of the swamp more closely resembled Kelly's original expectations.

As the boat hummed them closer to their destination, shadows seemed to threaten. The trees appeared to loom, gauging the right moment to hurl their webs of moss to ensnare the insignificant travelers. Every birdcall seemed to echo and mock Kelly and Nick's progress through the smooth, silent water.

Leaning back, she spared Nick a look. He seemed oblivious of it all. His hard profile told her that he had pulled back into some dark, dangerous place Kelly had once sensed existed. The thought suddenly came to her that had this man chosen to walk the other side of the law, he would have been just as determined, just as formidable, just as potentially lethal a foe as he was her ally now. The thought made her shiver, and her eyes caught the tense movement of a muscle working in his jaw. She understood. She could only pray that Jean was all right.

Fifteen minutes later the skiff rounded the bend and the shop came into sight. There were no squad cars on the premises, and the whole place had a disturbing air of abandonment about it. Deliberately Nick cut the motor. As he took up one oar and Kelly the other, she thought everything seemed too quiet. Carefully she paused in her stroking to ease her gun from the small of her back where she'd tucked it.

Nick quickly anchored the boat to the dock and stepped ashore, reaching down to give Kelly a hand.

"I'll circle around to the front," he whispered. "Give me five minutes, then approach. When you get there, wait for my signal."

Kelly nodded, feeling an icy calm of purpose steal over her.

"Stay alert and keep your eyes open, sweetheart," Nick cautioned softly. Kelly nodded, expecting him to take off. When he hesitated, staring down at her intently, Kelly looked up, intending to ask, "What?" The word was trapped against her lips by the soft kiss Nick placed on her mouth. He was gone before she could react.

Taken off guard, Kelly stared after him as he darted around the back of the building, his gun held in a two-handed grip.

She shook herself, recalling her wits, and bent her head to study her watch to check the time. As she ticked off the minutes, her eyes did a constant scan of the area around her. She couldn't hear anyone moving about, and she took that as a good sign. Finally the requisite minute ticked off and she made her way, with stealth, around to the front of the building. A beam of sunlight broke through the clouds overhead, distracting her slightly as it cast a glint on the metal of the shop's door frame.

There was no signal from Nick. Gripping her gun with a steady hand, she braced the other against the wall beside the door and leaned over just enough to get a look inside through the mesh. There was no sign of Nick. But neither had she heard any gunfire. He'd had more than enough time to check out the shop. What was wrong? she thought, her heart accelerating.

Taking a deep breath, she eased open the screen and as it squeaked, quickly ducked in, flattening her back against the inside wall.

"Nick?" she called just above a whisper.

No answer.

She raised her voice just slightly. "Nick!"

"Over here."

The absolute desolation in his voice frightened

her as nothing else could have. Tracing his voice to the back of the store, she moved lightly until she reached the back row of shelving.

"Oh, God, no," she whispered, letting the gun fall to her side.

Nick sat cradling Jean's body. Blood stained his hands and his pants, but he was oblivious to it. His eyes were red and anguished. She watched, her own throat tight, as he wiped automatically at a damp track on his cheek. Then he looked up at her helplessly.

Kelly echoed his cry with a soft gasp. It hurt to see him humbled, as she suspected he never had been by such naked anguish. Not knowing what else to do, she dropped to her knees and put her arms around his trembling shoulders, trying to absorb some of his pain.

How long they sat that way she didn't know. All she knew was that the way Nick leaned into her body, absorbing her strength and comfort, told her more eloquently than any words that another barrier between them had crumbled. The wail of approaching squad cars finally broke her embrace. Without a word, his tears long dried, Nick got to his feet, then cast a last look at Jean. Kelly followed him to the door.

The next few minutes passed in a haze of routine questions. Yes, they knew the deceased. No, they didn't know of any enemies. Yes, Nick had spoken to him only minutes before the murder, before Jean said he heard someone in his shop. Yes, they would come into Olmston to give their statements. Finally it was over. They both stood numbly as the ambulance bore Jean's body away and the police finished sealing off the crime site.

There was nothing to do but go back to the cabin. Nick turned and started walking toward the dock. Kelly took his hand and kept step with him.

The journey back to the cabin was a silent one. Nick still said nothing and Kelly let him alone with his grief.

What did Joey have to do with that old man's death? Because instinctively, she knew that he did. Nick said that Jean had been trying to tell him that some stranger was in the shop asking questions. Who could it have been, and why had Jean's death been necessary? Whatever Joey was involved in, it was frightening to think that it had reached far enough to kill an innocent old man more than seven hundred miles from its origin.

When they arrived back at the cabin, Nick went immediately to the front closet and dragged out a suitcase. The police had been unsure how long settling Jean's affairs here would take. While he packed, Kelly placed a call to Sheriff Brower.

When she hung up the phone, she walked around the sofa until she stood before Nick. He slumped against the cushions, his left arm resting upon the leg slung across his knee. His held his jaw in a tight three-fingered grip.

"Brower wants you to know how sorry he is, Nick. He's agreed to let us lie low for a little longer. After that, we have to make contact with the parish authorities and bring them in on the search if Joey hasn't surfaced."

No answer. His eyes just rested dully on her face.

"I'll get my things so that we can leave," she said quietly.

He nodded and let his gaze return to some invisible point behind her.

It didn't take her long to throw her things together, and before she knew it, Nick was locking up the cabin and they were on their way for a final time across the bayou. As Kelly watched the cabin fade from sight, she had the feeling there was still unfinished business here.

She closed her eyes against a sudden wave of pain. Though she had known him for an impossibly short time, she ached over the gentle old man's death. As the boat drifted away and Jean's cabin disappeared, Kelly had a clear premonition that she would be seeing this place again. Death, it told her, had only just arrived.

10

While Kelly and Nick drove back into Olmston, an old man was fulfilling the first part of a promise seven hundred miles north.

Earl Mack had been used to stares in his younger days. When he was king of this turf, he expected the stares of envy and respect. Today he still got the looks, only now they were likely to be followed by "you old rummy." He mostly ignored the gibes, seeing as how they were true.

And on those rare occasions when he traveled beyond his old turf, like now, the stares that said "vagrant" bothered him even less. He knew he looked like one, with his tattered clothes and his tired, lined skin. But he still had what counted, his sense and some means, thanks mostly to Nick. And this afternoon, as he walked into an eastside Sedgwick branch of the United States Post Office, he fingered the key in his tattered coat pocket and thought of the letter of less than two weeks ago that had put it there:

Mack,

I know we ain't heard from each other in a long time, but I got a favor I want to ask you anyway. You were always a loyal friend in the old days, and since you're still alive to call your own shots in that cesspool you live in, I figure you still ain't too bad a pick for someone I can trust. This key here belongs to a post office box, address enclosed. In the event of my death, which I sincerely hope ain't gonna come, I want you to use it. When you get what's inside, guard it with your life and remember your friends in high places. You'll be the only one who knows unless you choose to tell. And if you don't, well, consider it the final will and testament from a great man who even at the end, served his city well.

Jackie

Even before he had opened the letter, Earl had made himself some room to think about it. He'd moved from his apartment and kept Nick away with that story about going to Chicago to see his brother. He hadn't wanted to know what was inside the letter. He knew shit when he smelled it, that was mostly how he stayed alive these days, and this letter stank to high heaven. But old Jackie had bought it, and as he had pointed out, Mack was, in the end, a loyal friend.

So here he stood, patiently looking up and down the rows of metal boxes along the wall until he found the number he wanted. He knelt down, which took some effort nowadays, and turned the key in the lock.

Somehow a notebook was the last thing he had expected to see. He pulled out the plain, beige-covered booklet and started to leaf through the pages. With each page he turned, his stomach grew colder and his hands started to shake. Now he understood the silent fear that had been running up and down the streets since Cain got shot. And the real purpose behind Nick's questions.

Jesus, he thought, suddenly looking around, maybe there were eyes on him now. No, there weren't, he assured himself. No one who was threatened by what he held in his hands knew he was here. Or did they? he thought, glancing quickly at the patrolman propped in the corner who idly returned his look. Rising with some difficulty from his knees, Mack tucked the booklet under his coat, well out of sight, and got the hell out of there.

He was thinking of his friends in high places, all right. He was thinking how he'd never wanted to get in touch this bad, not even when his shakes had been at their worst. Of course, right on the heels of that thought came the mental anticipation of dollar signs and the booze he would buy. But that was secondary, he thought, digging the bus fare out of his pocket. The first thing he had to do was get rid of this by putting it in the right hands. Nick was the one he needed to see. In fact, the bus could wait. He needed a phone.

He slammed down the receiver two minutes later and peered from the booth out along the

street. Gone? What a time to be gone. Damn! Nick
sure could pick 'em. But wait, there was another.
He debated. This stuff was too important to un-
load on someone who could screw up. But on the
other hand, despite his declined circumstances,
Sandy was still a friend, he guessed. After all, they
still went back a long way. And Nick was his son.
And once, Sandy Abella had been a good cop.
Maybe deep down, he still was.

He climbed on the bus, mapped out his changed
destination, and sat back to wait. He guessed if
Jackie had to go, he would have wanted it to happen while he was doing the snooping he had always done best. As for himself, after he dumped
this legacy, Mack wanted no part of it. He was an
old man. But he still preferred his status of "living" legend.

Nick drove them straight to the police station
where they both gave statements. He also gave
Kelly his tacit consent to withhold the fact that
they were cops until it became necessary to do so.

By the time all the formalities were finished,
darkness had fallen and, bone weary, they
searched for a hotel.

Not far from the outskirts of town, they found a
charming little two-story hotel boasting fewer
than a handful of rooms. Actually, upon booking
in, they discovered it was really a small antebel-
lum home that had been converted into a bed-
and-breakfast some ten years ago. The soft-spoken
owner assured them she had one room available
to rent and they took it gratefully. Kelly didn't

bother to correct the assumption that they were a married couple. Neither did she comment when Nick signed the register that way.

As they were led up the stairs to their room, she could feel Nick's eyes on her. She wasn't naïve. There was every possibility that when this night was over, nothing between her and the man at her side would ever be the same.

The door closed behind them and they were left alone. Kelly's gaze slid away from Nick's watchful one, and the first things she saw were two double beds that sat adjacent to the beautiful floor-to-ceiling French windows that dominated the tastefully appointed room. She recalled last night and its conclusion and her tongue deserted her, so she walked over to the curtained windows and discovered they overlooked a wrought-iron balcony.

"Is this all right?" Kelly heard Nick ask behind her. She was slow to give her answer. Beyond surface approval, the question encompassed much, much more.

"It will do," she said neutrally. Despite what Jean had said, things were too complicated for her to do otherwise. When she heard the bathroom door quietly shut behind her, followed shortly by the dull roar of the shower, Kelly relaxed a little, feeling some of the tension leave her stiff neck and spine.

She pulled the French windows open wide and was immediately assailed by the sweet, delicate scent of flowers. She was charmed to see that the balcony was furnished with a small table and two padded chairs of black wrought iron. At either corner of the balcony sat huge iron tubs of lush red roses. The balcony overlooked a charming vista of rolling green lawn that sloped down to an honest-to-God bubbling brook that was landscaped with wild lilies and vibrant bougainvillea. The tableau was dominated by a huge old live oak tree, dramatically draped with the ever-present live moss.

This lovely old estate house, the room, its grounds, created a backdrop designed for lovers. Kelly wished wistfully, even guiltily in that moment, that she and Nick weren't here under such tragic circumstances, that by some twist of fate they could be the carefree lovers to fit the scene. With a sigh she turned back toward the room.

She walked over to the armchair where he had stowed their cases and lifted hers, hefting it over to one of the beds. She started pulling out toiletry articles until her hands paused.

She had been packing so fast she hadn't realized she'd included this nightgown. Of vibrant, floral paisley, it was styled like a full, mid-length slip with a camisole bodice. The difference was that unlike an ordinary slip, it and its matching wrapper were made of pure silk. At the time she bought it, she'd considered it strictly a luxury and indulged herself without regret. She'd known that it was the kind of lingerie worn for a lover. But she had no lover and bought it simply because of how feminine it made her feel. The last thing she wanted to wear tonight was anything that enhanced her vulnerable feelings.

The bathroom door opened and Nick stepped

out. Kelly clutched the gown to her breasts, her thoughts making her anxious. He had donned pajama bottoms of some dark blue masculine print. His chest was bare and still dotted with droplets of water that clung to the soft hair fanning his skin. His water-dark hair glistened black with the same moisture. His eyes were saying things to Kelly's, and she couldn't move.

"It's all yours," Nick said with an odd little smile. "I hope I left you enough hot water."

Kelly smiled slightly in return. Swiping up her cosmetic bag, she moved past him into the steamy room, shutting the door behind her with a soft click.

Gathering her hair under a shower cap she'd found packaged in the corner of the medicine cabinet, Kelly unbuttoned her shirt, shed her jeans, then stepped under the shower nozzle. At first she let the hot, pulsing water swirl caressingly over her skin. Gradually, when the water and steam began to do their work, she felt more of her tension drain away. Lifting the scented cake of soap from the dish, she leisurely began to lather herself.

After she rinsed away the soap, she remained under the soothing spray, her back against the tile, her eyes closed.

In another moment, I won't be able to stop.

Her eyes fluttered open and she shut them again, willing her mind to empty.

Then why are you angry?

I'm not angry, sweetheart . . .

With an agitated flick she shut off the taps and

dispersed the sensual memories into the steamy mist of the stall. She dried her body briskly, then slipped on her gown and belted the wrap securely around it. The rest of her toilette was completed after she had brushed her hair until it was a gleaming mass fanning thickly around her shoulders. When there was nothing left to do, she opened the door and stepped into the bedroom.

Her gaze went automatically to the beds and the travel clock between them. She'd spent no more than fifteen minutes in the bathroom and was perplexed. Both of them had nearly been asleep on their feet when they arrived, but both beds were empty. Moving farther into the shadowed room, she saw why. Curled deeply into the plush depths of the tufted easy chair, his feet supported by the equally plush matching ottoman, was Nick. He was sound asleep. She stood looking down at him and longed to smooth the lock of hair that had fallen against his brow. Even in sleep, it was still creased with tension. But she didn't. She never had thought much of tempting fate.

Hours later, when the call of an owl awakened her, Kelly rolled to her side to see if Nick had ever gone to bed. That the bed beside hers was as pristine and unwrinkled as it had been when she'd lain against her own clearly told her he hadn't.

She sat up and focused across the room through the darkness. The chair was empty, its hollow depths illuminated by the moonwash spilling through the French windows. One of them stood partially open. How long had he been out there alone?

Perhaps it was because her body was still heavy with sleep, or perhaps it was because she could see him again as he'd been this ghastly afternoon, blood spattered and alone, cradling Jean's head against him. Her heart ached all over again, and this time she didn't question the prudence of her move. She just acted on instinct, needing to be with him.

When she found him sitting at the table, his bare feet propped upon the wrought-iron table, the hard lines of his face looked almost cruel against the serenity of the still, balmy night. Kelly wanted to break the silence, but she couldn't find the words that would soothe.

Almost immediately he sensed her and held his silence, hoping she would go away. When it became obvious that she wouldn't, he shifted in his chair to look up at her. He looked straight into her eyes and felt his belly tighten.

"We will catch him, Nick. Jean's death won't go unavenged."

"What good is vengeance? It can't bring him back to life. That old man was the closest thing to a real father Joey and I ever had. He was the best friend my family had. Goddamn it, he didn't deserve to die because of us!"

"No, he didn't. But then, no one ever deserves to die at the hands of another. Brooding like this won't make things any better."

Nick's lips twisted. "Believe me, at this moment, it won't make things any worse."

Kelly heard his pain and answered it instinctively. "You need to rest, Nick." Her voice was as soft as the wind stroking the night.

"Go back inside, Kelly."

She gave him the only answer she could give. "No."

"You know what will happen if you stay out here." He saw Kelly shiver, though she stood her ground. He could so easily give them what they both wanted. But if he did, there was a good chance that he would only be giving her sex. And he knew that if that turned out to be the case, when the heat of the moment passed he would only have hurt her, maybe himself too.

"If I come inside, this time it won't end with a kiss. Do you understand?"

"Yes. I understand." She took a breath. "I understand that Jean was right, that life is transitory. He said while it lasted, not to complicate the things that were simple. Well, the simple truth is, I can't deny what I feel any longer. I'm not even sure I still want to, and that, more than anything you could say, scares the hell out me, Abella."

Nick turned his head back toward the night. He was silent for so long that Kelly thought he was going to keep ignoring her. When he turned toward her again, she stood there snared by the yearning in his eyes. The expression he wore was of a naked longing so intense it robbed her of breath.

"What are you saying?" he rasped.

She knew with absolute certainty that what she

was about to say would be the truest words she had ever spoken in her life.

"I want you, Nick."

"Oh, God, sweetheart, I want you too," he echoed. *But I don't want to need you!* his heart railed in return. Then he couldn't think anymore because already his legs were shifting until he stood tall and warm before her. Already his arms were reaching for her. Already she was melting against him, as if her bones would dissolve into his. He tried one last time to pull away, but when he looked intently down at her and saw the shimmer of moisture swimming in the bottomless depths of her eyes, he saw that despite her words, she was fighting a battle too. And losing.

They were both losing. The awareness humbled him, and he knew, as surely as the sun would rise tomorrow, that he too could fight himself no longer.

"Kelly, Kelly . . ." The words tumbled from his lips. And then he couldn't speak because she was reaching up to mesh the softness of her mouth with the warm firmness of his.

Strangely enough, the first kiss between them was very gentle, fragile, almost reverent somehow, as if the commitment of words they could not speak was being made by hearts that had never ceased to listen.

Kelly trembled beneath the gentleness of his lips. She had seen the hard hunger in his eyes, had tasted the wildness of his passion once before. That now he was making the obvious effort to restrain himself at the moment of her surrender shattered her. She knew by the way he was touching her that he understood that she was not taking this step lightly. And in a flash of clarity she guessed this was the reason why he had stopped last night. That sensitivity drew her deeper toward an emotional intimacy with him than anything that had gone before.

The depth of her feelings suddenly made her bold in a way that in the past she had never thought to be. Wanting to have the taste of him on her lips, wanting to absorb the very essence of the heart she felt beating strongly against her trembling breast, Kelly broke the kiss to pull away from Nick a little. She brought her arms from around his neck just long enough to reanchor them at his waist.

She could see the pulse beating at the base of his strong brown throat. As delicately as if she were seeking to gentle some proud, magnificent beast that drifted within her reach, she touched her tongue to that throbbing point. When her gentle exploration became a soft, sucking kiss, the raw sensuality of it drew a deep groan from the very depths of the man before her.

Kelly felt the change in him at once. She felt herself swept up into the hard-muscled strength of his arms and carried purposefully back through the French windows to her bed. He paused just once along the way to nudge the doors open wider so that the moonlight spilled fully upon the softly rumpled sheets.

Kelly was dimly aware of her feet touching the carpeted floor, then of night air touching her overheated skin as she felt her gown being swept from her. His soft exclamation of pleasure at her nakedness became a mental imprint she vowed to carry upon her heart. Then the cool sheets were at her back and she was watching him hook his thumbs into the low waistband of his pajamas before he slowly, deliberately, peeled them off.

She was awed by his magnificence as he stood proud, unashamedly aroused, before her. Her eyes dropped hungrily down the tall, tanned hard-muscled beauty of his torso, trailing the path of silky body hair that fanned lightly down from his broad chest, past the corrugated muscles of his hard abdomen that contracted with the tenor of his breathing, down to the point where the silky pattern fanned out densely to the firm, sinewed column of his thighs.

The thick, hardened proof of his need rose boldly, and Kelly knew a moment of fear. Before, emotion had overwhelmed her so swiftly she hadn't thought. Tonight her awareness was more controlled. She had not been with another man since her husband's death, and her heart skittered helplessly at the thought of the unleashed masculine power she sensed this man was capable of.

He saw the flicker of apprehension in her eyes and guessed at its cause. Wanting above all else to give her pleasure, he sought to put her at ease by lying down gently beside her and pulling her trembling body into his warm embrace.

"Nick, I . . ." Kelly stumbled. She felt awkward and embarrassed. "There hasn't been anyone since Jeff. I . . ."

"Shhh, it's all right, sweetheart. It's all right. I won't hurt you." He hugged her tight and reached up to brush a curling strand of hair from her brow. Then he replaced his fingers with a feather-light kiss. "I'd die before I'd ever hurt you," he whispered and realized he'd made the vow as much to himself as to her.

And then he was nudging her gently onto her back, bringing his own body over hers in one smooth motion until he was looming above her. The fullness of his weight rested upon his extended arms and he was careful to keep his lower body still and relaxed between her parted thighs.

"I won't hurt you," he repeated. "We have all night." But the feel of her soft thighs cradling his own, the delicate scent of her arousal blending with the muskier scent of his, the soft little panting breaths she took before he let his lips mingle and play with hers were driving him crazy. He prayed he had the control to keep his promise.

At the easy, unhurried way Nick was kissing her, Kelly felt the nervous tension seep from her body. She started to kiss him back, letting the rhythm of her breathing slow to echo his, letting her shy, pink tongue lazily tangle with the bolder wetness of his. She was rewarded when his mouth become more insistent at the gradual surrender of hers.

The heat within her began to rise again, and as it did, Kelly ended the play by angling her head up from the pillow to kiss him fully. Nick returned the kiss hotly, then in a flash of movement rolled

them over until he was on his back and she was
lying on top of him.

He was urging her to be the aggressor, Kelly
realized with surprise. The sheer need for air
forced her to break the kiss. As always with this
man, she felt herself spinning out of control. She
raised herself from him until she was kneeling
astride him, the pressure of his desire a hot, hard
brand against her stomach.

"Oh, Nick," she moaned, "how do you do this
to me . . ." Her words were swallowed as Nick
rose up to recapture her lips in a hard, open-
mouthed kiss. Kelly whimpered.

Her arms were clutched tightly around his muscled back, and she could feel his sweat dampening
her palms, could feel the beads of moisture on his
chest and belly mingling with her own.

"Oh, baby, baby, I can't believe this," Nick
groaned. He dragged a trail of burning kisses
down Kelly's throat until he reached what he
sought.

Kelly gasped as she felt one hard-tipped breast,
then the other, being pulled into the hot, wet cav-
ern of his mouth in a strong, sucking caress. She
shifted restlessly, wanting to get even closer to
him. But no matter how she tried, she couldn't get
close enough. Desperate and lost, she unwittingly
began to rotate her hips against the hot, moist
juncture of Nick's thighs.

"Nick, please . . ."

"I'm here, love." He was as desperate as she to
end the agony. But even through his urgency, an
awareness pierced the fog of his desire, and he

knew that this joining with her was something more than the quick, feverish mating he had feared it would be.

With no other woman had the sharp pleasure of his physical senses ever taken on this fuzzy edge that made him feel as if he were merging, really *merging* with her. The sensation was incredible and heightened his awareness of her, increased his need to be joined with her, miraculously dulled his fear of doing so. He couldn't have taken more pleasure from the soft, warm, willing perfection of her body, or the eager, wanton way she was loving him back. But on a higher level he was experiencing something deeper. He felt as if he were sinking into her soul.

Kelly was also sinking, burning until she feared this torment would turn her to ashes on the spot.

"I . . . I can't stand this," she sobbed. "Help me, I need you . . ."

"All right, sweetheart," he said.

Kelly felt Nick's hands drop down to still her hips. Her eyes tracked the jerky motion of his Adam's apple as he swallowed once, then she was mesmerized by the tense, pleasured look tightening his sweat-dampened face. As he entered her that first tiny bit, she felt the pinch of his invasion and was powerless to stop a gasp from escaping her lips.

Nick, understanding instantly, fell back, pulling her with him, keeping their bodies partially joined. He could barely draw breath as he said, "You control the pace, love. Take as much of me as you can. Or as little. I won't hurt you."

Kelly's eyes misted. She was overcome by the sensitivity of this man, of how unselfishly he was restraining his own needs in order to make this experience meaningful for her. She'd never felt cherished like this during sex, and still, she'd thought she knew what making love was all about. But now, loving this man, being loved by him in return, was showing her that she knew nothing.

Like nothing else she'd ever done in her life, she wanted to leave him with no doubt as to the depth of what she was feeling for him, what being intimate like this with him meant to her.

She braced her hands against his heaving chest and pushed down slowly until she absorbed him inch by slow inch. She felt Nick's fingers digging into her hips, and his grip was slightly painful as he urged her on. But she didn't care. She was too aware of the unbearable sensation of her wet softness absorbing his warm hardness until finally she rested fully upon him and he lay nestled completely inside her.

When she began the slow, measured undulation of her hips, Nick thought that he would surely die. Sliding his eyes closed, he turned his head sharply against the pillow and let her ride him, fighting doggedly every male instinct within him that urged him to spread her flat on her back so that he could drive into her and find a quick, hard release for this conflagration in his loins.

Kelly watched the strain settle across his features, felt the barely controlled pumping of his hips, and knew, as only a woman can, the dilemma he was in. A purely feline smile settled across her lips, then faded, as eventually she was forced to increase her pace as the beat of her body dragged her deeper into its relentless grip. Again and again she sank against him until she felt deep within herself the first tiny pulsations that heralded her release.

Nick felt them too, and with a low cry he held her hips in his damp, shaking grip while he thrust deeply, over and over, up into her shuddering body. He watched her head fall back, the lovely shimmer of her hair as it spilled across her back and shoulders, and felt a fierce male pride as she fell into that throbbing void of pleasure.

"God . . . God!" The words spilled from his tightening throat as he felt himself rushing toward his own fiery climax. "Kelly, look at me. Look at me!" he begged desperately.

Caught in the grip of her own pleasure, Kelly struggled to make sense of his words, to do what he asked. But when the peak of her spasms gripped her, her mouth opened on a wordless cry of ecstasy. It was only with a superhuman effort that she was able to drag her head forward and lock her stunned eyes to his. He looked wild, intense, out of control, and Kelly gloried in her womanhood.

At the sharp pleasure etched into Kelly's face, Nick let the force of his release thunder through him. His entire body convulsed with it, and he was powerless to stop his hoarse cry of pleasure from echoing through the room, just as he was powerless to stop his hips from arching off the bed to thrust one last time into the woman above him.

He felt the weight of her as she collapsed bone-lessly against him. For a very long time, he lay unmoving in the aftermath, content as he had never been before, to hold a woman, this woman wrapped closely against him, pressed fast to his quieting heart.

Kelly wasn't aware of how much time passed as they lay entwined, their tired, damp bodies cooling as the night passed around them. She pressed a kiss to his breast and knew that she had never imagined anything like the peace that engulfed her now. If the world ended at this moment, she thought sleepily, she'd be content to stay right where she was with no regrets. She thought she heard him mumble something and raised her head a little to look at him. But he didn't repeat it. His thick lashes lay still against his relaxed face; his breathing was regular and even.

"Nick?" she whispered anyway. But he didn't answer and Kelly was mildly disappointed. But she couldn't begrudge him the utter contentment that softened his handsome features completely for the first time since she'd known him. And she couldn't deny the joy of knowing she had put it there.

Smiling softly to herself, she snuggled closer and succumbed to a deep, peaceful sleep of her own.

Something warm and pleasant was stroking up and down her spine. Opening her eyes, she saw Nick propped on his elbow, facing her, an ab-sorbed expression on his face. The windows, which had been left open last night, permitted the first blushing light of dawn to filter into the room and across the bed upon which they'd slept away the night in each other's arms.

The trailing caress of his fingers, up and down, caused her eyes to flutter, and she hummed a soft purr while she snuggled back into his chest.

"Hey, where did you go?" His breath was a whisper against her hair.

"To heaven, I think," she returned drowsily.

Nick could feel the curve of her lips against his chest, the soft soughing of her breath as it gently tickled the hair there. He silently echoed the thought and tried to pretend for a little while longer.

While she had been sleeping, he'd savored the chance to watch her as she lay there totally relaxed and unaware. He'd tried to imagine what it would be like if he could begin his mornings knowing irrevocably that she was his, if there were no shadows hanging over his life, no implicit reminders of how she was bound by duty to potentially destroy his brother. Would his life ever be simple? Or would this moment, this morning, these moments out of time become the purest bits of happiness he would ever know?

Kelly could feel the melancholy that enfolded Nick, and she guessed some of what was causing it. The beauty they had shared during the night had, for her, been a revelation. But she didn't fool herself into thinking they could continue to evade the real world.

Somewhere out there, a killer was tracking

down the brother of the man she loved, a man who for all she knew was a killer himself. And if he was, she would by necessity be the instrument of his destruction. And she knew that while Nick's logical mind would have to accept the right in that, his emotional mind would never let him fully accept the destroyer. Kelly tightened her arms around him, a sudden desperation driving her to hold him close to her even while their newly found discovery of each other was threatened by circumstances beyond their control.

"You can't know how special last night was for me, Nick," Kelly began, needing to bind him even closer to her with words that suddenly seemed completely inadequate to express what she was feeling. "I've never felt as close to another human being as I felt to you. As I feel to you now."

She loved the way Nick's hand ceased its lazy play to settle at the small of her back. She relished the way he drew her flush against him, the way his lips dropped a soft kiss upon the top of her head, unmistakable indications that he was in the process of grappling with profound emotions too.

"I don't want to let you go," he said almost desperately. He'd never said that to another woman, never even come close to meaning it as he did now lying here with her. "You've become very important to me, Kelly."

Kelly's heart sang at his words.

"No more important than you've become to me." A shadow crossed her face. "But is it enough, Nick? The world won't go away."

No, Nick agreed, it wouldn't go away. But they

could hold it at bay for a little while still. For this morning, he would have this joy, cherish this woman who had quietly stolen into his heart.

Kelly readily met and matched the hunger in his kiss. She recognized what Nick was trying to do, and even if deep in her heart she wished he had said the words to match what he was so eloquently trying to express, she was fully aware that neither had she.

Perhaps they were both still too vulnerable. Both had known the pain of rejection and loss in their lives. At this moment, perhaps it was easier to take without demanding. Perhaps . . . and then she couldn't think anymore because she was melting, dissolving into the magic and utter pleasure of his touch.

She eagerly opened herself at his insistence and sighed as her body took him easily, fully. She welcomed the strong, steady rhythm of his thrusts. She rejoiced in the crush of his weight against her breasts. She pressed her lips to his throat, then dug her hands into his flexing buttocks in shivering reaction to the sensual abrasion of his hairroughened skin against hers. And finally, just before sanity fled, just before her pleasure took her, she reciprocated the tensing of his body as his deep groan of fulfillment blended simultaneously with the softer cry of hers.

11

Kelly closed the phone book, punched in the numbers, and settled back against the headboard to wait for her call to be put through.

"Fort Polk Information. Civilian or personnel?" the operator asked.

"Personnel, please."

Kelly heard a series of clicks, then another voice droned onto the line.

"Personnel locator."

"I'm trying to reach a Sergeant Robert Stevens."

"Just a minute, please." The voice paused, then said, "I have a listing for a Major Stevens."

"Fine." While Kelly waited for the number to be relayed to her, her eyes wandered carelessly about the room. Nick's complimentary glass of grapefruit juice sat warming on the breakfast tray with the rest of their used dishes. After their hostess had left the tray an hour ago, he'd wrinkled his nose and declined the compliment, thank you. Kelly smiled.

Her smile dimmed at what they'd discussed before he left. Nick had suddenly remembered where he'd heard of Andrew Malone. He'd been a soldier in Joey's army division while he was stationed in Louisiana. Joey had mentioned him once or twice in connection with some incident there that Nick couldn't clearly recall now. But he hadn't had to for Kelly's mind to start working.

She had thought back to her own musings about the army duty all three of Cain's bodyguards had shared and the question of whether there wasn't a connection to the Cain murder now. Nick had told her the name of Joey's division, and a couple of conversations later she had the name of its former commander. Now she waited for the number, hoping Stevens was still at the base to provide a link.

"Ma'am?"

"Yes?" Kelly took down the number. "Thank you." She punched in the number and the phone was picked up on the second ring.

"Army Post," a pleasant, young male voice answered.

"I'd like to speak to Major Robert Stevens, please. Is he in?"

"Just a minute, ma'am."

"This is Major Stevens. How can I help you, ma'am?"

"You don't know me, Major, but I'm a Sedgwick, Indiana, police investigator. I'm in Louisiana in connection with a case, and I'm wondering if you would have some time today to see me. I have a few questions about some men who were formerly under your command."

"What men?" The major's voice was noticeably wary.

"They were enlisted between 1983 and '87. Their names are Joey Abella, John Butler, and David Robbins."

Kelly didn't expect the silence that answered her. Perhaps this blind call was going to pay off after all.

"I'm not at liberty to discuss anything about those men unless you can present me with some paperwork that tells me I have to. With all due respect, ma'am."

"I see," Kelly said carefully. "I'm just interested in casual information, sir—what they were like, how they got along with the other men, things like that. Nothing confidential, really."

"I'm sure, ma'am. But like I said, you'll have to show some authority for me to do that. And from the looks of my calendar, the rest of this week doesn't look too good for me."

What, exactly, had put his back up? "Very well, Major." She heard the door opening behind her. "I'll take care of the clearance and you'll be hearing from me."

Kelly replaced the receiver at the same time two large, cool hands pushed the hair up from the back of her neck to make way for a warm kiss at the base of her nape. She shivered pleasantly when she felt the tip of his tongue lick her skin just before he released her hair and walked around the bed to face her.

"Any luck?" Nick asked, laying aside the newspaper he had gone out to get.

"I got a very interesting response from Stevens. By the way, he's a major now."

"Uh-huh," he said, sinking down on the bed beside her. "I'm listening." He reached for her hand, placed it on his thigh, and stroked it absently while she talked. Kelly was finding, to her delight, that Detective Sergeant Nicholas Abella was very definitely a toucher.

"I didn't have a chance to tell you about my own thoughts concerning Joey's days in service before you left. I don't understand the Malone connection, but I have been playing around with some ideas."

"Go on."

"Remember back at the cabin my telling you how Joey, Robbins, and Butler had all served in the same unit at the same time, and how it struck me as just a little coincidental that they had all ended up as bodyguards for the same man? Well, after you told me about the connection between Joey and Malone, I got to wondering if Stevens might not be able to shed a new angle on the situation."

"And did he?"

"Well, I'm not sure. That is, the good major didn't enlighten me with anything he said over the phone."

"But," Nick said, reading her, "you did pick up something in what he didn't say, is that it?"

"Yeah, that's it. What did Joey tell you about the time he spent down here in the service?"

Nick released her hand and got up to walk to the window. He looked out at the sky, which was a perfect, pristine blue. "Just the usual army stories. Most of it male boasting and swagger, you know. Aside from mentioning the fact that it was pretty wild he had pulled bodyguard duty with his old army buddies, he never told me anything especially notable about that time." He turned his back to the window and faced her. "Why? Tell me what you're really thinking."

Kelly looked down at her lap and raised a hand to rub absently at the side of her neck. "Maybe I'm just grasping at straws. Maybe nothing . . ."

"What?"

"I don't know," Kelly said a little impatiently. "If I knew, I'd be doing something constructive instead of sitting here stammering at you." She got up to walk past him out onto the balcony. The view was soothing, and its beauty reminded her of all that had transpired the night before. She turned to face him. His arms were folded across his chest, and he watched her, his expression noncommittal.

"I don't want to argue, Nick. I'm sorry I snapped. It's just that time is running out, and I feel like there's something staring me in the face that I'm just not getting."

Nick took a seat at the little wrought-iron table and lit a cigarette. "You said yourself that their military records are clean. No citations for disciplinary action show up. So in essence you're grappling with a gut hunch, babe, and you know there often is no solid explanation for that. I say we go talk to this guy and check it out."

"We'll need to get clearance from the authorities down here first. I need to call Brower so that he can take care of it for us.''

Nick nodded. ''You make the call. I'll go check us out. Get your things together, and we'll just make it a round trip from the base back to the cabin.''

''All right, fine,'' Kelly said, watching him stub out his cigarette. He got up to leave. ''Nick?''

''Yeah,'' he said, pausing to lean against the length of the window.

Kelly walked over to him, curved her hand around his neck, and brought his head down for her kiss. ''Be careful out there, hmm?''

One side of his mouth hitched up and the dimple deepened just before his lips met hers. ''Sure thing, sweetheart. Wouldn't want to ruin your day.'' The kiss was long, wet, and thorough, and Kelly was breathless when he released her and walked across the room and out the door. She'd never thought any man could make her feel the way he did. And none ever had. Not even Jeff in their good days. Everything was going to work out, she told herself. It had to.

It didn't take long for Kelly to make the call and get the interstate jurisdiction clearance she and Nick needed. With Brower's reluctant approval, Kelly was still able to hold off on having Joey declared an official suspect. No warrant was issued yet for his arrest.

So it was a little before noon when they left the hotel and picked up the necessary credentials to get them in to see Stevens.

They made it to the base in a little under an

hour. As they were waved inside the gates, Kelly looked around thinking how unspectacularly uniform military installations managed to stay. The scenery might have varied from climate to climate, but in essence only the names really changed.

Stevens's office was located just off the central area of the installation at the operations post. The secretary who greeted them showed some surprise as she seated them, offered coffee, which they declined, and went inside to tell the officer he had waiting visitors.

"The major will see you now."

"Thank you," Kelly said and preceded Nick into the office. The small room was sparsely yet tastefully appointed in a very understated, very correct military manner. An American flag stood displayed in the corner, and beside it was a glass case filled with honorary plaques and medals. Behind the major's desk hung a picture of the president, and to the side of that was a single, large window shaded by louvered blinds the same beige color that dominated the rest of the room.

The major himself, a distinguished-looking man of early middle age, rose and walked from behind his desk, which was crowded with a framed display of family snapshots. The introductions were made, and Stevens showed mild surprise at learning that Nick was Joey's brother.

"Please be seated. Officer Wylie, I'd like to apologize right off the bat for being so rude over the phone. But you see, your call was a little disconcerting so soon after Joseph's visit yesterday."

Kelly could hear Nick's indrawn breath, and she made an effort to conceal her own surprise.

The major continued. "I hadn't seen or heard from him since his discharge, and frankly, I was a little taken by surprise to have another inquiry from you about the same matters so soon after his. I was just being cautious."

"Yes, Major, of course. What specifically did Joey want to ask you about?"

"If I may ask, is Joey in some kind of trouble with the law? I'd be surprised to hear it. He was an exemplary young man while he was under my command."

Kelly skirted a little. "As I told you over the phone, my reasons for wanting to know about your conversation have to do with an investigation back in Sedgwick. Beyond that, I'm not at liberty to go into details, but some input from you on some specifics would be helpful."

Stevens was too experienced to miss the skillful way his question had been deflected. "Actually, he was here to ask me to substantiate a rumor that got established a long time before he ever joined my division."

"What rumor was that, sir?" Nick asked.

"Well, it was kind of strange, really. It involved a fight and a nickname that was given as a result. You may or may not know, but of the three men you mentioned in your phone call, Joey was the last to join my division back in those days. This fight took place before he was transferred to me. To tell the truth, I'd almost forgotten about it until Joey brought it up."

"Who was the fight between?" Nick prodded him.

"A smart-mouth private named Andrew Malone and David Robbins."

"Go on," Kelly said.

"You understand that none of it was substantiated then, which means it certainly can't be substantiated now.

"It was late after a Christmas party on the base, and the men were having a good time. Robbins, Butler, and some more men who had grouped together were coming out of the mess when they ran into this private, who was apparently feeling mean and spoiling for a fight.

"The story goes, somebody had smuggled in some illegal liquor, and supposedly Robbins was just drunk enough to give Private Malone the fight he wanted. They say when it was over, the private was literally eating dust."

"So, it was a bad fight. What made it special?" Nick asked.

The major rubbed his jaw. "Well, no one wanted to get a citation, of course, so nobody confirmed that there had been any fighting going on. Nevertheless, whispers started about what supposedly came after. The story goes, the next morning at dawn, one of the men went into the latrine and found the private huddled in a corner stall, 'hysterical and delirious.'

"They say he was nursing his thigh and muttering something about 'that butcher, that butcher.' Well, when the other man pried the private's hand away, he got a look at what Private Malone was talking about. About a centimeter up from his knee, a tiny mark curved something like a crude scorpion's tail had been carved into his skin. He said it had been Robbins.''

"Good Lord,'' Kelly said. "Did Malone ever press charges?''

"Didn't even try. Later that morning he claimed he'd been drunk and babbling, and said something about giving himself a tattoo. In time, the story died down to nothing. Nevertheless, Robbins acquired the name 'Scorpio' with the men who knew about it. By the time Joey got here, the nickname and the supposed incident with Malone had become something of a joke. Lots of the guys laughed; nobody much took it seriously.''

Something unpleasant was lodged dimly in the back of Nick's mind. "And what happened to Malone?''

"Nothing. That is, he served his term and was discharged honorably about the same time as Joey, Robbins, and Butler.''

Kelly looked over at Nick. His face was bare of emotion. What was he thinking? She turned her attention back to the major. "Is that all Joey discussed with you, sir?''

"Well, yes, if you discount a stroll down memory lane.'' He turned his attention to Nick. "I must say it was nice to find out Joey had become a police officer. Fine material for it; you must be very proud of him.''

Nick smiled distractedly. "Yes. Major, didn't you ever question Robbins yourself about that incident?''

The major looked surprised and seemed to consider the question. "I never really took that story seriously enough to press it. After all, if there had been anything to it, Malone would have pressed charges, wouldn't he?"

"Well," Kelly said, uncrossing her legs, "we won't take up any more of your time, Major. You've been a great help."

"What, that's it?" He smiled and spread his hands wide. "I don't feel as if I've done anything. There must be something I can help you with that's more useful."

"No, sir," Nick said. "We appreciate your help. Thanks for your patience."

The major shrugged, looking slightly bemused. "Well, if you're sure. It was my pleasure. Sergeant Wylie." He shook her hand again.

Nick didn't miss the way the major's eyes discreetly ran over her. He'd taken her arm, ostensibly under the guise of ushering her out of the office, before he knew it. The secretary smiled at them on their way out.

"All right," Kelly said in the car. "What were you thinking in there?"

Nick lowered the window and deftly fingered a cigarette out of his pocket and lit it before he spoke. "A crazy thought of a coincidence with a case a year ago."

Kelly turned sideways in the seat, tucking a leg beneath her. "I'm listening."

Nick watched the road through the shaded lenses of his glasses. He was suddenly loath to even voice what he was thinking. He took a couple of drags. "I was working a case, serial killings, all having to do with the murders of assorted street people, most sharing the M.O. of bizarre stabbings."

"Bizarre? How?"

"Sadistic. Not just delivering the death blow, but maiming, torturing, mutilating. Of course, aside from the messy inconvenience of the killer's showing the department up by leading the city's finest on a long chase, the brass wasn't all that broken up about avenging the victims. They were official scum of the earth—drug dealers, pimps, thieves, petty criminals. People who wouldn't in the scheme of life be necessarily missed. For months the killings went unsolved. And then we got a break.

"Some little old guy who couldn't take a nap because the TV in the next apartment was too loud put in a call. My partner and I were in the area, so we decided to take it. When we got there, I heard fighting behind the door and I made a forced entry. Inside was a sixteen-year-old hooker, a screaming baby on a corner couch, and a doped-up trick holding a knife at the girl's throat." Nick took a deep drag.

"We ran the guy in and it just so happened his prints matched some others we had lifted from evidence that had been confiscated from some of the crime scenes of those serial killings. It also so happened he was an ex-cop who had been kicked off the force years ago. All the way to prison, he kept singing about how the work wasn't done, about how the scum of the earth had to be purged.

"That last day in the courtroom, I'll never forget it. He looked straight at me and said, 'The righteous will carry on.'" Nick spared a glance at Kelly, who sat riveted. "'The righteous will carry on.' I never understood it, and because the killings stopped, I guess I eventually dismissed it."

"Until today," Kelly supplied.

Nick took a last drag off the cigarette and flicked it out the window. "Yeah. One of the recurring elements in some of those killings was the funny kind of wound the killer would cut into his victim's skin."

Kelly swallowed.

"That's right, babe. It was serpentine and pretty damned similar, it sounds like, to the one Robbins allegedly inflicted on Malone."

Kelly's tone was hushed with dawning realization. "You said *some* of the killings were noteworthy because of those stabbings, that the convicted cop's prints were found on evidence at *some* of the crime scenes." She watched Nick's stark profile. "But all of those victims weren't mutilated, were they, Nick? And that cop's prints weren't found at the sites of the victims who were."

Nick said nothing, and after a moment of consideration Kelly didn't judge. She could understood all too well the pressure Nick and other detectives working the case must have been under to pacify the public, to produce a clear culprit, even if they suspected that culprit might not have been working alone.

The cold fact was, the killings had stopped after Nick and his colleagues had successfully taken one more murderer off the streets. She didn't need to hear Nick's frustration over maybe having overlooked something, anything in his grasp that could have netted more. It was the frustration of every good cop.

They drove on in preoccupied silence until Kelly said, "I can't believe David Robbins could be the psychopath he would have to be to have been involved in those murders. I mean, how could he be that sick and function around normal people every day without ever letting it show?"

"I don't know. Jesus, I can't begin to know. David is a friend, for Christ's sakes. He's one of us." Nick ran an agitated hand through his windblown hair. "Look, let's not say any more. Let's just think about this for a while."

Kelly saw a muscle start to tick in Nick's cheek. The dread in her heart was in perfect sync with what was in his. She remembered what Nick had said about considering his fellow officers on the force his family. If their suspicions about Robbins were true, she'd be shocked, but she wouldn't be disillusioned. For Nick's sake, she held off verbalizing any more speculations.

It was well past dusk when Nick parked the car behind Jean's store. The ride to the cabin was just as silent as the latter part of the trip from the army base had been. Walking through the door of Jean's house almost felt like coming home, and Kelly dropped her purse wearily on the sofa.

Nick laid the keys on an end table behind her and let her know he was heading straight for the shower. When he emerged, his hair was still a little damp and he had shaved. The cleansing, however, had done nothing to erase the shadows beneath his eyes.

"Come on," Kelly said, walking into the kitchen. "I've broiled a couple of steaks and heated some rolls and vegetables. You should eat something."

Nick gave her a somewhat distracted glance and did as she invited. The dinner was a melancholy one. Neither of them could shake the awful suspicions that lurked in their minds. Nick offered to clean up afterward, and Kelly gladly let him while she went to take her shower.

Forgoing a pair of shorts, she chose instead a thin, knee-length cotton skirt and a matching cropped top. Nick was in the living room, standing in front of one of the windows. He'd drawn the curtain back and stood gazing out into the moonlit night.

"You know, if Robbins is culpable in those past crimes, a criminal history would put him in a whole new light and affect the suspicions surrounding Joey," Kelly mused aloud.

"Is that supposed to help?" Nick's voice was hard. The lines of his face were no less so when he dropped the curtain and turned to face her. "Or don't you even care? Would it really matter to you to exchange one dirty cop for another? Yeah, Joey could be innocent, what the hell? You could just round up another to take his place, right? Over. Finished. Job done."

Kelly's anger flared over the unjustness of his attack. "How dare you say those things to me?

Who the hell do you think you are, Nick? The last righteous cop? Do you think you're the only one who's affected by a dirty cop's stain on the department? Do you think you're the only one who bleeds when he's cut by the betrayal of a 'brother' on the force? Where do you get off speaking to me as if I have no feelings or capacity for compassion? No more honor than to play with people's lives for the hell of it so long as my 'job' is done!''

Kelly had to fight the kind of accusations Nick had just leveled every day of her professional life. Ordinarily she could deflect them. But after all they had shared, the words had hurt abominably coming from him, even despite the fact that she knew he was striking out in pain.

Nick's face was as tight with anger as hers. She wasn't surprised when he turned from the window and slammed out into the night. But she felt the vibration of the shuddering door in every fiber of her body.

When the tears came, she let them. What was she doing? How could she have let herself become so vulnerable to him? Did she even really know him?

She had thought she was beginning to. But the man she believed she was coming to love wouldn't have lashed out at her just to ease his own hurt. But he had. Just like Jeff. She'd promised herself a long time ago that she'd never stand for it again.

The tears fell harder. But it wasn't the same, an inner voice said deep down inside her. It couldn't be the same because she'd come to realize over the past weeks she had never loved Jeff with half the intensity with which she loved Nick.

The truth was, she'd been able to distance herself from Jeff because deep down she'd known she hadn't loved him enough to fight to reclaim him. Yes, it was true to an extent that the job took him away. But if she'd made it clear to him that she was completely there for him emotionally, especially during the bad times, wouldn't he have had more courage to fight to regain control of his life? Wouldn't he have had more desire to fight to reclaim her?

Was she making the same mistake now? Pushing away the man she loved because she couldn't advance beyond her own scars? Her own vulnerabilities? And this time, the love was stronger, the stakes much higher.

She looked toward the window. He was out there alone. What must he be going through? Everything familiar around him was being turned upside down, and she was letting him bear it as he always bore his disappointments. Alone. Scrubbing her cheeks, Kelly pushed away from the sofa and walked out into the night to search for Nick.

She saw him silhouetted on the jetty, his knees drawn up, his head resting upon them. Kelly dried the rest of her tears until, clear-eyed, she took the steps that were needed to go to him.

She stood beside him letting herself calm some more, then she sank down beside him. His head was turned away from her. She let her eyes drift over his hunched shoulders, let her senses absorb his dejection. Reaching out, she laid her hand on his shoulder.

"I'm sorry," she heard him say, though he kept his head averted. "I didn't mean to hurt you. You're the last person in the world I want to hurt." Slowly he turned his head to look at her. The fingers of the moon touched the silvery moisture spiking his lashes. "Everything is falling apart," he said in a shattered voice completely unlike him. It tore at Kelly's heart. "My friends are my enemies, my brother is a stranger, the man I loved as a father is dead. Right now, you're the only thing that's real to me, and even knowing that, I can't stop pushing you away."

"Nick, don't," Kelly whispered as her throat tightened again.

"You're the best thing that's ever happened to me." He shut his eyes. "But I'm scared to death at how vulnerable that makes me feel. I don't want to lose the miracle of having you, I don't, but something deep inside me can't stop shielding, can't stop trying to screw up what I feel for you."

"No, no, darling. Don't." Kelly pulled him close. When he unfolded his arms to haul her tighter to him, she sank willingly, wanting to be close against his heart. Suddenly she was terrified too at how helpless she felt before him.

"I need you," Nick whispered. "Don't leave me, don't leave me . . ." Her lips were crushed beneath his and her heart constricted as she felt the moisture on his face wetting hers.

Pulling him down there on the secluded dock beside her seemed the most natural thing in the world. She sighed when his lips sank to her throat and softly nuzzled, she trembled when his hands found her soft breasts and their tautened peaks, already aching for the fingers that caressed them. And when she would have pushed him away from her to lower her hands to his body to gift him with a similar caress, she protested softly when he held her hands at bay.

"No, love," he whispered. "Lie still."

"Nick," she said in a breathless whisper, completely overcome by the emotion she saw shining from his golden eyes. Her lashes fell and she moaned with helpless pleasure as she felt his hand drift upward along her trembling legs, stopping here and there for a soft pat, a softer caress. His other hand was playing a similar tune on her naked midriff as, one by one, he unfastened the buttons that blocked his way to what he sought.

When her breasts were naked and free to the shifting shadows of the night, the balmy air touched them but briefly before the wet warmth of Nick's mouth blocked even that errant caress.

Kelly's hands sifted through his hair as his hands continued to stoke the fire that burned for him deep in the core of her belly. When his hand climbed to her thighs, her body tensed with helpless anticipation, then it arched with helpless pleasure as the kneading palm of that hand found its rest against the warm moisture of her desire. A small tug and the scrap of silk was discarded, a deft twist and her skirt effortlessly followed. He smiled tenderly at the sensual anguish in her eyes.

She needed to touch him, to return something

of the beauty he was giving her. But when she moved her hands to do it, she found them blocked again.

Nick grasped both of her wrists in a firm yet gentle fist, then he dragged them away from his body, away from hers, until they were anchored where he wanted them. She felt the rough bite of the wood scrape softly against the tender backs of her hands as they twisted and turned and sought to be free.

"Let me, love," he whispered again. "Just enjoy it. I want to do this for you."

His lips settled upon hers and rocked easily back and forth until he had her gasping. When his tongue plunged suddenly and deeply into her dewy mouth, she met it and battled its ferocity with her own. A shuddering groan was wrung from him, and Kelly triumphed at last to have this small advantage in the play in which she burned to be his equal.

And then, as if bent on retribution, Nick shifted his legs and slowly began to thrust the hardness straining beneath his jeans against the aching, ready juncture of her thighs. Kelly moaned beneath his mouth, then wrenched hers away mindlessly as the cold metal snap of his pants beat a maddening counterpoint against the heat that suffused her skin. She felt the roughness of his denim, arched helplessly against it, until the thrust of her hips was sweetly matching his. The raggedness of his breathing told her that for both of them, the end of the game was near.

Then, just as she felt the knot in her belly uncoil

and surge to spring free, Nick stopped the motion and cupped her with his trembling hand, catching her on the very brink of the release her body craved. His words were barely audible, his breathing was shallow and forced.

"It's going too fast, sweetheart. Be still, I want to make it last for you, I want—"

But it was too late. Kelly's body was too close, and seeing that her pleasure wouldn't be stopped, Nick slid a gentle finger deep inside her and stroked, stroked at the nub of her desire, stroked at the heart of her pleasure until she was like a helpless wild thing, shivering in the throes of her passion.

At the pinnacle of her release, her shoulders rolled from the dock and her open, gasping mouth was stroked with his tongue, filled with his kiss, until the world tilted, then righted again. She drifted slowly, slowly back down to reality.

Kelly's heart was still thundering when she opened her eyes, and the tenor of her breathing refused to still when she saw that Nick wasn't finished.

One by one, he was slowly releasing the buttons of his pants. He was deliberate, his control tremendous as he straddled her thighs. He appeared to be utterly calm, but the pretense was negated by the bead of sweat that trickled from his temple and the slow, heavy heaving of his chest.

A muscle ticked in his cheek, his golden eyes shuttered, and Kelly knew a moment of fear as she lay at the mercy of this unsmiling lover. At last when he had finished, he parted his pants, but he didn't remove them. Kelly found the sight of the jeans gloving his hard nakedness more thrilling than if his desire had been bare and free.

Slowly he lowered to her and she gasped at the raw sensation of his hot, heavy, hardness probing at her woman's flesh. Closing her eyes in anticipation, she heard him mutter, "Hold on," just before his tongue pierced her lips.

The thrust was hard and he touched her womb, but he didn't begin the motion until he had braced one hand against the dock and cushioned her in the cradle of his other. She wrapped her legs around his thighs and had barely gripped his shoulders before the pounding movement of his hips began.

The pace was fast and the coupling was rough, but it drew Kelly into a dark, wild ecstasy she had never experienced before. Over and over he plunged into her body, his pace never slackening, the power of his thrusts never waning. Through her delirium, Kelly had the impression that he was deliberately branding her, that he was claiming her body and soul, that he was giving her his in the most basic, masculine way he knew how.

Then suddenly his hands were clenching and his body was tensing, and Kelly felt an impossibly strong climax rushing upon her. When the waves broke over her, Nick used his mouth to muffle her scream. She felt her nails digging into his flesh, but she couldn't soften the bite. Nick's hips were jerking, and as she felt the liquid fire of his passion jet into her, she released his mouth from hers to give him the gasping breaths he needed.

When they both came down, Nick pulled her into his arms. Neither could speak for the longest, hushed moments. The night air gentled them as their heated limbs slowly cooled, and gradually, Kelly felt one of the hands that stroked her back rise to cradle her jaw. Her chin rested on the damp warmth of his chest and she looked, as he wanted her to, deep into his eyes.

He tried to speak but couldn't.

Kelly watched his struggle and offered him only what she sensed he could accept. "It's all right." His body had just told her louder than any proclamation what was in his heart. Maybe one day, he would be able to, too. He gathered her blouse around her to shield her from the breeze, and she was content to lie in his arms for a little while longer.

At some point they gathered their things and headed back to the house hand in hand. There was no question about where Nick was going to sleep tonight, and as Kelly scooted to the center of the bed, she snuggled deep into the warmth and security of his arms. Her last conscious thoughts were of a smiling old Cajun who had given her a priceless piece of advice.

The noise woke Nick first. He gently eased his arm from beneath Kelly's head and sat up on the edge of the bed, listening. There it was again, a rattle at the door.

"What's wrong?" Kelly asked sleepily behind him.

"Put this around you," he said, reaching automatically for his discarded shirt he'd draped at the foot of the bed. "Where's your gun?" he asked just above a whisper.

Fully alert now, Kelly slipped the shirt over her shoulders and buttoned it rapidly. She reached over to the nightstand and pulled open the top drawer. When she'd pulled out her weapon and checked it, she climbed soundlessly from the bed and met Nick at the bedroom door.

He raised the muzzle of his own gun to his lips, motioning for her to stay where she was and to be alert for his signal. Kelly nodded and watched him step barefoot out into the darkened house.

Nick didn't make a sound as he stalked down the length of the hallway. When he was a hair-breadth from its opening, he stopped, pointing his gun upward at shoulder level. There it was again!

Whoever was there was in the house, and if he judged it right, the intruder stood a mere arm's length away from him. Another moment and the intruder would be stepping into a single beam of moonlight. *That's right*, Nick thought, *just keep on coming and I've got you. Just two more steps. One more . . .*

"Don't move." Nick had the gun cocked and jammed beneath the man's right eye. His other arm was a strangling band around the coughing man's throat. And so he was completely surprised when he heard his choking intruder rasp, "Jesus, man. Chill. You wouldn't shoot your own brother, would you!"

12

Nick's grip didn't relent. His answer, like his warning, was given in the same dangerous purr. "I might, if he put me through the hell you have." Abruptly he lowered the gun and gave Joey a slight shove away from him. The exasperated anger in his eyes nudged Joey back another step.

"Nick," Kelly said, emerging from the shadows behind him, "is it all right?"

"Yeah, it's cool. Come on out. I want you to meet someone."

Joey's attention sharpened as first one long, shapely leg, then the other, stepped through the shadows until Kelly emerged, a vision with a cocked gun, rumpled shirt, and cloud of lush red hair. She stood dead-eyed and steady behind Nick.

"Holy Mother, who are you?" Joey breathed.

"She's the IA officer who's here to bust your ass unless you start talking." Nick stepped past his brother, and as he did, lightly tapped the younger Abella's chin to close his mouth.

"Excuse me," Kelly murmured, seeing that the threat of danger had passed. "I'll be right back."

Joey nodded belatedly as he watched her turn and vanish back into the shadows. "Man, you ain't exactly been slumming while you've been waiting, have you?" He cut the rest of the teasing immediately when his eyes drifted back to Nick. The fierce warning behind those jeweled, yellow chips was clear. "You're serious, aren't you? She is a cop."

"Like I said, brother. Sedgwick Internal Affairs. And as far as what else you're thinking is concerned, don't. What you've been doing and where you've been is the issue, and I'd advise you to start talking."

"Here, here," Kelly said, entering the room again. This time, she was more sedately attired in a loose, white T-shirt and butter-soft jeans. "Did you kill Peter Cain, or didn't you?"

Joey's attitude was completely serious now, his intent to convince his brother and this woman that he was innocent. "No, I did not. I was only the witness."

Nick asked the question. "Then who did?"

Joey looked from one to the other. He wanted them to read the utter sincerity in his eyes. "David Robbins. David Robbins killed Peter Cain."

Nick released the breath he had been holding. Kelly did the same and reached unknowingly to caress Nick's hand, which rested on the sofa's back. Joey pondered the absent gesture, wondered what it could mean, but held his question until the immediacy of this crucial moment had passed.

"I think we could all use some coffee," Kelly

said. "Why don't we go into the kitchen while I make some."

The two men followed her and were seated at the table a short time later as she set down mugs all around. For a while they just sipped, each composing individual thoughts and questions. Kelly raised her eyes to study Joey. She welcomed the opportunity to do so unobserved.

He sat with his hands cupped around his steaming mug, obviously deep in thought. Had she not known he was Nick's brother, she surely would have guessed at some relationship between them. While they did not really look alike, their resemblance was strong. The same tall, rangy build was apparent, though Joey was a little thinner than his brother. And the same dark curling hair was worn just the slightest bit longer against Joey's neck.

He lifted his eyes and caught her watching him. She didn't avert her gaze. But neither did he, and she saw another way in which the two brothers were alike. Joey Abella possessed that same quality of stillness that could have the object of his attention wondering if he was poised for retreat or preparing to strike.

"All right," Kelly said, lowering her nearly empty mug. "Now we talk."

"Jean's dead, isn't he?" Joey said simply.

"Yes." Nick's answer was stark. "Suppose you tell us why."

Joey pushed his mug away and hung his head above arms stretched wide across the table. "Oh, God, it's my fault. I shouldn't have gotten him involved, but I was desperate. When I called him, he insisted on helping. He said no one hunting me would expect me to skip town with an old man. He made fleeing with him and staying at the cabin sound so much easier than trying to sneak out of town on my own." He shook his head again. "I wasn't thinking straight or I never would have agreed to let him help smuggle me out."

Kelly allowed him his grief for a moment before she pushed again for an answer. "Who else were you hiding from, Joey? Help us make some kind of sense out of why Jean had to die."

When he looked up, Joey's tears had dried and a hard anger had sharpened his features. Kelly knew it had overtaken his pain.

"They call themselves the Society," Joey said. "They're a group of police officers—men, women, patrolmen, detectives—all self-appointed vigilantes who have declared themselves the last resort to a system that fails."

The righteous will carry on. . . . Who do you think you are, the last righteous cop? . . . This thing is bigger than Cain, Nick. Watch your back, it's bigger than Cain. Like an ugly refrain, the words flooded through Nick's brain. He closed his eyes. Jesus.

"They said they were dedicated to nailing the dirtiest of the dirtiest, the everyday scum out there on the streets," Joey said. "Their targets are the habitual offenders, the ones who always manage to walk away from the law, no matter how hard we try to keep them jailed. The ones who eternally slip through the cracks."

In a way, it was like listening to Jeff all over

again, Kelly thought sickly. But instead of functioning by Jeff's motto, "If you can't beat 'em, join 'em," this group of fanatics had chosen to beat them—and at any length. "But if their targets are habitual offenders, why in God's name did they target Peter Cain?"

"This is all very complicated. I need to start back near the beginning."

"We've got nothing but time, Joey. Talk," Kelly urged.

And so he did.

Sandy Abella finished reading the document in his hand and laid it in his lap. His eyes sought the bottle on the table at his side, but he resolutely dragged them away. More than he ever had, he needed his wits about him now. It was the dead of night, yet he couldn't have been more wide awake as he remembered the events of yesterday. He'd been in a fog when Earl Mack had shown up at his door. In fact, he'd been certain he was dreaming, a conviction reinforced by the disapproving gaze he'd caught from a neighbor who happened to be walking along the street as Earl, in his tattered glory, stood at Sandy's door.

"Mack? How did you get here?" Sandy had asked while he leaned partially in, partially out of his front door.

"Don't matter," Earl had answered. "What counts is what I got to say. You gonna let me in or you gonna keep giving your neighbors a show?"

Sandy had stepped aside. Mack had taken an appreciative look around. He noticed the old, lived-in comfort of the home, taking in the cozy groupings and collections of aging objects still carefully maintained throughout. Someone took good care of him, Sandy knew Mack had been thinking, though from the look of Sandy's reddened eyes and rumpled clothes it couldn't have been Sandy.

"Can I sit down or what?" Earl asked.

"Of course!" Sandy answered, reminded of the manners that had deserted him while he was adjusting to the idea of having Earl Mack standing in his house.

Earl selected a chair by the sofa, planted himself gingerly, and reached into his coat to pull out the notebook. He tossed it at Sandy.

"Start reading that, then we'll talk. Oh, and by the way, it ain't mine." Sandy had read and grown more distressed by the moment. Dates, times, detailed accounts, all documented as they had been witnessed. The document was incredible and meticulously compiled in a way that only a habitual informant could construct. He'd gone through three pages before he looked up at Mack. "Have you read this?"

"Enough to get the drift," the informant answered. "The nest is full of snakes, friend. The question is what are you going to do?"

"Wait a minute," Sandy said, running a trembling hand along his unshaven jaw. "Wait one damned minute." His eyes fell on the bottle. With barely a glance at Mack, he reached out and grabbed it. When the burning had subsided, he said, "How do I know this is real? How do I know what's in it is true?"

"Remember Jackie Cabot?" Earl asked.

"Yeah, of course. All us old-timers remember him. He was killed not long ago." At Mack's level nod, Sandy grew cold. "For this?" he asked, holding up the book. "You're saying he was murdered for this?"

Earl reached into his pocket again and rummaged around until he pulled out the letter.

Sandy read it and laid it down beside him. His eyes moved over the notebook again. "Why haven't you gone to Nick? Why have you come to me?"

"Nick ain't here," Earl answered bluntly. "Looks like you're elected."

Sandy's hand scraped his jaw again. He got up to pace. Earl observed the restless habit. He'd seen it a million times in Nick.

Eventually Sandy stopped to stand behind the back of the sofa. His fingers gripped the cushions hard. God knew why this responsibility had fallen on him, but it had. Now it was up to him to remember the kind of cop he used to be, the kind of cop he had to be again. "I'll need to keep this letter for verification. Evidence. Do you understand?"

"Yeah, I hear you," Earl said. "But I don't want to be involved, Sandy. I'm an old man and I want to stay that way."

"I'll do what I can, but the police may need you to give some sort of formal statement for the record. The details of the process can be worked out later." Sandy looked around the room as if he were searching for a sign of what to do next.

"Kind of hits you in the gut, don't it?" Earl said, making his own clumsy attempt at consolation. "The daily stuff, the cowboy stuff is bad. But the murder of the prosecutor, and by one of his own men, too." He shook his head. "What is this world coming to when the players on the good team start killin' each other off?"

"Why, though?" Sandy said. "This"—he waved the book—"gives the facts, but it doesn't give the reasons. What could Cain have been even doing there that night in the alley?"

"You really have lost touch, fella. Was a time when you kept your ears to those things whether they concerned you or not."

Sandy snapped impatiently. "If you've got something to say, Mack, say it. Go ahead and spit it out."

"All right. Word on the street was that maybe the prosecutor was tending to his habit. And I don't just mean of showing up in the dead of night at places he wasn't supposed to be. I mean habit. As in illegal. As in addiction."

Sandy felt himself sobering up very quickly. He walked back around to the front of the sofa and sat. "How long?"

"I ain't sure. All I know is, I heard he had it when he got into office."

"This is incredible," Sandy said, shaking his head. "If a county prosecutor of this state was into making street deals, how could he keep dangerous dealing like that so successfully hidden?"

"Because he didn't. He had his own private messenger boys who made contact with his sources."

For a span of seconds, Sandy couldn't bear to ask. "His bodyguards?"

Earl calmed the man's worry. "No, not Joey. Here and there, over a period of time, the other two were spotted being a little too friendly with types they shouldn't have been on speaking terms with. Still, nobody would have known if those suits hadn't made the mistake so many of them do, if they hadn't thought of their suppliers as dumb junkies."

"What do you mean?"

"Even junkies have ears, friend. And memories. Really good ones, on occasion, when it's men of importance who talk. And when you're a 'dumb' junkie who's laughingly patted on the head for providing for one of your 'betters,' well, loose words are likely to cling to your brain. They're likely to be shoved away in the old future reference file, you know?"

"Joey had to know. He's a good cop. What kept him from revealing what he knew?"

"That I can't answer for you."

The two men sat in silence for a while until eventually Sandy noticed Mack's eyes darting more and more frequently to the bottle. He got up and when he returned from the kitchen, he set down a glass on the table.

"Obliged," Earl said as he poured himself a measure and swallowed long and deep. He poured another.

"So who can you trust? Who you gonna give it to?"

Sandy leaned his head back and thought. Who was it safe to trust? Only one man's name kept coming back at him over and over. "Anton," he said aloud. "If anyone's honest, he is. I'd stake my life on that."

"Yeah, well," Earl said, getting up, "you may just have to." He reached the door and opened it. Just before he stepped through he said, "Don't forget, I never gave you that book. I ain't got no intentions of endin' up the second dead snitch."

Former Private First Class Andrew Malone awoke with a start. His heart was pounding, his forehead dampened with sweat. Lying utterly still, he moved his gaze around the pitch-dark bedroom of his apartment, trying to see what had awakened him.

He saw nothing but darkness, heard nothing but the silence of the Louisiana night pressing down on him. Cautiously Malone turned his head against his sweat-dampened pillow and saw that the bedside alarm read 4:47 A.M.

He dragged himself upright against the headboard and linked his arms behind his head, fighting the impulse to flood the bedroom with light. Something had crashed to the floor outside his room.

Swallowing back the knot of fear in his throat, he groped beneath undershirts and jockey shorts in his night-table drawer for a small, deadly Beretta.

With the pistol in hand, Malone eased the covers aside and slid soundlessly to his feet. The bedroom door stood slightly ajar as always. He eased it open wider, pulling back from the darkness. Steadying the gun in his right hand, he inched his other around the corner and along the wall to the light switch while he took a deep calming breath. He flicked on the light and gasped as brightness flashed across the room.

The apartment was empty. From the front door in the living room to the shuttered French window bordering the east wall of his dining room and kitchen, it was empty.

Malone lowered the gun and sagged against the doorway in relief.

He'd thought it was Scorpio.

He walked into the kitchen, laid the gun on the table, and switched on the coffeemaker, thinking how for one crazy instant he'd been convinced Scorpio had gotten in.

Ever since the phone calls had started two weeks ago, ever since that hateful voice had started harassing him out of the blue, he'd started to fear for his life. Why the harassment had started after all these years, he didn't know, which made it all the more unnerving. Unnerving enough to cause Malone to vanish out of Olmston without a trace, he hoped.

He'd guessed back in the service that David Robbins was crazier than a hoot owl on Blue Monday. But he'd never been able to prove it. And later, after Robbins had threatened his life if he ever told of the attack in the latrine, he'd been too frightened to try.

The strident buzz of Malone's alarm shattered his apartment's silence. He wiped the cold sweat from his brow and hurried to shut off the jarring noise, then shuffled back to the kitchen to put away the coffee things. Despite the caffeine, he was still in a sleepy daze as he turned to go get dressed for work.

He was walking toward his bedroom when his bare foot pressed down on something sharp in the carpet. Wincing, he stooped to see what it was. Digging his finger into the deep pile, he probed until he found a tiny chip of porcelain. It was small, but he was able to make out a familiar blue-and-rust mosaic pattern. It was the pattern on the coffee table lamp sitting next to him.

He ran his hands over the cool, smooth surface of the lamp and felt a tiny nick at its base. With unsteady fingers he slid the chip into the nick.

The fit was perfect.

Terror hit Malone like a steel fist.

He rushed to check all outer points of entry, then he turned toward his bedroom to check the balcony windows there—and saw the dirt tracks. God, how had he missed them? But it wasn't that realization that tightened the knot in his throat. The tracks stopped at the threshold of his bedroom door. That butcher had wanted him to see.

Skirting them, Malone dodged into his room, locked the door, and called the police. When he hung up the phone, he was tight as a wire.

He sank heavily down on the rumpled sheets,

leaned his head against his headboard, and tried
to get control of his restless imagination. He had
to get the hell out of here, had to get dressed, he—

The gun! His head jerked up. He'd left the gun
on the kitchen table!

He was across the room in seconds. Snapping
back the lock, he wrenched open the door,
sprinted to the kitchen, and grabbed the weapon.
When he turned, he almost collided with the knife
at his throat.

Stunned with shock, Malone felt the gun
knocked from his hand and his body spun around.
An arm was hammerlocked across his throat in a
bone-crushing grip, the hairs on Robbins's skin
below his short-sleeved shirt moist with sweat.
The rubber gloves he wore were in contrast dry
and horribly cool. The knife was at Malone's jaw.

"Hello, old buddy. Nice to see you. Stop strug-
gling! Another move and you die."

Malone's eyes blazed and his anger rose at being cornered in his own home.

"You should have checked your closets." Robbins's voice was awful in its calmness.

"What the hell do you want, man?"

"You're in the way, buddy, you're an old sore
just waiting to erupt."

Malone started to sweat. "What are you talking
about?"

"Destiny, Andrew. You're in the way of my
destiny. I've structured my life and those around
me with a purpose. If that purpose is to be successfully carried out, I can't afford to have anyone

walking around who could blemish it with wild, poisonous stories smearing my good name."

"Are you—" Malone sweated a little more freely —he'd almost said "crazy." "Nobody believed that story about us then. Why would anyone believe it now? It happened too long ago."

"Apparently not long enough. For some reason Joey Abella—remember him?—has been snooping around the base. Three guesses why, and I'll tell you now it's not for auld lang syne. Fortunately nobody there can do anything but reiterate the rumor. You, on the other hand, can substantiate the fact."

"Listen!" Malone said. "I'll—I'll do anything you want. I'll go anywhere you want me to go. Just don't kill me. Besides, if anything happens to me, what's to stop Joey or Stevens from getting suspicious and making that link to the past you're trying to avoid?"

"Joey is going to die. Stevens is expendable too. Anyone else's two cents would be pure speculation, and besides, why should anyone think your death is any different from a million other random assaults that happen every day?"

Malone despaired. How could he reason with a madman?

The knife started to move. It drew a thin streak of blood. Robbins's words fell like gentle rain against Malone's ear. They were whisper soft, a promise of death. "We're through stalling. You really do think I'm crazy, don't you? You really think that I don't know the police are coming."

The whisper flattened to a monotone. "I told you one night long ago not to play me for a fool, boy."

"Please. *Please*," the terrified man begged.

"I'm sorry, Andy. You're too dangerous to live." The knife slashed.

Malone choked as the blood surged from his throat. The killer behind him escaped out the back as his choking victim sank to the floor.

It seemed like hours, though it must have only been seconds before the pounding on the door exploded through the apartment. Malone was nearly unconscious, but some last burst of energy, a desire to live, gave him the strength to inch his hand over to the lamp cord beside him. He yanked and the crash of the porcelain sounded beautiful to his ears. The door crashed inward as the police rushed forward.

The doctors told him later it was that crash that saved his life.

Robbins fought against the impulse to speed. He even commended himself for slowing a bit when he passed a rushing squad car that passed him going in the opposite direction.

He pulled into the first gas station he came to, shoved the bag holding stained gloves and the towel he'd used to wipe his arms beneath the car seat for later disposal, and walked to the self-serve window to pay for his gas. While he was there, he got the bathroom key. As he calmly pumped his gas, he looked up and smiled at the pretty cashier who watched from the station window.

Inside the bathroom, he slid the key into his

pocket and walked to the sink to turn on taps until the hot water gushed into the bowl. He slowly rotated his forearms under the punishing stream to take away any faint, lingering residue. Letting the water do its work, he raised his head to look at his reflection in the cloudy mirror.

His eyes scanned dispassionately over smooth, even features, distinguished only by a sandy mustache. He guessed most would call him handsome. Maybe he should ask the flirtatious cashier, he thought with a smile. His blue eyes looked untroubled and clear. That was good, he thought, his business was almost finished here, and he couldn't let anything go wrong now. His eyes lifted to the sandy strands of his hair.

His smile widened as he fingered the wig. His touch dropped to the false mustache and he laughed.

It was a funny thing about even features. You could disguise them, play them up or down as you chose. He thought of how Nicholas had looked right through him beneath that Cajun bastard's shop in Nashville that day. He thought of how he'd had to kill that old man anyway to keep him from alerting Abella and the woman that he was in the area looking for Joey.

He also thought of what he hadn't bothered to tell Malone, that Nicholas and the Wylie woman would die too, then there would be no one living who could convincingly link David Robbins the police officer to the shadowy Scorpio figure from the past. Butler's loyalty was unquestionable; it always had been.

After this fallout with Cain was cleaned up, he wouldn't need the disguise anymore. He would be protected by his band of brothers as loyally as he would protect them. Though they were only a dozen now, they would grow and everyone who mattered on the force would understand that he and the Society provided an invaluable service.

The Society was clued in to the only real way to eradicate the filth from the streets. A higher justice than courts had to exist, a stronger retribution unanswerable to court rules that were subject to the fallibilities of men had to prevail.

Cain had understood that once. He had understood when rules had to be bent to keep the walking scum off the streets. And he had been a man of influence and power, a great ally. Until, like Joey, he'd shied away, unable to stomach the attrition of war. Of course, he mused with disgust, Joey had never really been one of them, he'd only pretended, then conveniently bolted before he had been called upon to prove his mettle.

Cain had also turned on his warriors, listened to the brainwashed masses who whined about lenience and victims' rights and police brutality. He'd ignored the basic survivalist truths of selective force and total vengeance. Those were the only real regulators of evil in today's society. Those who understood that in this world were princes. Instead, Cain had lost his soul and launched a purge against his brothers.

He turned the water off. The activities of the Society couldn't resume yet, but soon they would. The temporary obstacles had fallen one by one.

Cain was gone. Malone was gone. There were four more. He was sure Joey had made contact with his brother and the woman at the cabin by now. But soon they would be gone. Stevens would follow. The Society would resume—and flourish.

13

"Man, are you crazy!?" Nick demanded. "I've seen you do some harebrained things in your life. But this, I swear, has got to be the worst. Or didn't you think that maybe you could get killed?"

"I told you, Nick," Joey said. "I didn't know they were this vicious. Hell, I didn't even know if they were real vigilantes. I mean, I dig Dirty Harry as much as the next guy, but I never thought I'd be working in a precinct full of clones from Central Casting."

Kelly smiled in spite of herself. "All right, Joey. So you say you overheard some cowboy locker-room talk, got suspicious, and in order to check it out, wangled yourself an invitation to some of these vigilante meetings, right?"

"That's about it. And I probably wouldn't have done that much if John Butler hadn't been one of the ones talking. Since we had a minor history in the army together, I guess I just got curious to see if all of his militant talk was for real or if he was just blowing smoke."

"When did you find out he wasn't?" Kelly asked.

"It was at the third meeting at his house. One of the guys started talking about Cal Owens, a kid who just finished doing some token jail time for purse snatching. He's an in-and-out repeat offender who's been a career criminal since he was seventeen."

"So what's the story?" Kelly asked.

"About a week after his latest release, Owens was hospitalized for massive contusions, internal injuries, trauma, you name it. The bottom line is, aside from the medical jargon, somebody beat the living crap out of the kid, which is noteworthy because the first thing he started yelling was police brutality."

"You're telling us that these Society members exacted some sort of retribution on the little punk?" Nick asked.

"Let me finish," Joey insisted. "Two days later, when I'm hanging out in the café around the corner from the precinct, who should walk in but John Butler. David was on duty with Cain that night.

"So I motion John over and we start talking about this and that when he brings up the Owens kid. 'He's a little punk,' I said, 'but all the same, it's still too bad he got busted up that way,' to which John replied, and I quote, 'The little punk ought to be grateful he's not dead. The next time, he might be.'"

"Well, that's a pretty callous attitude," Kelly said. "But you and I and a hundred other officers hear posturing just like it every day. Besides, Butler was probably right, the kid probably will end up a victim of the streets."

"Uh-huh. That's what I thought too, so I just mumbled something and kept eating my sandwich. It was what he said next that bothered me."

"Nick and I are on pins and needles, Joey." Kelly poured herself another mug of coffee.

"He said, next time that kid's number came up, he might be the one holding the slip. I asked him what he meant, and he said there were some around the precinct who were willing to go that extra step to see that justice was done."

"That could still be taken a lot of ways, Joey," Nick said. "What convinced you that John was talking about something extreme?"

"Well, he didn't say anything, he just encouraged me to come to the next meeting that week. So that following Friday I showed up, expecting what I'd seen so far, swagger and bluster."

Joey fell silent and Kelly raised her eyes to Nick. She silently seconded the apprehension she saw creasing his brow. She looked back at Joey. "Tell us about it."

"It was at a guy named Charlie Ryan's house. You know Charlie, Nick. Works in Dispatch. Used to come over to visit Pop in the old days. Well, I was the last to get there and things were low-key enough at first. Plenty of beer, pretzels, sandwiches." He laughed mirthlessly. "I think his wife even made some cookies. Regular Rotary Club shit. Then they brought out the pictures."

"Pictures?" Kelly asked, leaning in toward

Joey, wanting to hear every word he was telling them.

"Mugs of about forty, fifty people. All neatly arranged in a dime-store photo album your grandma would be proud of. It was Charlie's own private rogues' gallery of criminals. Pimps, thieves, prostitutes, dealers, you name it. Well, I still didn't get it, but I figured if I kept my mouth shut, ears open, and smile ready, I'd find out soon enough. And I did, unfortunately.

"Some guy, a patrolman I don't know, started talking about target practice. Well, others joined in, but for a while nobody said outright exactly what they were talking about. Then Charlie flipped to a page in the middle and urged the fellas to give themselves a cheer for another target hit and job well done. I couldn't believe what I was hearing, so I looked over his shoulder to see who he was talking about. His finger was resting on a mug of Cal Owens."

Kelly leaned back in her chair and rubbed her arms. She felt very, very weary.

Nick pushed himself away from the table and walked over to the refrigerator, where he poured himself a tall glass of ice water. He propped his hip against the sink and emptied the glass in one long swallow. "You had an obligation to come forward, Joey."

Kelly shifted her eyes from Nick back to Joey. He was absently turning a fork over and over against the tablecloth.

"Yes. I know that was my first option," he said.

"Then why didn't you take it?" Nick asked mildly.

"Because even then, I knew I couldn't be sure who in the department was involved. I mean, Christ, if Charlie Ryan could be involved with those nuts, anybody was suspect."

"You could have come to me."

"Yeah, right, to let you take over for me again, big brother?" He shook his head at Nick's wounded look. "Now, don't get me wrong. I'm your brother and I love you. But sometimes you can be just a little, well, overprotective. Not your fault, it's just the way you are about people you love."

Nick's eyes flickered to Kelly.

"Besides that, you didn't know the game or the players. I didn't want you talking to the wrong person just to end up without backup in some dark alley one day."

"So after that incident," Kelly said, "you play-acted like you were a loyal inductee-wannabe and the group eventually accepted you? Just like that?"

"Correct," Joey said. "Oh, I could tell some of the guys, including Butler, were a little uneasy with the quickness of the judgment. But David pushed for me, saying he could vouch for me on account of how we went back to the army and all. I guess I just got lucky nobody was uneasy enough to challenge his decision."

"What was your motive for getting in? What did you plan to do with what you knew?"

"I carried a concealed recorder. I figured after I

got enough incriminating conversation, I'd have a leg to stand on when I reported what was going on to brass. I'd have proof that not only did the group exist, but that David Robbins was generally acknowledged as its leader."

"Obvious question, Joey," Nick said from across the room. "Where are the tapes?"

Joey sighed in frustration and disgust. "They disappeared after Cain's murder."

"Disappeared? How?" Nick demanded.

"I don't know!" Joey snapped, his voice rising to match Nick's. "I can swear that nobody knew I was taping anything. In fact, I know they didn't because if they had they would have been gunning for me long before now. The only thing that makes sense is that after Cain's murder David figured I must have had something on the Society and acted on the guess.

"When he saw me that night trying to warn Cain out of that alley, he wasn't pretending to be shocked. I wasn't misinterpreting the rage on his face. Afterward he must have sent someone over to my apartment to make the search. And unfortunately, whoever it was that beat me there was pretty damned thorough, snatched my alibi, and here I am."

"You still haven't explained how Cain came to be in that alley in the first place," Kelly pointed out.

Joey looked grim. "You know those rumors that were circulating a few months ago about Cain, about his alleged links to illegal drug sources?"

"Yes," Kelly said wearily, not liking where this was going.

"Well, he didn't have any organized links. But he definitely had a problem. He used David and John Butler to connect with suppliers."

"Joey," Kelly said, "I hope you know that if you beat this murder rap, you are still going to be in some very major trouble. What you've just revealed about Cain amounts to major-league aiding and abetting. How can you justify not blowing the whistle on him?"

"Morally, I can't," Joey said. "But strategically, I felt it was imperative to let things go on as they were for a while. I wanted to stay in good with David. Peter wasn't even aware of the group, but his hard-core stance against crime still made him a hero in the Society's eyes. Just the three of us knew about his addiction. If that addiction was suddenly made public, David would have known it was through me. I would have been out like a shot, and no one would have been in a position to keep tabs on those vigilantes."

Kelly sighed impatiently. "Well, I don't like that glib little explanation one bit, but for the sake of progress, I'll allow it. Go on. How was Cain lured to that alley?"

"You're going to like this even less. You know that crackdown on the alleged police brutality Peter initiated? Well, that didn't sit well at all with David and the others. As a matter of fact, I don't think I've ever seen David more livid than he was at that last meeting before Peter was killed. He was actually ranting about betrayers, and destroyers, and painful purges had to be made for the sake of the good.

"I'll always regret that I didn't understand the extent of his rage even when it was staring me right in the face. After that meeting, David pulled me aside. He told me that as much as it pained him, something was going to have to be done about Peter. He'd been thinking about it, he said, and had finally reached a solution."

"Which was?" Nick asked.

"Blackmail. The plan was to blackmail Peter over his drug addiction. If he didn't yield on the crackdown, then 'in his own best interests' he would be exposed. David said, so Peter would have no doubts as to who was in control, he wanted to intimidate Peter by issuing the ultimatum off his turf.

"David said the plan was to get Peter to the alley on a pretext. He said he was going to tell Peter that a witness he'd been cultivating on some hot case or other was ready to meet and talk on neutral ground. David knew Peter could be a zealot and that if he made it sound like the meet wouldn't go down any other way, Peter would meet the contact there. David said he'd assure Peter he'd shadow him for protection. Sure enough, Peter fell for it. The glitch occurred at my birthday party.

"Everybody was having a good time when John drops in for a second after his kid's play. He walks up to me and starts talking about how everything with this crackdown was going to be taken care of that night. Well, of course, I thought I knew what

John meant. Even when he started talking about the threat of the prosecutor being removed permanently, I still didn't connect it with murder. It wasn't until after the party, about thirty minutes before the shooting, that I got an awful feeling that it was all going to go wrong.

"I wasn't panicking yet and I called Peter, but he wasn't answering. I knew then that David had been lying. When I got to the alley, I was too late. You know the rest."

Neither Nick nor Kelly said anything immediately. All three were silent and a bit overwhelmed.

"So then," Kelly said, "David is here in Louisiana, looking to silence you. And you're running, trying to stay one step ahead of him until you can figure out a way to accumulate some sort of evidence against him, in lieu of the tapes, that will help in your exoneration, am I right?"

"Nail on the head, Sergeant."

"That's why you went to Fort Polk asking about this Scorpio thing?" Nick asked.

"You got it, brother. As they say, there's more than one way to skin a cat. But I swear, David is one particular cat who seems to have more than nine lives."

"And this Scorpio thing," Kelly said, "you remembered the Malone incident and the M.O. quirk surrounding those serial killings, didn't you? You already had buried knowledge about what Nick and I had only just pieced together. So your strategy was, if you couldn't provide anything on Cain's murder rap, perhaps you could link David to other killings?"

"That was my thought, yes."

Kelly smiled. "It just might be very feasible."

"You know, the one person who can corroborate the link is Malone. I wonder if we can find him?" Nick said.

Kelly looked from one brother to the other. "We can try. Let me get on the phone and see what I can dig up."

A short while later, what she'd dug up was a police report on the critically wounded former PFC Andrew Malone. He was currently convalescing in the Sisters of Mercy Community Hospital, eight miles from Fort Polk. Kelly hung up the phone and faced the other two.

"Well?" Nick asked.

"He's alive. Barely. It seems our knife-happy friend has already beaten us to him."

"We could have trouble."

"Well, don't keep me hanging in suspense. What do you mean?" David Robbins rubbed the piercing throb at his temple. He had a nauseating headache, and watching the fatally dull life of downtown Olmston through his motel window wasn't helping.

"There's a buzz in the precinct that something major has developed on the Cain shooting. I think a link has been found, but I can't get anybody in position to find out."

This was not what Robbins wanted to hear. "Could you possibly be more specific, or is that beyond you today?"

"No need to get snippy. That's the point I'm

trying to make. I don't have any specifics, just a tune-in on a buzz."

"Anything to do with Joey? Can you tell me that at least?"

"I'm not sure, but I don't think so, at least not directly. I think this concerns something else. Are you sure you didn't leave any evidence, anything that could be traced?"

The quick anger that rose inside him at Butler's impertinence only made his head throb harder. "Don't you question me! I told you no."

"All right, all right, calm down. I didn't mean anything by it. It's just that I get itchy when I can't read what's going on around me. And I get doubly itchy when what's going on might concern me."

"Well, do you have any suggestions, or did I just call to hear the voice of doom?"

"Yeah, I do have one. I been thinking about Sandy Abella. Seems to me that he's been overlooked an awful lot in this thing. I mean, he is the father of two of the principal players. And even though he drinks, I can't see ruling him out completely as someone who ought to be watched."

Robbins actually felt his sight beginning to blur. "All right." It was an effort not to gasp. "Do whatever you think best. Use whatever resources you have to. I should have everything wrapped up down here within the week, then I'll be coming home."

"Good enough. Hey, are you all right? You don't sound good."

"Yes. I'll be in touch." He nearly dropped the phone in his haste to get it in its cradle. Ah, God, the pain had never been this bad before. He groped blindly for the wallet he'd thrown on the nightstand along with his keys. Locating it by feel because it hurt to focus his eyes, he pulled it to him and rummaged around its folds. He threw papers to the floor, to the bed, anywhere they landed when he grew desperate to find what he sought.

At last he touched the tablets and pulled them out almost frantically. He stumbled to the bathroom doorway and had to pause for a minute to lean against it. Then, with a super effort, he shuffled inside, where he groped for a courtesy plastic cup and turned on the tap.

When he had swallowed the codeine, he stumbled back into his bedroom and all but fell onto the bed. Within minutes, mercifully, he felt his eyelids drooping and his senses emptying as blessed, blessed relief overtook him.

Kelly stood just within the door of the intensive care unit where Andy Malone lay. Although the three of them had made the journey together, only one of them had been given permission to go inside the room.

And so here Kelly stood along with a duty nurse whom she had persuaded to accompany her to act as a witness. At this moment, Kelly was just having a hard time pushing down the horror of imagining what it must have felt like to actually live through having your throat cut.

She stood by the bed, trying not to let her eyes dwell on the heavy packing that swathed Malone's throat. She quietly pulled a voice-activated cassette recorder, a pad of paper, and a pencil from her purse.

"Mr. Malone," she called softly.

Slowly, hesitantly, the man's eyes opened to focus without recognition on her face. She tried to smile reassuringly.

"Mr. Malone, I'm Sergeant Kelly Wylie of the Duncan County, Indiana, Internal Affairs Branch. I just want five minutes of your attention and then I promise to go away. It concerns David Robbins. Is that okay?"

Malone took a minute to respond. At his barely perceptible nod, Kelly was relieved he was going to cooperate.

"I have a pad and pencil. The doctor's told me you can write to communicate. So to make it easier for you, how about if I just ask you some simple yes-or-no questions?"

Again the slight nod.

"Good. Here, please take these." When he had taken the pad and pencil and lay waiting, Kelly asked, "Did you know a man by the name of David Robbins between the years 1983 and 1987?"

A pause while Malone's eyes held hers. She could sense the slight agitation there and feared he was going to refuse to respond after all. But then the pencil scratched across the paper. He had printed the word *Yes*.

"Did you have an altercation with Robbins during the Christmas of 1983, an altercation that resulted in the mutilation of your leg, a mutilation committed by David Robbins?"

Again the scratch. *Yes.*

"Did he acquire his nickname of Scorpio as a direct result of the style of mutilation he inflicted upon you?"

Scratch. *Yes.*

"During that Christmas episode, did Robbins in any way threaten your life?"

Scratch. *Yes.*

"Was David Robbins responsible for the attempted murder that put you here in the hospital?"

Scratch. *Yes!*

"You're doing beautifully, Andy. Now just one last question. Would you be willing to testify in a court of law against Mr. Robbins in regard to the events that took place in 1983 and this recent attack?"

Scratch. *Yes! Yes!!*

Kelly smiled, snapped off the recorder, and glanced back at the nurse. "Thank you," she told her before turning back to Malone. "Thank you again for your cooperation. I'll be in touch later when you're feeling better. Be well." She reached for the pad and pencil and turned to leave.

Nick and Joey rose from their hard, plastic waiting room seats as she approached. "Bingo. Mr. Malone has signed, sealed, and delivered the link of those serial mutilations to our Scorpio killer. One more corroboration and we'll strengthen that link."

This was the hardest, Kelly thought later, standing inside the Orleans Parish morgue waiting for the coroner to see them.

"You may go in now," the pretty young receptionist told them with a smile. Her amiability grated on Kelly; it seemed jarring in such grim surroundings.

"Come in, come in. I'm Dr. Eric Skyler. How can I help you good people?"

"We called ahead, Doctor. We're here to find out some information about a body you received a few days ago—the body of a Jean Le Beau."

"Ah yes, Ms. Wylie. I remember your call. As a matter of fact, I've got the file out and ready here. Now, let's see." He seated himself behind his desk. "What would you like to know?"

"My question concerns the wound, Doctor. I'm wondering if you found anything unusual about it?"

The doctor shuffled through his papers for what seemed like forever. Kelly looked over at Nick and Joey and read their discouragement. She was already focusing on tackling another angle when the doctor spoke up, surprising them. "Ah, here it is." He pulled out an ordinary, yellow Post-it-size square of paper. "I'm afraid I'm sometimes a little unorthodox in my record keeping.

"There was something just a bit unusual, a mark on his neck just below the collar. Couldn't quite make out what it was supposed to be at first, but when I looked closer, I made it out to be snakelike or something. Damndest thing, never seen anything like it in all my years."

Kelly felt a rush of sadness, but also of undeniable relief. "Thank you, Doctor. There's just one more thing. We may require your testimony about your medical findings on Mr. Le Beau in a court of law."

"Oh. Well, of course."

The doctor's eyes twinkled and Kelly wondered cynically if it had anything to do with his relish of being involved in a "big-city" homicide case.

Back at the cabin, Nick let the phone ring five times.

An unease he couldn't explain was urging him to dial home. He was about to hang up when Sandy picked up on the sixth ring.

"Hello."

"Sandy?" Nick said hesitantly. He hadn't heard his father's voice sound this firm in years.

"Nick! Lord, am I glad you called. Joey's in the clear."

Nick sat down hard on the sofa. How could Sandy know anything? "In the clear? What are you talking about?"

Sandy told him briefly about the notebook that named Robbins as Cain's murderer and that he intended to turn it over to Brower. "I'll explain the other details when you get home. Just take my word for it for now." Sandy waited impatiently for his older son to fill the silence across the long-distance line.

"This book contains names?"

"Well, only a few, but Robbins's is one of them. That's what I'm trying to tell you. Jackie Cabot came through one last time. And the book's comprehensive, Nick. I mean comprehensive as in, as soon as some interviews have been conducted in the Acre and around town, indictments could be handed down soon. The important part is that Joey is likely to be the key witness to back things up. He's got to be here to make it stick."

"Yeah, all right, Pop. Calm down."

"Yeah. Oh, and, son?"

"Uh-huh?"

"Things are going to change around here. I've been forced to take a good, hard look at myself these past few days. And, like I said, things are going to change. Starting with my boys. Hurry home. I've missed you."

"Sure, Pop. We'll do that." Nick sat thoughtfully for a while before he reached behind him to hang up the receiver. What had gotten into his old man?

When Nick hung up the phone, he met the waiting looks of his brother and Kelly. He told them about the conversation.

"Thank God," Joey said. "Robbins's time is running out, and with what we have and what we know, it's got to be safe to go home. When do you think we can leave?"

"The sooner the better," Kelly said.

Nick nodded his agreement. "Let me call and see if I can't book us a flight out of here tomorrow morning."

14

After Nick made the reservations for early the next morning, Joey headed for the deck to gather his things for the flight home. When he'd gone, Kelly walked over to Nick's outstretched arms.

"Is it really almost over?" she said. She was unutterably relieved but also a little frightened that the afterward she'd tried not to dwell on was at hand. Nick's arms tightened.

"Yeah, I really think it is." His voice held a touch of melancholy. He pulled away from Kelly, though he didn't leave her arms, and cast a telling look around the cabin.

"He died trying to protect someone he loved, Nick. I know that's not much consolation right now, but if you hold on to it, maybe in the future it will help."

"Maybe," he said, pulling her tight once more. He sighed.

And what about us? she wanted to ask. *What about our future?* But since she wasn't sure she could capsulate things any more clearly than he, she didn't have the courage to ask.

He dropped a kiss on the top of her head. "I

guess I might as well go secure everything outside so we'll be ready to go in the morning. Why don't you check out things in here, then we'll all turn in early. I have a feeling we're going to need our sleep."

"Will do," Kelly said. "And, Nick," she called just as he was about to step outside. She hadn't known what she was going to say, but whatever it was was stalled by a trace of that same guarded look he'd worn after they'd made love last night on the dock.

For a moment she got the feeling he didn't want to hear what it was she had to say, and a weight settled in her chest. It remained even after he smiled. "Hurry back, hmm?" She tried to make her smile seem genuine and promised to try later to convince herself she hadn't seen an almost imperceptible look of relief cross his face.

"Only as long as it takes, babe." The door clicked shut behind him.

Determined to push aside questions she'd have to deal with later, she watched him through the curtains as he hopped from the deck down to the boat to go through an engine check. She stood there for a few minutes until he finished and wandered off to inspect the grounds, then she started to the bedroom to get her own things together.

Where was Joey? He was being awfully quiet. Her step slowed, and for no good reason, she felt the hair on the back of her neck rise.

"Don't breathe," she heard from behind her as a hand covered her mouth. Her heart started to thunder as she felt the cold, razor-sharp point of steel press into the side of her throat.

David Robbins laughed softly. "Yes, I can see I surprised you. Otherwise that man of yours never would have left you alone. And the one in the bedroom back there would never have let his guard down."

At Kelly's muffled protest, Robbins laughed again. "Shhh, shush, you beauty, I didn't kill him yet. I merely incapacitated him. He should come to just in time to see you and his brother die."

Reacting to the menace in his voice, Kelly jerked against him and the point of the knife pressed deeper against her throat.

Robbins chuckled coldly. "Come on!" He was rough as he pulled her into the living room. He dragged her in front of the couch, then shoved her down. Faster than seemed possible, he ducked around the back of the sofa and grabbed a painful handful of her hair from behind. The horrible knife was at her throat again, but this time Robbins poised it horizontally against her skin.

"Go ahead and scream and I'll cut you now. Makes no difference to me, since you're going to die anyway."

Kelly had seen a gamut of irrational behavior in the course of her career, but little had disturbed her the way the calm smoothness in this maniac's voice dropped to an emotionless monotone.

"I have to kill you, you understand. All of you. The Society depends on my leadership. I can't have that position threatened by nasty secrets out of the past. Do you understand?"

All she understood was that she'd never been this frightened in her life. She'd seen firsthand what this man could do.

Kelly refused to give him the satisfaction of answering, and he jerked her hair so painfully that tears sprang to her eyes.

"Don't use that condescending silence on me like I'm crazy!" he growled. "You'll only make me mad, and I'll kill you quicker."

"Please," Kelly choked, trying desperately to control the tremor in her voice. "You can't get away with this. Brower knows about Cain." She didn't know if Sandy had made that true yet, but she gambled Robbins wouldn't doubt it.

His voice was frighteningly calm. "It doesn't matter what you've told him. Without Joey to validate it, he can't treat it as truth. And I know for a fact there was nothing else left in that alley to incriminate me. Try again."

Kelly shuddered as he raised the knife and used the flat of its blade to stroke her hair.

"You won't believe it," he sounded contemplative, "but it makes me sad about Nick. I've always liked him. He could have been an incredible asset to us." His voice turned silky. "But even if things had turned out differently, you still would have corrupted him, wouldn't you? You, with your Judas sentiments and your seductive ways . . ." The knife continued to stroke. "Such beautiful hair, I'll bet he loves your hair . . . I was watching you two through the window before he left."

His breathing was roughening, and Kelly's

blood turned to ice as he lifted a few strands with the blade, then let them fall.

"Does he breathe in its temptress fragrance . . . tangle his hands in it . . . stroke it like this too . . ."

The movement of the knife seemed obscene as it moved from her hair to her cheek, down her throat until finally he let it rest just above her breast. Idly, the point of the blade toyed with a button.

"Maybe I'll sample what Nicholas surely has tasted for himself . . ."

"Oh, God, please! Don't." Fear, cold, clammy and primal, swamped her. But beneath it a black fury began to rise.

"That's right," he said with a sudden vicious jerk of her hair. "Beg!" his voice was cruel. "Let him walk in and see you begging. I'll enjoy it that way more, I'll—" Kelly heard his sudden cry of pain at the same time his hand slackened on her hair and clutched convulsively at his temple.

She used the moment to act. She sprang away from the cushions, her target her pistol inside the oak table beside the door. Her fingers actually made contact with the drawer when a million needles of pain shot through her scalp; she screamed as her head was snapped back brutally by the vicious yank on her hair.

Robbins slammed her to the floor, and she almost screamed again as she felt a hard knee rammed into her back. He was breathing heavily upon her.

"Bitch! I can see I'm going to have to kill you now!"

Kelly's head was angled painfully to the side, and she actually saw his arm swing up and hover, ready to descend. Her gaze was riveted with fascination on the deadly glint of the knife, and she gave an involuntary sob, fully prepared to die.

An explosive crash rent the room as the front door was kicked open and Nick dived through in a roll, his gun a hair trigger away from killing the man holding her.

"Drop the knife, you fuck, or I'll blow you to hell!"

Robbins hovered indecisively, the knife still poised in the air. A slow smile spread across his lips. "I have nothing to lose. I can squeeze the life out of her now with the pressure of my knee. Or I can kill her quickly with the point of my blade. It makes no difference to me." Even as he said the terrible words, he increased the pressure against Kelly's back.

Kelly was in agony. His knee felt as if it would crush through to her spine any minute, and she was helpless to hold back a tortured gasp of pain.

Nick, fully prepared to fire, gave Robbins one last warning. "Let her go or you die."

Robbins's smile only widened.

Nick started squeezing the trigger—but the satisfaction of firing the shot was denied him when Robbins's face suddenly contorted with pain. The pressure of his knee slackened, and just before he fell heavily to the floor, an expression of shock registered on his face. Nick rushed forward to help Kelly shove Robbins's hateful weight from her.

Not trusting the killer's seemingly lifeless sprawl, Nick touched a hand to his neck and, as he did, noticed the thin stream of blood trickling from his ear. Aneurysm, he realized dispassionately, and then Kelly was in his arms.

"Nick, Nick," she sobbed as he gathered her close and buried her face in his arms. "Oh, my God . . . oh, my God, I've never been so scared in my life!" She gripped the hard-muscled strength of his arms, unable to let him go.

"Neither have I, sweetheart, neither have I. Jesus, when I heard your scream . . ." He hugged her closer. "But it's over now. Nothing can hurt you."

"Joey!" she gasped.

Nick looked stricken. Kelly was right behind him as he raced out to the deck. They both halted at the threshold, Joey's inert body paralyzing them with dread. His back was to the door, his hands tied behind him. Nick moved jerkily, as if his legs had turned to wood, until he was kneeling over his brother.

Kelly's heart was in her throat as she watched Nick turn him over. For a moment she didn't breathe—then Joey's eyes fluttered open. She sagged with relief and moved into the room until she was kneeling at Nick's side helping him untie the rope Robbins had knotted. Thank God Robbins's sadism had backfired this time. He'd been serious about postponing Joey's death in order to make him watch theirs.

When the last knot was released and Joey was free, Nick gathered his brother into his arms. The younger man was groggy, but he managed to mumble something and return the embrace. As they held each other, obviously shaken at how close death had come, Kelly looked on until the moment became too private. She rose and backed away, leaving them alone.

Back in the living room, she stood over Robbins's body. His face was serene except for that thin trail of blood. She averted her eyes and dialed the police.

Sedgwick Airport was blessedly sparse as the three of them disembarked and walked through the arrival gate. They'd gotten very little sleep the night before after all.

It had been hours after the authorities had come that all the immediate details surrounding Robbins's death had been handled sufficiently to allow their departure from Louisiana.

Now it was early afternoon, and they were concentrating on gathering their luggage before they met with Brower, whom Kelly had phoned previously with their flight information. She'd only had time to say that Joey was innocent and that David Robbins was guilty, and then there hadn't been time for anything else because they'd literally had to run to catch their plane.

Now they were walking down the concourse when surprise stopped them. Brower was coming directly toward them.

"Joey," Brower said, stopping within arm's reach. His face gave nothing away.

"Sir," Joey answered. He didn't attempt to extend the greeting. Kelly watched him glance down, distinctly uncomfortable.

Brower nodded to Kelly and Nick, then his gaze went back to Joey. "Come here, boy!" he said gruffly, pulling Joey against him.

Brower's hug was firm, and when Joey leaned away, Brower continued to grip his shoulders. The affection in his gaze was clear, but a somber light entered his eyes as he shifted his attention to include Nick. He let Joey go.

"I've got bad news. Sandy's been hurt bad. He was rushed to the hospital last night. They've got him in critical care."

Kelly saw blank incomprehension register on both the brothers' faces before varying degrees of reaction set in.

"What the hell happened to him?" Joey ran an agitated hand through his hair. "Will he live?"

Brower's tone wasn't encouraging. "He was shot. His chances are better today, but . . . the doctors still don't know."

Kelly had been watching Nick. His stillness was in stark contrast to Joey's tense agitation.

"Come on, I'll explain on the way." Brower led them to his car and nothing more was said until after they left the airport.

"John Butler did it," Brower said as he negotiated the heavy afternoon freeway traffic. "We've got him in custody now."

Kelly turned to Nick, who sat in the back beside

her. His face was expressionless. The shell of aloofness that had descended at the airport didn't crack. Kelly squeezed his hand along the seat, and he didn't pull away even though his detachment disquieted her.

"You wouldn't believe how much shit has hit the fan over the last twenty-four hours. . . ." He started to tell them about the notebook he had in his custody and was forestalled by Kelly, who told him Sandy had already alerted Nick to the book's existence. In return, Brower told them that Butler had agreed to plea-bargain, using an exchange of Society members' names in return for any leniency that information could secure.

"A patrolman in that damned group had apparently been keeping an eye on Earl Mack soon after you two were seen meeting with him in the Acre," Brower told them. "Earl must have been followed to Sandy's house the day he turned over the book."

Brower explained that Butler said he wasn't told until yesterday that Sandy had been visited by Mack. But prior to that, the officer who trailed Earl must have said something to somebody running scared inside the precinct because Butler started hearing uneasy rumblings involving Cain and internal conspiracy.

"He must have panicked, but since whispers hadn't spread to the top levels yet, Butler figured he still had time to try to get out of Sandy what, if anything, Earl had told him."

According to Butler's statement, Brower told them, Butler had said that when he got to

Sandy's, Sandy wasn't home, so Butler forced his way inside and was in the midst of a random search when Sandy surprised him by appearing from the back of the house. Sandy had a gun, but Butler, years younger with reflexes not dulled by booze, had rushed him. They had struggled and the gun had gone off twice, the first time wounding Butler, the second time almost fatally injuring Sandy.

"Neighbors called the police, and the two were taken to the hospital. In a day or so Butler will be released from observation into our custody. Some of Sandy's professional instincts must have been functioning, because when he was brought in, he had the notebook on him, tucked inside his shirt."

The rest of the ride was quiet. For the time being there didn't seem to be anything to say when each one of them knew it was only a matter of time before the city was shaken by a police scandal far uglier than Cain's murder. They knew it would be a long time before they themselves recovered.

At the hospital, Nick and Joey were directed immediately to Sandy's critical care unit and Kelly accompanied Brower to the floor's waiting area. Brower got them both coffee and Kelly accepted hers, grateful she was wearing comfortable jeans and sneakers. She knew they were in for a long wait.

Fifteen minutes later Nick and Joey came down the hall. Strain was evident on both their faces, but Kelly could detect nothing more distressing, so she assumed, and the brothers confirmed, that

Sandy was out of immediate danger and holding his own.

An hour later, Brower left with Kelly's assurance that she would meet him at the precinct later to file the necessary formal report. In the wake of everything that had happened and Sandy's condition, Joey was given leave to stay at the hospital a while longer before coming downtown to issue his formal statement.

Since his initial check on Sandy, Nick had accepted two cups of coffee from Kelly, but other than that, he had refused offers to get him anything else with little more than absentminded courtesy.

Kelly was a little hurt, but she knew him well enough to understand that the deep, inner defense mechanism he used to guard the very core of himself had kicked into place. And though he was being uncommunicative, he hadn't completely withdrawn. The occasional looks he threw her told her he was reassuring himself she was still there, and she fully intended to come back as soon as she had finished with Brower.

The rest of the afternoon passed with Nick and Joey taking turns with Sandy. Joey was in there now and Kelly couldn't put off leaving for much longer, so she walked over to the window to let Nick know she would be gone temporarily.

"I have to go in for a while, but I'll be back as soon as I can. Are you going to be all right?" She soothed her hand up and down his arm. He looked down at her, reluctant gratitude softening his eyes.

She wanted to reach out and take him in her arms, but his reserve held her away. Instead she reached up to touch his cheek, wanting to tell him she loved him, wanting to tell him she did so with a completeness she hadn't thought she'd ever be able to offer a man again.

But she knew he wasn't ready to hear it, and she sighed. Would he ever even be able to surrender to what was in his heart? Was he even able to at least say the words to himself? Because whether he chose to accept it or not, he revealed the essence of what he was resisting with his every look, every touch.

She had finally found her man to believe in. The irony was, maybe he just didn't possess the ability to believe in himself.

Nick let her draw her hand away, watched her affection turn to uncertainty. He wanted to reach out and pull her back, tell her that only her presence had been holding him together from the moment they'd heard Sandy had been shot. Instead, he damned the shroud around his heart, the barrier that refused to free him to tell her what she needed—no, what she deserved to hear.

He hadn't expected the raw pain that had hit him with the news about Sandy. He hadn't expected to be winded by the loss he'd braced for when he arrived at the hospital, certain Sandy lay dying.

Once he'd asked himself if deep down he still had any love left for his old man. Consistently he'd told himself he hadn't. How much he'd been deluding himself had only now been brought home to him.

Was love really so ungovernable, so unpredictable, that a man had no conscious defenses against it until the presence of it hit him like the proverbial ton of bricks? He'd loved his mother and she'd walked out on him. He'd loved Jean, and now Jean was dead. Looking out for his little brother gave him the satisfaction of believing there was some outlet for his affection that he could protect if not necessarily control. But an unblinking part of him saw the limitations in that. He watched Kelly walk away from him and realized the time had come when he wanted more.

He wanted another kind of love in his life, the unselfish, unconditional kind that Kelly had opened up to him.

With Kelly he had glimpsed the joy to be had in surrender and in giving, in needing as well as in taking. She was patient, but she wanted some sign of intention from him, and no woman was patient forever. No man had the right to expect her to be.

The bottom line was, he was going to have to decide if he had the courage to take a chance on love. But he couldn't until he resolved this fear of rejection that had ridden him most of his adult life.

For the rest of the week, the days took on a pattern. Nick and Joey spent all the time they could at the hospital, and Kelly made a point of joining Nick there to support him whenever she could.

Joey had since made his statement, and Butler had been released from the hospital into police custody. With the aid of his cooperation, Jackie's notebook, and Joey's corroborations about what he'd witnessed, with the denunciation of David Robbins's and the Society's vigilante doings, suspicion surrounding him was totally dispersed.

Also, with the testimony and corroboration of an assortment of street people and determined witnesses, indictments were handed down and arrests were made. An autopsy had revealed that David Robbins's mental instability had likely found its roots in the distant past. Both the tumor in his brain and the aneurysm that had ultimately killed him had been frighteningly advanced.

By the middle of the next week, Sandy was released. And Nick all but disappeared from Kelly's life.

He didn't call, nor did he come by her house, and the hope that had sustained her faith in believing their relationship had a future was lost. She hadn't been prepared for this loss that was infinitely harder to deal with than what she had suffered with Jeff.

By the end of the second week she was crying for him. By the end of the third, she was damning him, angry with him for driving them apart, angrier at the fate that made her fall for men who seemed destined to leave and hurt her in the process.

"If you've got some time, Kelly, I'd like to see you later today."

Surprised at a call from a detective named Alan Parsons one late-September morning, Kelly put down the receiver and gazed out her office window. Who was he, and what did he have to say to her about Nick? After work, she arrived at the bar around the corner from the precinct where they had agreed to meet.

She was beautiful, Alan saw. But then, he had expected that. What he'd been apprehensive about was the depth of her feelings for his friend. He took one look at her tense face, at the reluctant hope in her eyes, and was relieved.

Alan introduced himself and bought her a drink. When she was seated, he asked bluntly, "What's going on between you and Nick?"

Taken slightly aback, Kelly took a sip of her drink. "I'm not sure I understand what you mean."

"He took a leave of absence a few weeks ago to retreat to his cabin in Brown County. I talked to him before he took off and got some of what had developed between you two." Kelly looked away restlessly. "Yeah, Nick had that same look before he left. Listen, I don't know what he said—or, knowing Nick, what he didn't say to you before he left. But I'll tell you one thing, he cares for you."

Kelly's gaze drifted back to him. She read the genuine concern in his eyes and in that moment accepted that he really was Nick's friend. "Maybe so, but if he can't tell me that, what's the use? It takes two to make a relationship work. Without that combined commitment, no matter how strong, love eventually withers up and dies."

"Then tell him so."

Kelly was impatient. "He's not a child, Alan. I won't force anything from him that he's not ready to give. Besides, if he can't, maybe it's because whatever he feels just isn't deep enough. Have you thought about that?'' Kelly hated the pity that entered Alan's eyes, hated the finality of it.

He rubbed his hand across his face. "Oh, well, it was worth a try. I just thought that maybe one of you . . . well, there are some things that just aren't meant to be, I guess.''

Afraid that if she sat here one more minute she would disgrace herself by succumbing to tears, Kelly got up to leave. Alan reached out to gently clasp her wrist.

"And then on the other hand,'' he said with an enigmatic smile, ''I could be wrong.''

The sun was setting and another summer dusk was settling before him.

Nick sat alone on his porch, his bare feet propped on the rail surrounding his cabin. He took another sip of coffee and concentrated on the deepening colors that enfolded him, absorbed the peaceful cacophony of birdsong and rustling leaves that whispered over him, tried desperately to focus on anything that would blunt the worst loneliness he'd felt in his life.

Which was only fitting, since he'd disappeared into isolation and by so doing maybe made himself the world's biggest fool. Even Sandy had said so. He smiled a little. Damn, the situation really was gone when Sandy's taking him to task made sense. But then—he let the smile fade—that assessment wasn't really fair anymore because, true to his word, Sandy was making an effort. His enrollment in Alcoholics Anonymous had been more than talk. It was real.

Nick took another sip and thought back to the surprising conversation they'd had two weeks ago.

He'd stopped by the house to check in on Sandy as he had every evening since Sandy was released from the hospital. Randolf, who'd been persuaded to play nursemaid for Sandy while he convalesced, greeted Nick at the door and gestured toward the back where Sandy sat reclining out in the back yard.

"Hello, Pop."

Sandy had winced a little as he shifted on the lounger, but his eyes were clear and his smile hesitantly welcoming.

"I've been waiting for you. Come over here beside me and sit down."

Nick sat and Sandy looked him over thoroughly. "You don't look good, Nicky. Haven't you been sleeping?"

How could he tell his father that he dreaded trying to sleep because every time he tried, he saw Kelly lying beside him, felt her body nestled warm and trustingly in his arms. "I've been sleeping okay, Pop."

Sandy hadn't looked as if he'd believed it, but in light of the fragile truce that had newly formed between them, he let it go. "I saw Joey last night. We talked about some things, this and that, nothing really important." He looked off into the distance at the sound of some neighboring kids playing on the other side of the privacy fence. Still looking away, he added, "And we talked about you."

Nick leaned forward on the grass and wrapped his arms around his bent knees. His father's voice held a tone Nick hadn't heard for many, many years, not since he was a boy still young enough to believe trustingly in it.

"Don't look at me like that, Nick, please. What's past is past. We can't go back, we can only move ahead."

"What did you want to say to me, Pop?" Nick acknowledged his father's appeal and yielded to it, just too weary all of a sudden to fight.

"Joey tells me you got a girl."

Nick said nothing, only turned his head to gaze out across the freshly mown grass of the yard.

"He says that she's different from the rest, solid. The kind worth having. I . . . I'm here to listen, son, if you want to talk."

"When did we ever really talk?" He didn't raise his voice; he didn't have to. They were both too sensitive to the truth in what he asked.

"Nick, there's something you've got to understand. Your—" He cleared his throat. "Your mother and I had problems long before you and Joey came on the scene. What you grew up seeing was just at the end of it."

Nick did look around at that, a little stunned at his father's candidness and a little uneasy too. He wasn't sure he wanted to face this confrontation with old ghosts, ghosts that had haunted them long enough.

"Your mother's childhood wasn't a good one.

Her parents gave her no reason to trust anybody as she grew up. She was skittish, always on her guard like some poor, mistreated animal when I met her not long before I went off to the war.

"From the moment I saw her, I sensed that beneath the shell she was sweet and kind and beautiful, someone worth getting to know, someone I could come to love. She was hesitant at first, but after I broke through her guard, we dated. A couple of weeks before I was shipped off, we got engaged.

"When I got back we got married, but things started to fall apart. The things I'd seen over in Korea froze something up inside me, and despite your mother's attempts, I couldn't let her in. She read my inability as rejection, and since she'd grown up with nothing but rejection, something inside her instinctively coped by withdrawing from me. Still, you came along, then I joined the force. By the time more years had passed and Joey was born, the force had begun to give me a solidity I couldn't find at home, and I deliberately spent more and more time there.

"Your mother gradually gave up trying to connect with me, and I just found it easier to let her."

Sandy sighed and turned to face his son. "I don't know, maybe we just weren't meant to find happiness together, or maybe we were but we just didn't have the guts to try harder for it. Even after I started drinking, Nick, I loved your mother, even after I saw how my self-imposed isolation was killing her love for me. But by that time, I couldn't break out. I'd convinced myself that it was just easier to let her drift away than to take a chance on winning her back only to have her say that nothing I could do could make her love me again.

"Jean tried to talk sense to me, but I wouldn't listen, until he gave up on me and left. Then, when Sara left, I lost everything, even the respect of my children, all because I'd been too stubborn to fight for love, in spite of everything, to ask her for a clean slate, take another chance."

A dog had joined the playful fray next door; it barked and the children laughed happily, as if each day was destined to be as carefree as the next, as if there were no such things as finality and regret and pity in the world.

"Say what it is you're trying to say, Pop."

"That the things most worth winning in this life are usually the ones you have to fight for. If you've found something precious, Nick, don't let it slip through your fingers because you're afraid to take a chance. The only sure thing that will happen is that you'll find yourself alone in your old age with nothing to console you but bitter what-could-have-beens."

He'd had no response for his father then, but he'd since been thinking about it a lot, chiefly that everyone was ultimately responsible for his own decisions, his own choices. One of the only things life guaranteed was that mistakes were going to be made. The ability to overcome them and cope the best way you could was what ultimately separated the men from the boys. Seemingly it had taken Sandy all these years to realize that, but he finally had done it, and that was at least a start.

Did he have the courage to do the same? The more he was apart from Kelly, the more he was coming to believe that leaving her had been the worst mistake he had made in his life. By some miracle he had been given a chance at real happiness, had found a woman who could share with him the kind of love most people spent their lives searching for and never found.

And he was throwing it away with both hands.

His feet hit the deck and he stood. Maybe there was still a chance to regain lost ground. And if it was too late after all, if she told him she didn't want him anymore in the end, at least he'd have the satisfaction of knowing the demons inside him hadn't won without a fair fight.

Six thirty A.M. A strange sense of déjà vu overcame Kelly as the sound of the doorbell died away. Everything happened almost the same way it had the other time she had been awakened and Gino bounded from the bed and she searched for her slippers before she went to answer the door. The only thing that was different was the thousands of butterflies that had invaded her stomach.

Kelly pulled the latch back, opened the door a crack, and felt that déjà vu come full circle. She closed the door, slipped the chain off the lock, and stepped back to let in the man she hadn't been sure she'd ever see here again.

No treat awaited him, and Gino seemed to sense the heavy moment in that uncanny way pets have. He padded over to the kitchen and lowered himself to the tiles, his baleful eyes peeking from beneath his hair as if to observe how the scene would unfold.

The nightshirt was different; this time it was striped and boasted the baseball team that was Chicago's finest. Was it possible she was even lovelier than when he'd seen her last?

"Why are you here, Nick?" Kelly held herself stiffly, her arms crossed around her middle as if bracing to ward off a blow. "If you've come to tell me it's over, you can save your breath—the message you've been sending has been loud and clear."

He hadn't prepared anything to say and realized with painful clarity that the crucial moment was upon him. Everything about her was unyielding, and he was suddenly terrified that her refusal of him might really happen. He resisted the urge to clear his throat.

"I came to say I'm sorry."

Kelly nearly flinched. She'd expected the words that would sever things forever. Instead he'd unbalanced her. "What are you sorry for?" she whispered.

Nick shoved his hands in the pockets of his hooded cotton sweatshirt. "For running away from you, running away from us," he told her with unadorned candor. "For being too much of a coward to see whether or not we had any kind of future before us."

"And?"

Nick looked down at his feet, then over at Gino.

She even saw him swallow once and died a little as she braced to hear good-bye.

"I love you."

This time she did flinch. She couldn't believe he'd actually said it. Neither could she sustain her coolness; what he'd said meant too much. Still, she needed to know more.

"I love you too, Nick. But what does that mean in real terms?"

And just like that, in a blinding flash, he knew. He took slow steps toward her until he was standing close enough to take her in his arms. But he didn't, not yet. He didn't want her to think for a minute the seductiveness of the touch was clouding his judgment.

"It means," he said slowly, "that I didn't even know how alone I was until you showed me what it meant to be wanted, there," he touched a fleeting hand to her chest, "there inside your heart. The truly amazing thing is, before you, I never thought I'd be capable of feeling that way too. But I do, sweetheart, and the reason is you."

Kelly caressed every inch of his beautiful, stubbled face with her eyes. It was tense with watchfulness.

"What's the rest, Nick?" The question and all it entailed was so delicate it could have floated away on a puff of air.

"The rest is—" Oh, God! this was hard! "The rest is, I want you. Tomorrow and the next day and the next. I want you for the rest of my life." He couldn't look at her. All the fears he'd ever had came crashing down to this moment . . . until he felt her arms go around him.

"Oh, Jesus," he breathed, returning her hug. "Does this mean you really want me back?"

"You foolish, foolish man," Kelly said, smiling against his shoulder. "It means I'll want you until I'm too old to want anything anymore."

"Lady, lady . . ." The words became a litany as he chanted them over and over again. He rocked her in his arms for a while, savoring the absolute peace, wondering how he had ever been afraid of this.

"Marry me, Kelly. Love me forever." The words slipped from him unbidden, soulfully, like a prayer. His happiness was complete when she answered it like an angel. His angel.

"Forever, darling. Forever and beyond."